LA

PASIONARIA

*   *the passionflower who bled for Spain*

*   *the historic Jarrow Hunger March*

*   *tragedy of niño's whose lives Franco stole*

John Davies

Order this book online at www.trafford.com
or email orders@trafford.com

Most Trafford titles are also available at major online book retailers.

Printed in Victoria, BC, Canada.

ISBN: 978-1-4269-1890-2 (sc)

ISBN: 978-1-4269-1889-6 (hc)

Library of Congress Control Number: 2010901221

*Our mission is to efficiently provide the world's finest, most comprehensive book publishing
service, enabling every author to experience success. To find out how to publish your book, your
way, and have it available worldwide, visit us online at www.trafford.com*

Trafford rev. 5/12/2010

 www.trafford.com

North America & international
toll-free: 1 888 232 4444 (USA & Canada)
phone: 250 383 6864 ♦ fax: 812 355 4082

FOREWORD

This novel is the latest residual trickle in the spate of literature, and dramatic Hollywood blockbusters, that emerged after the Spanish Civil War, a rehearsal for World War II. Author John Davies exposes how children were brutally stolen from their Republican mothers at the order of Nationalist leader Generalismo Francisco Franco. Join the infamous Hunger March from Jarrow, and on to troubled Spain, and read how the author gets to grips with the terrible atrocities that oozed like puss from a conflagration which pitched brother against brother, and father against son. The inhumanity, the hatred, and agony, of a war that also saw suckling babies torn from their *mama's* teats while their Republican parents were shot by Franco's brutal hit men making no pretence of being honourable soldiers.

PROLOGUE

Born in the Midlands I am as British as roast beef, despite now being a fully authenticated resident of Spain, a nation, frankly, that commends itself more to me, in modern times, than the UK.

But the characteristics of the Welsh race also run through me as rich as the seams of coal that once laced below the teeming mining valleys of the Rhonnda. The men that dug out the black gold from the bowels of the earth developed huge loyalty to their working class peers and inspired fierce courage. I inherited some of those characteristics from my father, Stan Davies, who worked in the bowels of the earth as a pit-boy. At 17 he volunteered to serve with the Royal Welch Fusiliers in the Great War winning the Military Medal and the Belgian *Croix de Guerre* for gallantry as a signaller sergeant. After demob he became an International footballer. Playing for Preston, Everton, West Brom and Rotherham. Making 18 international appearances. When Wales beat Scotland at Wrexham in 1922 he scored the winning goal against Scotland before taking over from the injured goalkeeper, Peers, for the last 20 minutes. The kind of grit that had prompted many older collier colleagues from the previous decade to lay down their picks, shovels, and, indeed lives for the Republic in the Spanish Civil War between 1936-39. I thank my father for teaching me about loyalty to the working class. As always I am grateful to my late wife, Rosa, and to Renate Roncevic, who have always been there for me and to my faithful manuscript reader Beryl French.

John Davies

AUTHOR'S ASSURANCE

Although this novel is a work of fiction the events depicted really happened but not always in the same chronological order.

Some of the characters have been given fictitious names to protect the identity of any ageing victims of General Franco, or their relatives, who are still alive. There is no doubt about the raw courage that pulsed through the ranks of the International Brigades drawn from the working class, including hundreds who in Civvy Street had previously diced with death while toiling underground in the appalling and antiquated coal mines of the world.

What is not in dispute while General Francisco Franco was the central figure in the Nationalist victory, and the peace that followed, the icon of the Republican cause was Dolores Ibárruri Gómez, famously known as *La Pasionaria*.

So be it-I take the risk of being accused of arrogance by linking myself, a humble journeyman of the pen, to one of the world's great writers, Ernest Hemingway, who also wrote of *La Pasionaria* in his famous novel about the Spanish Civil War, *For Whom The Bell Tolls*. The only epitaph that fits iconic *La Pasionaria*, who died of pneumonia in her nineties, is: *"She dedicated her life to fighting for the working men and women of Spain ."*

In fairness although Franco was passionately Spanish so were his Republican enemies. Although he sanctioned thousands of atrocities after the Spanish War there is little doubt that Republicans would also have killed on a massive scale had they prevailed.

That is the very nature of the gruesome beast called 'Civil War'.

1

Dai Powell, a former miner and university graduate from the Rhonnda Valley, was staying for a short holiday with a former Rugby football team mate, George Stewart, an unemployed shipyard welder, when he was sucked into helping in making a slice of industrial history in the autumn of 1936.

The Communist Party of Great Britian had rallied workers throughout the country to fight for their rights in the middle of a global recession which had hit British miners and ship builders savagely. Many of the coal mines had been put on short time and hundreds of colliers sacked when unemployment benefit lasted only 26 weeks leaving the Assistance Board to make paltry relief payments for long-term unemployed before brutally referring them to merciless Poor Law officials who frequently evicted them from their homes. That was the situation that Dai Powell and his family in their Rhonnda pit village of Ynswen were faced with.

A similar tragedy hit the depressed area of Jarrow a small town at the mouth of the River Tyne near the heavily industrialised City of Newcastle. The town's only significant employer, Palmer's

Shipbuilding, was established in the 19th Century transforming Jarrow into a boomtown where a quarter of the world's big ships were put together and launched on the muddied waters of the Tyne. After the Great Depression Jarrow became a ghost town occupied by men and women without any employment whatsoever.

This was the topic of conversation that engaged the two lads, who had played Rugby League football for a semi-professional side in Yorkshire, as they slowly sipped their Newcastle Brown Ale, a delightful elixir a local brewery first produced in 1927.

'*The situation is getting really serious I am telling you Dai lad,*' George Stewart confided to his Welsh pal. '*The Jarrow Borough Council are organising a protest against the Government demanding that they reinstate the local shipyard. They are calling for the town's unemployed to march to the House of Commons and hand in a petition with thousands of local signatures demanding action.*

'*The Borough Council want to call it a "crusade" to distance it from the Communist Party- supported National Unemployed Workers' Movement who have organised similar marches. They don't want the Council to be linked with Communism. But I don't think a piece of paper, with hundreds of signatures on it, is going to impress that bloody pig, Prime Minister Stanley Baldwin, do you? But I will have to play my part and join the March.*'

Dai Powell took a thoughtful swig of his Brown Ale before replying: '*Look George it's our turn on the dartboard. When we have finished our game we'll have a long talk about this . I have got some thoughts of my own about what is going on in this country particularly in the Welsh coalfields where thousands of miners are out of work and their kids dying of malnutrition.*'

After a couple of games they lost the next one and sat down at a table again.

'Have another brown ale on me George,' Dai invited his pal. *'I've still got a couple of bob left from this week's dole money. I don't know if I have told you before but I am a paid up member of the British Communist Party. Although I am not very impressed with the Party in Wales because of its weak leadership I think that international Communism, as an ideal, offers the best solution for the downtrodden, unemployed, under-paid and, generally abused, manual workers of the world.*

'I am very drawn towards what the Communists are doing for the Republican cause in the Civil War against the insurgent Nationalists, who are supported by the German National Socialists and Italian Fascists. The Communists in Spain are inspired by a crusading woman, Dolores Ibárruri, known as La Pasionaria, who called the nations to arms when the Civil War began three months ago with the clarion cry: " We especially call upon you, workers, farmers, intellectuals to assume your positions in the fight to finally smash the enemies of the Republic and of the popular liberties. Long live the union of all anti-fascists! Long live the Republic of the people! The Fascists shall not pass!"

'What a contrast to the wishy-washy speeches made by the British Communists. That woman passionately believes that one day Communism will take control in every country of the world where the workers get a raw deal from employers who bully them, underpay them, and throw them to the dogs when they get too old to work!' The fervent Welshman then made an urgent proposition to his Geordie mate.

'When the march to the House of Commons, from Jarrow by unemployed workers starts on 5 October I intend to join them,' said Dai Powell. *'Then when we get to London I will make my way to the coast, probably cadge a lift on a fishing boat across the British*

Channel and then wind my way through Europe to Barcelona and volunteer to fight for the Republicans. George, I know, like me, you've got one of the new British passports and I'd love you to join me.

'You will be striking a bigger blow for the working class than taking part in half a dozen marches from Jarrow to London!' George Stewart spent a sleepless night when they got back to his parents tiny home where Dai Powell was staying as a house guest. He knew it would be "make your mind up day" on the morrow.

2

In fact *La Pasionaria's* impassioned battle cry speech, appealing for the defense of the Second Spanish Republic, delivered at the Government Building in Madrid on 19 July 1936, was even more stirring than the short extract so admiringly expounded by Welsh miner Dai Powell in a Jarrow pub.

'Workers! Farmers! Anti-fascists! Spanish Patriots! Confronted with the fascist military uprising, all must rise to their feet, to defend the Republic, to defend the people's freedoms as well as their achievements towards democracy!' she smashed home her defiance against General Francisco Franco's National Army which had been flown back from Morroco to quell the Republicans and oust the Government.

'Fascism shall not pass, the hangmen shall not pass! Workers and farmers from all Spanish provinces are joining in the struggle against the enemies of the Republic that have arisen in arms. Communists, Socialists, Anarchists and Republican Democrats, soldiers and other armed forces remaining loyal to the Republic combined have inflcted the first defeats upon the fascist foe. The whole country cringes

in indignation at these heartless barbarians that they would hurl
our democratic Spain back down into an abyss of terror and death.
However. They shall not pass!'

Dai Powell's abridged version of *La Pasionaria's* dynamic
oration, however, was enough to convince George Stewart what he
had to do as he writhed sleeplessly weighing up his options.

* * *

Mabel Stewart did her son and his pal proud when she produced
a slap-up fried breakfast the following morning despite having
to eke out the sparse funds available from the paltry dole money
received each week by George and his 50-year-old father, Sam, an
unemployed riveter.

'*Let's have a long stroll down to the harbour and walk this lot*
off,' George smiled patting his stomach. '*We can have a lunch-time*
pint at the Working Men's Club and have a long chat about things.'
Then, pulling his buddy's leg, George added: '*Oh, and by the way,*
Dai it's your turn to wash-up the breakfast dishes for Mum--I did
it yesterday remember. You'll find a pair of rubber gloves on the
sink.'

The two lads made a brisk and circuitous four mile walk
arriving, as if by some cunning plan, almost on the hour of midday,
the opening time for the bar at the Working Men's Club. They had
passed by the tragically idle shipbuilding yards and their derelict
cranes.

They had sadly noted the rotting scaffolds, the deserted hulks
of two ships under destruction when the effects of the Global
Depression began to bite. The results of that dire event that sent
thousands of workers on both sides of the Atlantic to line-up at the
dole queues and soup kitchens.

The human tragedy that was unfolding was underlined when the only humans they saw in the huge graveyard of ship building were a couple of ageing watchmen huddled into their corrugated huts and frying slices of bacon on a polished shovel over a brazier.

'*I don't expect that the owners of the shipyard are hungry,*' said George Stewart angrily. '*What do they know about the hardship suffered by men who worked so hard to make their bosses' rich. The desperate difficulties for honest workers hurtled into poverty through no fault of their own and striving against the odds to put food on the table for their suffering wives and little children. If anyone doubts that workers and bosses should be treated equally, then they should visit the ghost of once busy ship yards, or go to the idle coal mines and witness the pathetic sight of unemployed miners scratching through slag heaps for nuggets of coal to sell for pennies or heat their chilly homes.*'

There was five minutes to go before the Club Steward Bertie Milburn opened the bar at the Working Men's Club.

'*Let's have a game of darts,*' challenged George Stewart. '*Best of three legs with the loser paying for the drinks.*'

Dai Powell grinned and cracked back: '*You will only be able to blame yourself George-boy. You must love living dangerously!.*

The Welsh man won by two straight legs and showed no mercy for his luckless pal as he chortled triumphantly: '*Get your belly up to the bar and buy two Newcastle Brown Ales.*'

When they settled down at an iron-legged bar table savouring a badly needed drink exhausted after their long walk George Stewart admitted: '*I lay awake in the short hours of the night thinking about the talk we had yesterday. I have decided to accompany you to Spain and will volunteer to serve with the Republic Army in the Spanish Civil War. There are two weeks to go before they set off on what the newspapers are already calling the Jarrow Hunger March. If we, in the International Brigades, prevail in our task to help the Republicans win the Civil War and retain control of the Spanish Government we shall have struck a vital blow for unemployed workers all over the world.'*

Dai Powell was delighted with his friend's support and said: *'Without being too presumptious I thought all along that was the decision you would make. We had better start training tomorrow a 300 mile march to London will be a feat of endurance and we don't want to let anyone down!'*

That is what the two braves did at 7am every morning for the next two weeks until the historic march began. Togged out in garishly colours rugger shirts, knee-length shorts and, what was called in those days, plimsolls, they set off on a brisk seven mile run each day.

Ma Stewart's famous fry-ups which often included black pudding, and even kidneys on special days, were like giving strawberries to a donkey for two young athletic youngsters, when with sweat still oozing from their exertions they sat down at the kitchen table.

Succulent breakfasts they would both recall in the days of danger, devastation and devotion to duty that lay ahead.

3

Spain, like the rest of Europe, was experiencing the worst slump in its history and, as one shrewd money-man at the time cynically commented: '*When America sneezes the rest of the world catches a cold*!'

The Wall Street crash of 1929, however, was a lot more serious than a sneeze in Spain where by 1936 unemployment had soared above 30% in towns and cities which were soon to be drenched in their own blood. There was no dole in Spain where one million out of a workforce of three million were out of work. More than 70% of the people still lived on the land and 52% of them worked in agriculture which produced more than two thirds of its vegetables, fruit, almonds and olive oil for export. There was little or no industrialisation in progress.

Conditions for working people were worse for the Spanish than the underdeveloped Chinese. There were widespread reports that there were areas of poverty stricken Spain where the people were living on a sparse diet of root vegetables and boiled greens.

When the Spanish Republic was born in 1931 the workers and

peasants, after years of living under oppressive dictatorship, hoped that the country would be modernised and their living standards improved. That did not happen and the nation was ripe for anarchy and the Civil War broke out in 1936.

Paco Delgado, at 48 years of age, was one of 30,000 Asturian coal miners who went on strike. He had six mouths to feed on the paltry wages he had been paid by parsimonious pit owners.

It meant the family were on the poverty line as the country imploded into anarchy.

The Nationalists decided that the only solution was for the organised working class to be put down and they were backed by an army led by General Francisco Franco and by most of the country's wealthy employers.

The predicament of the Delgado family split them tragically down the middle. Paco was supported by his wife Maria Serra Delgado, his elders sons Carlos and Tomas who enlisted with him in the Republican Army while youngest son Rafa joined the Nationalist insurgents..

It left the prettiest Delgado of them all, 17-year-old black-haired Pilar, to make her own mind up on which way to jump.

The emerald-eyed beauty chose a non-combatant role in a war where women did fight alongside their men and were incited by the Republican ikon *La Pasionaria* to prepare buckets of boiling oil to throw over General Franco's army when the Nationalists attacked Madrid.

Pilar volunteered to be a nurse in a Republican front line surgical unit a brave decision for a genteel girl who it seemed at one time was destined to become a nun. For the next three years she tended the wounds of the harassed Republican soldiery. Held their hands while the surgeons amputated their limbs. Lit a last cigarette for men who no longer had any arms to do such simple tasks for themselves. Took dictation as dying soldiers whispered a last letter to their mothers.

Yet through all this horror Pilar never lost her feminity. She was an angel in the midst of hell deprived during the three year Iberian inferno of the romantic escapades that usually indelibly colours the life of teenage girls.

Neither did the pain of losing her two elder brothers, Carlos and Tomas, add a crust of agony to her gentle nature. She just went to the local church and asked the priest if he would say a Mass for the souls of the Nationalist soldiers who had pulled the deadly triggers.

Then came the acid test when an 18-year-old Nationalist warrior was brought to the battlefield surgical tent with a gaping hole in his chest. She sat through the night comforting him as he gurgled his way to eternity. It was if those suffering around her could hear the flutter of angels' wings in every act of compassion she made. As the horror of a Civil War unfolded setting father against son and brother against brother she never lost her composure.

It was a strange war that, incongruously, would throw together a Chapel going, rugby playing, unemployed coal hewer from the Rhonnda and a dazzlingly beautiful green-eyed daughter of an out of work miner from Asturias together.

No one should have been surprised. History has always shown that the abomination of conflict between nations often creates strange bedfellows.

4

On fifth of October 1936 an astonishing line-up of 207 Geordie men, most of them unemployed shipyard workers, plus one out of work Welsh coalminer, walked their way into history with a blistering hike from Jarrow to London.

Their Member of Parliament, Ellen Wilkinson, known as '*Red Ellen*', accompanied them on the gruelling 300 mile procession from the North East of England, through Yorkshire, Nottinghamshire, Leicestershire, Bedfordshire, Hertfordshire and North London to Westminster.

'*Red Ellen*' was as symbolic to the distressed workers of Jarrow as '*La Pasionaria*' was to the starving *trabajodoras* of Spain's Republican Movement. Sometimes the gritty '*Red Ellen*' marched proudly alongside her constituents in their campaign to rouse the government to find work in order for them to support their families by firing life into the pathetic paralysis of the idle Jarrow shipyard. At other times the Honourable Member for Jarrow would ride in the bus, fitted with cooking equipment and carrying ground sheets, that accompanied the marchers.

George Stewart and Dai Powell were nearly always at the head of the procession. Powell carried a rugby ball which they back passed to each other scoring a point when their pal occasionally dropped the oval leather.

At times Stewart would lead the singing with a Geordie anthem that accompanied the harmonica band lifting the spirits of the trudging marchers.

'*Whoa me lads you should have seen us gannin.*

'*All the lads and lassies there with smiling faces*

'*Gannin doon the Scotswood Road to see the Blaydon Races*'

Soon George Stewart would be melodiously joined by more than 200 other Geordies voices as, ignoring the pain of blistering feet, they tramped, more or less, 12 miles a day, for 23 days. No one has ever boasted that the men from the North East were noted for their singing and Dai Powell's Celtic hackles rose with ambition to prompt some Welsh Choral style harmonising.

When the larynx's of the marchers started to tire of their musical trip to the Blaydon Races Dai Powell's rich alto voice warbled clearly in the rich language of Wales:

'*Sospan fawr yn beri ar y llawr*

'*Sospan fach yn berwi ar y tan*

A'r gath *wedi sgrapo Jonni bach*'

Then as if by some prick of conscience he realised he was being rude to the comrades he was marching alongside by singing in a foreign tongue he powerfully sang the next stanza in English.

'*Sospan fach boiling by the door*

'*Sospan fawr boiling on the floor*

'*The cat's gone and scratched poor little Bill.*'

Within half an hour, miraculously, dozens of hairy-armed

North Easterners, were enthusiastically warbling a quirky song about a Welsh saucepan--in the English language. A choral concert that ended in raucous laughter.

> *'Mary Anne's little finger is better*
>> *'Poor Dave in his grave now lies deep*
> *' The baby in the cradle is silent*
>> *'The cat now in peace lies asleep*
> *'Sospan fach boiling by the door*
>> *'Sospan fawr boiling on the floor*
> *'The cat now in peace lies asleep*
> *'Mary Anne's gone and broken her finger*
>> *'And Davey the ploughboy's taken ill*
> *'The baby in the cradle is crying*
>> *'The cat's gone and scratched poor little Bill*
> *'Sospan fach boiling by the door*
>> *'Sospan fawr boiling on the floor...*

Dai Powell held up his hands as the singing stopped. Six accompanying mouth organ players gasped for air, dozens of Geordie's smiled as they heard the praise heaped on them by Dai, their self appointed choir master: *'Well done me boyos I haven't heard better singing than that in the Bryntor Congregational Chapel or at the local Band Club's Saturday night sing-songs . In fact my lads your performance would not have shamed the great St David's Concert Hall, Cardiff....*

There was a hush as one of the marching Jarrow men, way back in the line shouted cheekily: *'Thanks for the compliment Dai-- so you'll be buying the drinks when we pitch up for the night at Harrogate?'*

The quick-witted Welshman, however, not one to be bettered in a verbal joust, cracked back: *'Hold on lad. I only said you were good, not wonderful. In fact you'll be paying for me beer tonight if you want any further singing lessons from me.'*

5

The remaining five minutes of that day's march was drowned in laughter.Although George Stewart and Dai Powell put as much heart, effort and energy into the hunger march as any of the other 206 unemployed shipyard workers who had embarked on the gruelling 300 mile trek which according to the banners carried by the footsore walkers was officially called the '*Jarrow Crusade*', the two pals had a hidden agenda.

Under discussion every evening was how they would travel on to Spain, where they planned to volunteer and fight with the Communist supported Republican army's International Brigades after the Jarrow Crusade reached the House of Commons to lobby Parliament. They planned their future escapade at the Jarrow March's overnight stops at Chester-le-Street, Ferry Hill, Darlington, Northallerton, Ripon, Harrogate, Leeds, Wakefield, Barnsley, Sheffield, Mansfield, Nottingham, Loughborough, Market Harborough, Northampton, Bedford, Luton, St Albans, and Edmonton before their much acclaimed arrival at Westminster.

'I have made a couple of phone calls to the Communist party of

Great Britain,' was the surprising disclosure Dai Powell made to his pal. *'I was advised that the best way for us to get past the French border guards would be to get a return rail and cross Channel ferry ticket from Victoria Station, London to Perpignan in the South of France, a convenient back door entrance to Spain. A return ticket will support our claim that we are genuine tourists aiming to travel back to the UK when our vacation ends and not mercenary soldiers on a mission to play a part in the Spanish Civil War.'*

Despite their preoccupation of the perilous determination to play a vital role in the worldwide struggle by workers to be given jobs at a fair wage so that they could maintain their families with dignity, respect, free of oppression from bully-boy employers earning enough money to provide three nutrious meals a day for all, Dai and George were overwhelmed with the support the Marchers got from the public during their 300 mile safari down the spine of England.

As they marched at almost military pace the weary unemployed shipyard workers of Jarrow were astonished at the gift of dozens of pairs of new and strong boots donated by the public. They could have been trained by a drill sergeant of the Grenadier Guards judging by the cohesion, and precision of their marching. Wherever they stopped at the end of their day's march the local people were on hand to offer them a comfortable bed for the night, a plate of steaming stew and countless pots of strong tea. Many of them held blue and white banners proclaiming that they were: "The Jarrow Crusade for Justice".

The warm-hearted burghers of Barnsley in the South Yorkshire hinterland, painfully cognisant themselves of the perils of coalmining and the calamitous effect of unemployment provided a generously welcome surprise when they opened the specially heated municipal baths to the sweat-crusted marchers.

This wondrous gesture prompted Dai Powell to lead the marching choir to a lusty rendering of M*en of Harlech* as they headed next morning to their next port of call at the teeming city of Sheffield.

The stirring lyrics of *Rhyfelgyrch Gwr Harlech* floated across the heavily frosted dales of the picturesque West Riding as Dai Powell's mellifluous alto voice powered across the fields to spook pheasants, rabbits and badgers from the hedgerows causing minor stampedes amongst the small herds of cattle and bedraggled flocks of sheep.

Heroes, soldiers, rally
On the foe we'll sally
We will chase the hostile race
From stream and hill and valley
Conquest's banner proudly bearing
We'll exult in their despairing
Victory the shout declaring
Cambria live for aye!

The all-important petition demanding government aid for the stricken town of Jarrow signed by 11,000 citizens was always carried at the head of the procession and was extended with a subsidiary supplication as hundreds of people along the toilsome route scratched their autographs in brotherly support.

The vehement message of support around the world, circulated via a basically critical Press, towards the dauntless marchers after they completed the 13th leg of their long haul. It echoed from Mansfield to Madrid where *La Pasionaria* aimed another stimulating battlecry to workers around the globe.

'*The Communist Party calls you to arms,*' shouted the dramatic Dolores Ibárruri, dressed in sombre black, her sinewey arms stretched emotionally towards the sky. '*We especially call upon workers , farmers intellectuals to assume your positions to finally smash our enemies.*'

6

Several days before the Jarrow marchers had reached Westminster to confront Government Ministers in a bid to help unemployed men of North East England, in particular, and the country, in general, back to work, the Spanish Civil War had taken on a new sinister aspect on the blood-stained canvas of world history.

The reigning Republican's had been dealt a devasting blow to their chances of being able to continue in control of the country against the the Nationalists, when a group of right wing generals, led by General Francisco Franco, launched a military coup to overthrow the parliament which had been elected at the nation's 1935 general election the previous year.

Controversially , France, England and the USA had denied the Communist sponsored Republicans any military support. On the other hand Hitler and Mussolini made a pact with Franco. In repayment for military assistance two of the world's most evil dictators would take vast quantities of Spain's invaluable iron ore, copper and other essential raw materials.

On 29 October 1936, Russian tanks and aircraft were in action supporting the Republic Forces for the first time. This was more than matched when German and Italian bombers repeatedly dropped sticks of deadly bombs on behalf of the insurgent Nationalists in an evil intent of diluting civilian resistance. Loss of life apparently did not come into the equation. Hitler's barbarous aviators apparently used the tactics later when they blitzed London in the early says of World War II.

* * *

While wearily completing the next leg of their journey, from Mansfield to Nottingham, the dog-tired marchers passed through a section of Sherwood Forest, where the legendary Robin Hood was reputed to reign supreme, with his band of Merry Men. But there was no Robin Hoood to rob the rich to feed the poor on this famed March. There was just the largesse along the road dispensed by the ordinary big hearted public who came to their front gates and dispensed clean blankets, warm hand-knitted jumpers, pairs of new boots, bowls of piping hot soup with chunks of home made bread, bottles of beer and freshly baked sausage rolls.

A truly impressive exhibition of working class loyalty and affection for men they regarded as courageous and fully deserving of their support.

Although the Jarrow March was basically approved throughout the country by those on the left in British politics and treated as a boundary mark the Labour Party disagreed and, monstrously, the Trade Union Congress advised their members not to help the marchers.

Cornelius Whalen, who was the last surviving Jarrow Marcher, before he died at the age of 93, in September 2003 once put the dire situation in proportion saying: '*The bastards stabbed their own people in the back and the working class will never forgive them!*'

* * *

But George Stewart and Dai Powell did not let anything sour their pledge put their lives of the line in their allegiance to the global cause of Socialism as they sang and jigged their way to Marble Arch from Edmonton, Middlesex, and then on the last couple of miles.

Seemingly always destined to be the leader Dai shouted to the marching columns: '*Come on my bonny lads I taught you the song, now let the London buggers hear the last verse of Men of Harlech.*'

As the rolling thunder of more than 400 marching feet wheeling around Marble Arch, as if by some omen, past the site where the old Tyburn Gallows once stood, and where once the gory hangings and disembowelling took place of footpads, highwaymen, adulterers, religious martyrs, traitors, arsonists, counterfeiters, murderers and bizarrely in 1725, Jonathan Wild, an organised crime lord who might have featured in Mario's Hollywood thriller *The Godfather*, if he had still been around in the 20th century.

Those 200 Men of Jarrow might have felt a sore throat coming on if they had known that political agitators like William Fitz Osbern, the populist leader of the London tax riots was the first man to do the '*Tyburn Jig*' in 1196 after being dragged naked by a horse to the London gallows. Or the duel hanging of Michael Gof and Thomas Flamank, leaders of the first Cornish Rebellion in 1497, and the stringing up in 1550 of Humphrey Arundell the architect of the second Cornish Rebellion, which is often referred to as the '*Prayer Book Rebellion*'.

The Jarrow Hunger Marchers , although not summarily despatched at Tyburn, were contemptuously snubbed at Westminster by the Prime Minister of the day, pipe-smoking Stanley Baldwin who said he was too busy to meet them! Jarrow's unemployment problems never really recovered until after the start of World War II in 1939 when the nation needed steel workers again to produce arms for the struggle against Germany.

7

So with no qualms of conscience that they were leaving behind their families and home country without notice, and were off to fight in Spain in defence of the Communist-sponsored ruling Republican government, George Stewart and Dai Powell said farewell to their Jarrow March colleagues two days later.

'Those bastards at Westminister couldn't give a fuck about the situation of the unemployed in the North East. Wales, Scotland, Ulster, the Black Country and other industrial areas in the Midlands,' ranted George Stewart.

Dai Powell rushed to support that embittered proclamation saying vehemently: *'You're right Georgie lad. Those Westminster wankers don't give a shit that there are children in working class districts of Britain dying of malnutrition, rickets, tuberculosis, and other diseases associated with poverty--poor little bastards! There will have to be a revolution, and a lot of blood shed, in Britain, like there is in Spain at the moment, to put that right.'*

Now the two intrepid pals as they caught a bus across London to Victoria Station in those pre-WWII days before the advent later in the century of low cost air lines. They bought return tickets to Paris where Dai was hoping to get advice from the French Communist Party leader Maurice Thorez, the first man to visualise an international force of volunteers to fight for the Spanish Republic.

Only two months earlier Maurice Thorez set up a multi-national recruiting centre in Paris for the Spanish Republican army where volunteers were forwarded on to the International Brigades' training base at Albacete in Spain.

'Congratulations on the part you two men played in the Hunger March from Jarrow,' said the enthusiastic Thorez. *'Now I hope you can strike an even greater blow for world Socialism in Spain against the growing curse of Fascism.'*

The French Communist leader gave George and Dai two through train tickets from Paris to Perpignan on the Spanish border.

'From there you will be only an hour away from the Republic Army's base in Barcelona where you will be processed and transported for induction and training at Albacete,' Thorez explained handing over a bundle of francs to pay for their food on the journey.

As the train rattled on the six hour journey to Perpignan the two Brits stretched out in their otherwise empty compartment munching garlic sausage baguettes, washed down with bottles of strong French beer.

Their hunger and thirst satisfied, George and Dai placed their kit-bags behind their heads as make-shift pillows and settled down to the longest sleep they had enjoyed since they had left Jarrow at the start of the 300 mile march down the spine of England four weeks earlier.

'Sleep well while you can George my lad our big adventure

begins tomorrow,' said Dai Powell. *'You will find out soldiers have to snatch their sleep while they can.'*

The next 24 hours were a blur, passing through the French and Spanish immigration officials at Perpignan without any problems, arriving at the Republican base at Barcelona and rocking and rolling on an army truck to Albacete where, it seemed, they were not given time to breathe. They were inducted, examined by the army doctor, kitted out by the quarter master sergeant with brownish-tinged khaki of uniforms of the Republican Army.

The next stop was to the armoury where another sergeant handed them a rifle and bayonet each plus a box of ammunition and ordered to the rifle range. *'Bloody hell this a 303 British Enfield P14 rifle used before and during the Great War, so we are not exactly joining a modern army,'* commented Dai Powell as a corporal marched them up to the firing range where they spent an hour in target practise.

When they were marched back to their hut they learned what all the rush had been about. With 26 other English, Scotch and Welsh lads, who had been inducted that day, they were brought to attention be their beds when a Captain strode into the hut and informed them: *'Alright men stand easy,'* snapped the immaculately uniformed officer. *'Get a good night's sleep. Tomorrow you will be transported to take part in the defence Madrid. We have intelligence that a Nationalist force under the command of General Emilio Mola are keyed up to attack the capital and bring a quick end to the war. Good luck men. Fight with pride!'*

So two nervous Brits, George Stewart from Jarrow and Dai Powell from South Wales were about to go into action with the first International Brigade units to reach the front line fighting alongside German, French and Polish volunteers. '*This is it George lad,*' said the Welshman. '*There is nowhere to hide now!*'

Neither of them slept that night!

8

No young warrior goes into battle for the first time in their lives without feeling fear--the apprehensive Dai Powell and George Stewart were no exception as, with full packs across their backs, 303 rifles slung with fearsome 22 ½ inch bayonets attached, and steel helmets perched precariously, they crawled up to the front line on the outskirts of Madrid.

They soon knew they were in range of the barking fire arms of the opposing Nationalist invaders attacking the metropolis as the dum dum bullets screamed by their ears hitting the ramparts where they were holed up. Despite concerns by supporters of the Republic, or Loyalists as they were known, was that they were in danger of being outgunned, at the outset of the Civil War they still commanded the allegiance of half the nation's armed forces. Although the Nationalist insurgents were led by General Emilio Mola in this initial attack on Madrid the overall leader that emerged to lead the fascists during the three years war was General Francisco Franco and as *Caudillo* of peacetime Spain between 1936 until his death in 1975.

But the icon who inspired the Loyalists in these early days was the highly emotional *La Pasionaria,* eighth of eleven children born to a Vizcaya coalminer, in the Basque country, Antonio Ibárruri and Juliana Gómez. *La Pasionara* moved to Madrid at the outset of the Civil War to become the editor of left-wing newspaper *El Mundo Obrero (The World Laborer).*

Dai and George attended a crowded cinema in Madrid on the night before they were marched up to the front line and heard *La Pasionaria* make an impassioned speech when her first rallying cry in Spanish and English was heard after sneering against the hated fascists as they attacked Madrid: *!No Pasaran! (They Shall Not Pass).*

The test for the entrenched Stewart and Dai Powell came on the second day of the attack on Madrid when the opposing General Mola, most of the men at his disposal being units of the Army of Africa, ordered Colonel Jose Varela to attack the north-west wing of the Madrid defences.

During the following week the Nationalists pushed the Popular Army backwards until the first International Brigade units were called up to stablise the front line. The first time the two Jarrow marchers saw blood came when a green-uniformed Nationalist leapt over their rampart lifting his bayonet-attached rifle aiming at George Stewart's chest. With a quick and instinctive movement, as he spotted the danger facing his pal, Dai Powell fired his British Enfield P14 rifle from the hip. A remarkable shot for a rookie soldier in his first engagement which climaxed as the marauder fell like a log into the trench, an ominous maroon hole in his forehead oozing his life blood.

George Stewart was dazed, shaking with nerves, and near to

tears as he looked first at the dead body of the enemy soldier and then into his pal's eyes.

'Oh Dai, thank you, thank you,' he stammered. *'You know I once read the writings of the poet Wilfred Owen from the 1914 Great War in which he said:*

"'Christ is literarily in no-man's land.

There men often hear His voice: Greater Love hath no man

Than this, that a man may lay down his life- for a friend.'"

'Thank you again Dai for being with me today!

Dai Powell, modestly tried to brush away his friend's gratitude with a joke: 'Think nothing of it George bach! Just buy the beers when we get back to the canteen at the barracks.

The siege of Madrid lasted 15 days and ended in stalemate despite the Nationalists ploy to call up Hitler's Condor Legion to launch ruthless air attacks against civilians in the capital. After that bloody fortnight both sides were exhausted and it was clear to the Nationalists that any further frontal attacks on Madrid would be too costly.

George Stewart and Dai Powell were stood down with the rest of their unit and with the rest of the International Brigade were given a five day liberty pass to sample the delights of Madrid. On the first night the two mates got rolling drunk in the barracks canteen with George buying all the drinks, despite the not too convincing objections from Dai.

It was a source of humour to most of the International Brigade members in the canteen that night, having survived their first taste of enemy fire, that Dai Powell, despite surviving the siege of Madrid, should fall down the steps of the canteen and injure his leg.

The laughter was so loud that a threatening shout from the guardoom ordered the men to *'pipe down'* or they would find themselves being locked up for the night in the cells. But Dai was in deep pain as his pals staggered under his weight and lifted him to the base medical centre.

'What do you lot want?' queried the duty orderly as they propped the groaning Welshman on to a waiting-room chair. *'Our mate has hurt his leg,'* the International Brigadeers pleaded. *'He fell down the canteen steps and has injured his leg.'*

The orderly, a one stripe corporal, said cynically: *'Pissed out of his mind. Like the fuckin' rest of you I suppose. Leave him here and we'll look after him. You lot had better get back to your huts or you'll finish up for the rest of the night in the guardroom cells.'*

As the International Brigade men, including a rather reluctant George Stewart, sheepishly left the medical Centre the orderly turned towards Dai Powell: *'There is not doctor on duty here tonight . But I will call the enfermera who is in charge at the moment. She is a good nurse and will be able to deal with your problem.'*

Then turning towards the field telephone on his desk the orderly briskly turned the handle and waited for an answer.

'Hola, Hola,' he acknowledged the voice at the other end of the line. *'Is that Nurse Delgado? Oh yeah! Thank you Pilar but I have one of the International Brigade soldiers here at the Medical Centre who has hurt his leg. Can you come over, please ?'*

9

After 15 days helping Republican Army doctors in a medical station virtually working day and night with only snatches of sleep, assisting surgeons amputate limbs and other horrific, but too often unsuccessful, operations *Enfermera* Pilar Delgado was entitled to feel as shattered and exhausted as any front line soldier involved in the defence of Madrid against the insurgents.

As the duty nurse in charge of the International Brigade's medical centre the 18-year-old Pilar wearily dragged herself from her army cot, splashed cold water into her face to encourage a quick, if painful, awakening from the deep sleep that had mercifully enveloped her less than an hour earlier.

She donned her navy blue uniform, tied the starched apron adjusted the jaunty cap, threw her military issue red-lined cape around her shoulders, and lit the oil lamp at the side of the cot to illuminate her way across the barrack square *en route* to the medical centre.

Any reasonable person would have willingly forgiven her for

complaining as she faced an injured soldier who she soon diagnosed had sustained nothing but a badly sprained ankle.

'*Habla español?*', she asked the groaning patient, as she bent over to examine Dai Powell's throbbing foot.

The Welshman looked up sorrowfully as the effects of the four litres of *cerveza* and two glasses of *Fundador* brandy he had consumed began to wear off , exacerbating the pulsating pain.

'*No hablo mucho español,*' Dai Powell rejoined then, as he looked up at the pretty face of the young nurse who was tending his injury. *'I am sorry but I am English--or to be more precise I am Welsh.'* Pilar Delgado smiled broadly, indicating that she could understand English, and said: '*English is no problem because I learned it at school. You're from Gales eh! We know all about Pais de Gales in Asturias where I come from. My father and my two elder brothers work in the Asturias anthracite mines. What did you do before you came to Spain to fight with the International Brigade for the Republican cause?*'

Dai Powell was beginning to forget the discomfort of his damaged ankle as he began to appreciate how beautiful the nurse was. His pain dissolved in the surging tide of his testosterone.

'*I worked at the coal face at the pit in my home village in the Rhonda Valley,*' Dai explained, anxious to keep the conversation going with the emerald-eyed beauty.

But Pilar, as if she had decided that there had been enough chit chat for one evening got down to business again.

'*Well I have had a good look at your ankle and I am sure there is nothing broken,*' she said, adding with a grin. '*I'll just put a cold water bandage on it to stop the swelling. So you are going to live. But you would do well to take more water with your cervase in the future. I saw injuries a lot worse than that at the front line during the siege of Madrid. I cannot write you a note to excuse you duty although you will find it difficult to march. I'll speak to your drill sergeant and ask that you be given light duties for the next few days.'*

Dai seemed reasonably satisfied with Nurse Pilar's prognosis but could not resist making one last request.

'Is there anything in Republican Army regulations that say a common soldier may not ask a military nurse out for dinner one evening?' he said pleadingly.

Pilar Delgado had already decided that she was quite attracted to this Welsh lad, who with his ebony hair and deep brown eyes could be passed off as a handsome Spaniard. But her Catholic upbringing prevented her from appearing too bold.

'No there are no rules such as that,' she said. *But the fact is that I am here in the war zone, just like the other nurses to do a hard job. It is a fact that the Medical Service don't exactly approve of nurses liasing with soldiers. But I am a grown up woman and can make my own mind up. Let's wait until your ankle is better then ask me again. Neither of us know where we are going to be deployed next in this awful war!'*

10

Having successfully fended off the Nationalist attack on Madrid, orders were sent from the Republican Army heaquarters that the International Brigade, having performed quite creditably during the attack on the capital, should be given extra guerilla training to equip them as an elite front line force.

So issued with back packs containing dynamite, ammunition, and other explosives the multi-national volunteers were sent off on manoeuvres for two weeks designed to harden them up for all-out war against general Franco's insurgents.

In charge were special non-commissioned officers from the 81-year-old Guardia Civil of which 53% of their men stayed loyal to the Spanish Second Republic during the Civil War. Mainly long-serving sergeants they were as tough as US Marines, known as leather necks, or England's teak-hard SAS.

Even Dai Powell with his swollen and painful ankle was not allowed to miss the manoeuvres or as Sergeant Pepe Tejero shouted at him in fractured English: *'Listen Taffy if you think you are going to malinger and stay stinking in your cot   then you are fuckin'* mistaken. *I have assigned you to your unit's cocina during the manoeuvres. You will be discharging a most important kitchen duty during the next 14 days and that is peeling every patata, scrubbing the dirt off every cabbage, and washing the grease off all the cooking pans until your dainty fucking hands are bleeding like a stuck pig. Maybe that will teach you not to get pissed, like some nancy boy, and twist yout fucking ankle when your mates are going out on a battle manoeuvre.'*

Dai Powell was already barrack-room-wise enough not to argue with a top NCO like Tejero and swallowing his pride at the bollocking he had just been given, timidly answered: *'Aye Sergeant I'll do my best!'*

Segeant Tejero was not the man to let a common soldier have the last word, snapped back: *'You'll have todo better than your best if you don't want to be peeling potatoes for the rest of your bloody career with the International Brigade.'*

Later that night Dai and George Stewart lay talking to each other on their adjoining bunks.

'What a total bastard that Tejero is,' moaned the Welshman. *'I can't help that I hurt my leg.*

'It's a good job I am not going out for battle practise with you lads otherwise Sergeant Terejo might find the sharp end of my bayonet rammed up his asshole .'

But at eight o'clock the following morning Dai sat on a low stool outside the unit's mobile kitchen staring glumly at a five foot high mound of muddy potatoes. Looking down at the small potatoe peeler, its wooden handle bound with cord, he moaned in disgust.

'Fucking hell to peel all those spuds will take me a week rather

than a day,' he snorted. *'It'll be like trying to flatten the slag heap at the Bryntor Colliery with a teaspoon.'*

Enviously Dai watched his pal George Stewart and the rest of the British batallion march off to the manouvres desperately sad that he was missing out on the fun. The only respite from his drudgery and boredom came when Corporal Tom Adams, the 'cookie' in charge of the field kitchen, an 18 stone former foundry man from Sheffield, pittying the Welshman's sore and bleeding hands brought him out a mug of steaming hot cocoa.

'Here Dai, lad, get this down your belly before one of those Guardia Civil shit sergeants see it and put me to work helping you peel those 'taters.'

But what really made what had so far been a day of misery was the sight of a solid-tyred Field Ambulance pull up at the side of the parade ground where a medical unit had been set up under canvas. Out poured the driver, a medical officer wearing the three shoulder pips of a captain, and--a sight for Dai Powell's bloodshot eyes--the trim uniformed figure of Nurse Pilar Delgado.

Dai knew under military discipline it would go hard with him if he deserted his potatoe-peeling deployment and cross the holy of holy's in any army, the barrack drill square, to pass the time of day with the elegant *Enfermera Delgado*.

But in line with the old cliché that everything comes to him that waits, an hour later with the mountain of spuds, seemingly, only a tad lower than it was at 8am, Pilar appeared walking towards him on the circuitous route around the barrack square en route to the ladies room.

She was surprised when she saw him because she had not associated him to being there. *'Hola Dai,'* she trilled. *'I can see the army are keeping you busy.'*

Matching the humour that she had introduced into the repartee, the Welshman cracked back: '*Yeah, yeah Pilar darling. They say the quickest way for a soldier to work his way up to a General's star is by peeling potatoes.*

'*But it is lovely to see you darling. While we are both here why don't you accept the invitation that I made to you in Madrid to have a meal or a drink together?*'

Pilar Delgado had thought about that invitation several times since she had met Dai Powell in the batallion medical centre when the International Brigade had been stood down after the National insurgents' abortive bid to wrest the Spanish capital from the control of the Republican army.' For she was attracted to the dark haired, brown eyed lad who spoke with an almost melodious Welsh accent. Where a week before she had hesitated, she now was determined to follow her heart and get to know Dai Powell better.

'*But how can you get away from the camp here you are obviously a bit out of favour,*' she said. '*The job you are doing, peeling vegetables is usually handed out as a punishment to soldiers who have broken the regulations.*'

Dai, feeling a tinge of excitement that Pilar was about to soften her stance and accept his invitation for a date, said: '*Look I am not confined to barracks, or being punished for any misdemeanour. I am getting the usual bull-shite from the sergeant because you had advised I should be given light duties until my injured ankle healed. To be honest I would much rather be out on battle manoeuvres with my mate George Stewart and my other International Brigade comrades.*'

Pilar Delgado hesitated for a moment as she thought of a ploy that would enable her to arrange an assignation with Dai Powell that very evening.

'*Look Dai, I have an idea,*' she said eagerly. '*We, that is the Medical Unit I am here with today, are going to take the ambulance down to an aldea called Llano about seven kilometres away. Some 20 children of the village have already been struck down with chickenpox and the local has appealed to us for help to contain the epidemic. So the doctor in charge of the unit, and myself, plus the soldier who drives the ambulance, are setting off at 5pm for the village where we will be conducting a mass innoculation of the village children. You can join our expedition if you like--you will come in useful if only to make the coffee to sustain us while we are working.*

'*We should be free about 8pm and you and I could get a meal or drink at the village bar. I understand that the base have a truck laid on to return to the barracks at 11pm each evenng for any military personnel wanting to get back to the base.*'

It only took Dai Powell five seconds to agree to Pilar's suggestion and he said: '*Right a wonderful idea Pilar. I'll see you by the ambulance at 5pm.*'

11

As so often happens in civil wars the conflict between man and man, brother against brother, father against son, and exacerbating the human tragedy between sisters, mothers and daughters developed into somewhat of a lull for a few weeks after the Nationalists failed to capture Madrid.

Although there were signs during that period when front to front fighting had ceased there were still gory incidents which kept the pot boiling. Hitler's murderous Condor Legion launched a number of investigatory air attacks in support of General Franco's Nationalist forces who had been formally recognised as Spain's government by their allies Germany and Italy. It was a short fallow period of almost tit for tat incidents which kept the flames of hatred between faction and faction.

The Republicans retaliated against the Nationalist atrocities by executing, in Alicante, José Antonio Primo de Rivera, the leader of the Falange a group that aped the Italia facists, German nazis, and Belgian rexists that all claimed they welded the working class and fervour for nationalism together.

La Pasionaria was the Communist heroine who refused to allow any forgiveness towards the Nationalists. Always dressed in dramatic black she was regarded as a revolutionary saint by the working class. The Nationalists hated the Passion Flower and they spread a rumour that she had killed a priest by using her teeth to bite out his throat. The Catholic Church were not forgiven for many years for allying themselves with the Nationalists and only after General Franco's death in 1975 Rome and the Spanish state were truly reconciled.

The bitterness reached a crescendo again when Nationalist aircraft bombed the city of Barcelona recognised as a hotbed for the Communist cause.

But all of this brutality and detestation throughout a tragically split Spain did not overly bother the intrepid International Brigadeer Dai Powell and the beautiful *Enfermera Militar* Pilar Delgado on what was to be a bizarre first date.

Dai came out of the evening having earned a lot of Brownie points for helping Pilar and the army doctor as they set about inoculating every child in the stricken *pueblo* of Llano. First of all he gently took the babes in his muscular arms from their mothers cradling them fondly whispering sweet talk as he carried them to Pilar or the doctor for their injection and the returning them to the loving caresses of their worried Mums.

Then came the older children who he persuaded to line up with military precision, giving each one an encouraging pat on the back as he marched them up for their innoculation. The kids loved him and so did Pilar.

After the last innoculation against the dreaded chickenpox infection had been given Dai made a pot of strong coffee for the doctor, Pilar and their driver. Pilar got the OK from the doctor to stay on for an hour or so to have a meal in the village with Dai.

The doctor, equally as delighted as Pilar, with the way Dai had helped them with the inoculations agreed.

'*Of course Nurse that will be fine,*' said the medic. '*I'll deal with any emergencies back at the barracks until you return to the barracks on the evening truck. Oh and thanks Private Powell you were a tremendous help to us tonight and I'll commend you to your sergeant when I see him.*'

Arm in arm, as sweethearts do, Pilar and Dai strolled down to the village bar. The Welsh lad had collected his money at a pay parade two days earlier so he had a few pesetas to treat them to supper and a glass of wine when they reached the bar which was crowded with soldiers from the barracks. He spotted his pal George sitting on his own in the corner and beckoned him over to join Pilar and himself at their table.

As George Stewart accepted the invitation and sat down at the table Dai Powell introduced him to Nurse Delgado: '*This is George Stewart, my very best friend Pilar,*' he said warmly. *We have been to hell and back together over the past few months. It started when we set off from George's home town Jarrow, which is in the North East of England. With 200 other out-of-work men from the town we took four weeks to march 300 miles to London and demand the government take action to aid the unemployed.*'

Pilar was quite excited about the warm introduction of his pal and addressed her reaction directly at George: '*News of that epic Jarrow March reached the men in my family, all of them out of work coal miners, back in Asturias. They are full of admiration for men like you Senor Stewart and of course our mutual amigo Dai.*'

Stewart, hastening to make it clear that he did not want to appear rude, interrupted: '*Sorry to break your train of thought Pilar, but please address me by my first name George. I am fascinated that you come from coal mining stock. We are all in the class war together. That is why Dai and I volunteered for the International Brigade together in order to strike a blow for all the miners, and all the other downtrodden workers of the world.* '

Pilar continued her hard-hitting harangue against social injustice. '*We have a terrible situation here in Spain where we already have one million out of work. One million men without any income in a country where, unlike England, there is no unemployment money. The Chinese, supposed to be one of the world's most undeveloped nations, those working in the rice paddy fields, I mean, are better off than the labourers in Spain where, it is widely known, we have families living, on a starvation diet of root vegetables and boiled greens stolen from the nearest farms and fields.*

'*My father Paul Delgado is 48 years of age but looks like a bowed over man of 70 because of the backbreaking work he has had to do in the Asturias anthracite mines for the past 34 years. No wonder he went on strike against the conditions with 30,000 other anthracite miners.*

'*So we fight with the passion and bravery of our icon La Pasionaria for the cause of world Communism, or Socialism, call it what you like.*'

Dai Powell, did not hesitate to endorse the zealous emotions of his two friends, and said: '*Now there are other diabolical political factions like the Fascists of Italy and National Socialists of Germany trying to hang their banner to the cause of the world's workers. But don't let them pull wool over your eyes they are fighting for all-out totalitarian, dictatorial one-party government rather than give the workers a vote under a democratic system of elected representatives.*

'If the Republic lose this Civil War be warned Spain will be jumping from the frying pan into the Franco-and accompanying tyranny!.

'Now enough of this heavy stuff what do you fancy to eat. This bar's Menu del Noche is a home made estofado carne de vaca--a rustic beef stew George just to improve your Spanish.'

All three youngsters opted for the *estofado* washed down with a litre *jarra* of local *vino tinto* and a basket of crusty *pan integral*. All for less than it would cost for a pack of cigarettes back in England.

The attractive Spanish senorita, the ardent Welshman from the Valleys and the dour *Geordie* from the derelict shipyards of north east England gelled quickly and after what Dai Powell irreverently called the, *The First Supper,* reacted towards each other as warmly as the legendary Three Musketeers.

'Pilar how did your family react to you joining the Republican army medical service?' queried Dai Powell of the attractive nurse he was, albeit optimistically, beginning to claim as his *amiga* .

There was a quick dampening of the emerald eyes as Pilar turned away as if, for a moment, hoping that her new friend had not asked the question. *'Well my father was really proud that I wanted to do my part in the fight for Socialist values,'* she said with a sad shake of her head.

'My mother Maria Serra Delgado did not really say anything but I knew she approved what I had done when she gave me a big hug when I left home to join the medical service. I was not surprised when my two older brothers Carlos and Tomas congratulated me

and presented me with a real leather military holdall which they had bought between them.

'Now I come to the saddest thing for our family my youngest brother, Rafa, had become involved with the German version of national socialism and regards Adolf Hitler as a demi-god. He is only 18 and has gone and joined the Nationalist army and has split our family down the middle.

'It is not unusual in this cruel Civil War and I have heard of cases where father fights against his sons, were brothers on opposite sides aim their rifles against each other.

'The most poignant point of Rafa's decampment is to see my mother pull a warm shawl around her shoulders at dawn each morning when she goes to mass to say prayers for the soul of her youngest child .'

The bonhomie, the fraternal freindliness and harmony of their supper and depth of their discourse was abruptly ended when a squad of black bereted Military Policemen. The burly sergeant major in change shouted loud enough to silence the crowded bar: *'Listen up all of you. All military personell must return to the cuartel immediately. There will be several trucks from the camp here in the next quarter of an hour to transport you all back to the barracks. Once there you are advised to get to a good sleep because you will be called on parade at 9 o'clock tomorrow when you all be told of your next deployment. Good luck all of you please leave this village as quietly as possible, remember local people will be trying to get to sleep.'*

So Dai Powell's first date with the lovely Pilar Delgado came to a hasty end with a hurried kiss on the cheek as the three of themselves descended at the camp guard room from the truck.

12

More than 600 men from the 30,000 or so volunteers, of all nationalities, that eventually fought with the International Brigades during this hideous three year civil war lined up at dawn on the frost blanketed parade ground the following morning.

The British Battalion, consisting almost entirely of out-of-work blue collar workers, included 174 Welsh miners, who like Dai Powell, were well versed in street- fighting with policemen during their bitter industrial strikes.

They were addressed by the Colonel commanding the garrison.

'Having fought so gallantly a few weeks back to defend our beloved Madrid now is your chance for further glory,' yelled the dapper Republican officer who had served under the emerging Francisco Franco when the crack Spanish Foreign Legion were fighting the Moroccan mountain tribes in the late 1920's. He was one of the officer's who refused to turn his back on the Loyalist government of the day. It was in fact one of the strange facets of the

Spanish Civil War that a soldier's loyalty was often influenced by where, and what unit, he was serving with at the time.

'*The Nationalists, having failed in their recent attack on Madrid, are now trying to cut off the capital from the rest of Republican Spain,*' said Colonel Felipe Perez, rapping his mallaca cane against his highly polished riding boots. '*Our intelligence people say that the Nationalists are about to mount an attack on the Coruna Road, 40 kilometres north of Madrid. You will all be deployed to the site, we are informed, where the Nationalist will launch their bid to isolate Madrid from the main bulk of the Republican army. We will move as a defensive force to block the Nationalist ploy in a fleet of lorries, trucks, and other essential supporting units in three hours .*

'*Although the Nationalists claim the Church of Rome supports their cause I still send you in to battle with the humble message of God Go With You.*'

Dai Powell managed to wave to Pilar as she sat next to the driver when the ambulance moved off at the rear of the convoy of lorries wending its way towards the Coruna Road a one and half hours ride away. He sat next to his buddy George Stewart in the swaying truck, both of them a little pensive about what lay ahead although they had already experienced the trauma of facing enemy fire in the earlier siege of Madrid. '*Here we go again pal,*' said Dai, who earlier in the morning had been promoted to Corporal by his Captain for the help he had given to the medical unit at the pueblo of Llano the previous evening when every child in the village had been inoculated against catching the dreaded chickenpox.

By midday they had rattled through the desolate Spanish countryside. The morning sunshine although tepid was strong enough to tease away the thin frost that had peppered the tarmac of the parade ground during the cold hours before dawn. The soldiers were glad of the warmth from the greatcoats of those that were lucky to have been issued with them or alternatively the ponchos made of blankets of those less fortunate. They munched on the packets of stale rustic *pan integral* and rock hard *Manchego* cheese the cookhouse had handed each one of them to consume as *desayuno* on the move accompanied by 25 litres aqua to each lorry load

'*I'd give a day's pay for one of my Mam's fried breakfasts,*' said George Stewart nostalgically, prompting equally pensive support from his pal.

'*Four slices of crispy back bacon with two eggs turned over,*' said the salivating Dai.

George joined the wistful wail: '*Fried bread, and if we were lucky, plump pig's kidneys…*' Dai, not a one for etiquette, interrupted amusingly: '*…and black pudding smothered in baked beans that activate your bowels for the rest of the fucking day prompting the wind to blow free.*'

The repartee set their comrades laughing raucously and shouting irreverent jokes about '*farting*', as fighting soldiers tend to do, as they moved up to the front line. For some of them their destiny would reach climax sooner than any of them would imagine.

A convoy of 40 trucks travelling in close order was not a tactic that would have been used by any army in wars that followed when the emphasis would be more on air power. But war planes were fairly rare in the early days of the Spanish Civil War and those that were eventually in action were mainly provided by Hitler's Condor Legion and units of the Italian airforce who all flew on behalf of the insurgent Nationalists and made a decisive impact on the outcome of the conflict which really was meant only to be between Spaniard and Spaniard.

But the men travelling in the Republican convoy to the front line were not dwelling about such macabre dangers as Dai Powell led them in a round of *'Sospan fach'*. The song spread from truck to truck until almost the whole convoy echoed with a lusty chorus that would not have disgraced the Aberdare Band Club on a Sunday evening. The loudest noise came from the 174 Welsh miners who had enlisted in the British Battalion.

'... *Sospan fach boiling by the door*
'Sospan fawr boiling on the floor...
Then a tumultuous explosion rocked the slow moving crocodile of trucks as soldiers and their NCO's nervously lifted the vehicles' canvas sides to see what had happened.

In dire realisation that a disaster had occurred, through the mist of dust and smoke word spread that the leading truck had drove over a Nationalist planted land mine and including it's load of 36 International Brigades' warriors had bleen blown to smithereens.

The two former Jarrow Hunger Marchers were in the convoy's third truck. Dai Powell, with his brand new corporal's stripes already sewn on his tunic was the first to jump down and broke the shock of the moment by marshalling the men in his vehicle.

'*Come on lads,*' he shouted. '*Let's see if there are any injured who need help. Jump to it there is no time to waste.*'

The new responsibility of leadership fitted the Welshman as comfortably as a bespoke lounge suit crafted in the prestigious Saville Row. An attribute that would stand him in good stead long after the Spanish Civil War had passed into the annals of man's inhumanity to man.

Dai's squad were quick to the site of the badly shattered lorry and had calmly brought some order to the convoy before the senior sergeants travelling at the rear of expedition had made the tortuous struggle to the front of the long line of camouflaged heavy duty vehicles.

They laid out the dead. In detail 29 badly smashed bodies, or in some cases, tragically bloodstained fragments of human bodies. As his men dealt with the catastrophically crushed cadavers, of once doughty members of the International Brigade, Corporal Dai Powell, of the British Battalion busied himself administering emergency treatment to the survivors.

By the time the travelling ambulance had painstakingly crawled the one and half kilometres, from the rear of the convoy edging past nearly 40 parked trucks, Dai had laid out the seven injured soldiers in order with the most injured, in his opinion at the head of queue.

Enfermera Pilar Delgado was first to alight from the ambulance followed closely followed by Captain Alberto Godoy, the Medical Officer.

'I can see you have sorted the injured out in some sort of order Dai,' said Pilar. *'Tell me how you rate the worst of the those injuries it may save vital time and help the doctor if he has to conduct emergency surgery those most seriously hurt.'*

Corporal Powell, his khaki uniform badly bloodstained from lifting the injured men clear of the shattered truck and administering some first aid, considered Pilar's query.

'The lad at the front of the line, Craig Russell, as you can see has lost half his right arm, to the elbow in the explosion,' explained Dai Powell. *'He has lost a lot of blood and I just haven't got the facility*

to help him much more. Perhaps the Medical Officer should see him first and treat him before he succumbs from blood loss.

'Next comes a Welsh lad, a former coal miner like myself, who is suffering from what looks like severe lacerations to the head and chest. But he seems to be holding his own but is obviously in need of pain killers.

'The rest have varying degrees of cuts, bruises and suffering and at the end of line I have laid out three men who are not showing any injuries, or signs of bleeding, but seem to be suffering from concussion, obviously as a result of the explosion which we think was caused by a land mine planted by the Nationalists, who apparently seem to be have been informed that this convoy was moving to the defence of the Corunna Road.'

Having listened to Corporal Powell's assessment and after examining the seven injured men Medical Officer Godoy had decided what his plan of action should be. Looking at the soldier who was driver of the ambulance he barked: '*Snap to it Private Diaz, erect the portable tent as quick as possible. I will need it as an emergency operating theatre inside half an hour. Also get a fire going and boil as many pots of water as you can.*'

Then, looking at Dai, Captain Godoy added: '*Once again we have to thank you Corporal Powell. If you please I would like you to help me in the operating theatre where I will have to perform emergency surgery on the boy who has lost part of his arm. This will leave Enfermera Delgado to administer treatment to the other six injured men. So let's get to it, team.*'

Things began to get really organised in the next hour. The commanding officer of the Republican task force ordered 38 trucks to move forward passing the wreck of the lorry blown up by the land mine. One of those trucks, plus the 38 members of the

International Brigade travelling in it, was ordered to stay behind as an escort guard for the ambulance, the operating theatre tent and the Medical personnel

The Medical Officer ordered Corporal Powell to gently clean up Private Graig Rusell, the man who had unfortunately lost part of his right arm, and get him ready for surgery.

The doctor explained he had to tidy up the jagged end of the jagged stump on his severed arm, to avoid problems for the injured man later in life.

'I will need to amputate some 25 millimetres from the stump,' Captain Godoy told Dai Powell. *'That will given me enough skin to wrap round the stump leaving it smooth and tidy.*

'If all goes well the new stump will serve him well without trouble for the rest of his life. Physically he seems quite good under the circumstances and appears fairly stabilised. Your job will be to administer ether to him which is all the anaesthetic we have with us. The more modern anaesthesia range of drugs will be in the fully equipped mobile field hospital which will not link up with us until we reach the Corunna Road.

'But don't worry Corporal Powell ether has saved many a wounded soldier's life in the past. In fact Crimean War medic Nikolay Ivanovich Pirogov was one of the first military surgeons to use ether as anaesthetic in a battlefield operation as early as 1847. You will administer the ether on a towel to the patients nose under my instructions during the operation.'

13

Corporal Dai Powell performed his duties as a makeshift anaesthetist with calmness, doing a stressful job which he had been neither trained or prepared for.

His efficiency was so admirable that he impressed Captain Alberto Godoy of the Republican Army Medical Corps, who successfully amputated a piece of Private Craig Russell 's already severed arm to prevent gangrene setting in saving the unfortunate British Battalion soldier from a premature death.

For the second time in a few hours Captain Godoy commended the Welshman to his superior officers and Dai Powell joined the elite band of soldiers who were honoured by instant promotion to Sergeant on the battlefield during the siege of the Corunna Road. He also was later given the distinction of being the first British member of the International Brigade to be awarded the blue, gold and red striped Medal of the Spanish Civil war.

Pleased and proud with the turn of events Sergeant Powell was saddened to have to say farewell for the time being to Nurse

Pilar Delgado, who had been ordered to escort and care for the unfortunate amputee Craig Russell who was being repatriated to the French border on the first leg of his long journey back to England. Pilar departed with an ambulance carrying Private Russell back to Perpignan on the French frontier via the Republican stronghold of Barcelona.

For the first time Dai kissed Pilar with passion as he said goodbye. *'Look after yourself darling,'* he whispered. *'Get back to me as soon as possible. When we do get together we'll talk about getting married. Now I have met the girl of my dreams I am not going to let you go easily. I want to spend the rest of my life with you.'*

Nurse Delgado was just as fervent in her farewell and assured her lover. *'Don't worry Dai querido. All the officers in the Republican Army Corps won't be able to keep me from joining up with you as soon as I have escorted my paitient to safety across the French border. I love you Dai Powell and there will never be another man for me.'*

A brave promise made by lovers in the midst of war. Sincere pledges which were often cruelly dissected by the vagaries and twists of battle.

14

The Nationalist insurgents were obsessed with capturing the Spanish capital and, having failed in their frontal attack on Madrid three weeks earlier, they tried to cut off the Republican Army from the rest of the country where it enjoyed the greatest support.

The Nationalists intention was clear when their commander, General Jose Varela, headed his strong contingent towards the Corunna Road which stretched 25 miles to the north of Madrid. For 12 days between the 3rd and 15th January 1937 General Varela's forces held a seven mile stretch of the road against fierce opposition by Republican troops.

Sergeant Dai Powell's squad from the International Brigades' British Brigade suffered terrible casualties as the fighting grew ever more intense. A motor cycle despatch rider reached him where he was holed up in a dense wood half as mile from where Varela's attack force had organised their battle HQ. The terse message read:

"You are ordered to attack the Nationalist headquarters and loosen their advantage. You will lead the attack yourself, Sergeant

Powell, following the death of your Lieutenant in action yesterday. I will try and move reinforcements up to you as soon as possible. Good luck.

Signed by: Colonel Felipe Perez:: 13th January 1937"

Dai Powell knew that it would take a shrewd battle plan and a lot of luck to overcome General Varela' s task force. His first move was to call on his pal George Stewart. *'We have been ordered to launch an onslaught against the Nationalist's, and, like it or not, following the loss of Lieutenant Morgan by a sniper's bullet yesterday, I have been put in charge by Colonel Perez,'* explained the Welshman to his pal. *'But in order to establish a chain of command to take over if I am wounded or killed I am appointing you George as my assistant, or in army terms, my second in command, with the title of Acting Corporal. If we both come safely through the task ahead, I promise you I will get your promotion to Corporal ratified with the appropiate pay rise.'*

Dai and George sat up in their roughly made dugout all that night mulling over their situation and planning tactics for the imminent battle to prevent the hated Nationalists bid to capture Madrid

As Republicans girded themselves to defend Madrid for a second time in little more than a month the icon of the left, *La Pasionaria,* gave them another bloodthirsty slogan of: *'Better to die on your feet than to live on your knees at the mercy of the Nationalist murderers.'*

This coupled with *La Pasionaria's* stubborn *war cry of No pasarán*--they shall not pass.

* * *

George Stewart was not of the same resilient stock as his best pal and was the type of reluctant soldier who needed his NCO to give him a reassuring arm around his shoulder to help him dismiss his worries

'*You are quite different to me Dai,*' George admitted to the friend who in a short space of time had become his sergeant. '*You seem to have taken to soldiering like a duck to water. For me everything we are asked to do is a puzzle. Don't you ever any doubts about making the right decision when we came out to Spain a few months ago to fight for the Republicans? Have you ever thought that we are caught in a war started by politicians? Or that we are being used as pawns between the Nationalists, supported by Hitler, Mussolini and the Catholic Church on one hand or the Republicans backed by Russia and Communism ?*

'*I know we came to Spain to strike a blow for the working class, to bring an end to the curse of unemployment, poverty and starvation? Are we really doing any more for our fellow workers in Britain than we did when we walked 300 miles from Jarrow to London?*'

Sergeant Dai Powell took several minutes to consider his friend's choleric criticism of the situation they found themselves in helping Spaniards in a tragic fight to the death with their fellow Spaniards even, in many heart-rending cases, against members of their own family.

He delved into his rucksack and found a litre bottle of *Fundador,* and grabbing two blue-rimmed enamelled mugs and poured them both slugs of brandy large enough to have killed a rutting Spanish donkey.

Placing in front of them a tin of American *Lucky Strike* cigarettes, he had bought at a Red Cross van during the night he had spent in Madrid *en route* from the Medical Unit to link with their squad's present bivouac just four kilometres from the insurgent Nationalist front line.

'Look George we have come a long way together,' said Dai, trying to bring some stability to the turbulent thoughts of his friend.

'You are my closest pal. I hope it will always stay that way. I feel a part of your family for your mother and father treated me like one of their own when I stayed with you all at Jarrow. I too have had serious doubts about whether we have done the right thing coming out here to fight for the Republican army. Yes there is no doubt, to a certain extent, we are being used by certain factions. Until a few days ago I had the same doubts as you.'

Dai explained that his whole perspective of what they were fighting for when he spent a night in Madrid.

'If you recall I had to stay behind with the Medical Unit, helping the surgeon amputate the arm of the soldier who was wounded by the Nationalist land mine which also killed 29 members of the International Brigades,' he said. *'I stayed one night on the way at the Republican casa cuartel in Madrid before travelling on to join you here near the Corunna Road.'*

Dai Powell was settling into his story, eager to explain the wonderful experience he had that memorable night in Madrid.

'I have been waiting anxiously to share this extraordinary revelation with you,' he said warming up to his impassioned disclosure. *'You remember the Medical Officer, Captain Albertto Godoy, who amputated that unfortunate boy's arm and who I had helped to innoculate the children in the village of Llano the previous evening? Well he also stayed over in Madrid that evening and invited me to join him and listen to a speech that the most eminent*

Republican of them all, Dolores Ibárruri, known by everybody as La Pasionaria, was making a political speech.'

Sergeant Powell admitted he was enthralled with *La Pasionaria*, totally under her spell and emphasised her dedication: '*Never in my life had I ever met a woman like her. It was akin to love at first sight. It is strange to say but it felt like an orgasm. Not the kind of romantic feelings I have for my beloved nurse, Pilar Delgado, who I hope to marry one day. But a sensual obsession for a 41-year old woman, old enough to be my mother, whose every word completely captivated me.*

'*She preaches fervently the opposite message than most of the world's democratic leaders are issuing and warns that the emergence of facism in Germany and Italy will eventually be globally catastrophic. A total opposite view, for instance, adopted by Neville Chamberlain, England's new prime minister who believes that appeasement is the way to deal with Hitler.*

'*It is imperative, is the message she preaches so ardently, for the well being of the Spanish people that the Republicans, who she supports, resist the Nationalist insurgency and prevent the nation from having to don the yoke of facisim under a dictator.'*

Dai Powell described *La Pasionaria's* appearance.

'*I could not help but be moved by her looks and sincerity,'* he stressed. '*Although she was dressed in sombre black with a peep of rope sandals below the hem of a long dress. Yet she had the poise and dignity of a highly bred duchess, rather than the eighth of eleven children born to a poverty-stricken coal mining family at Gallarta in 1895,* in the Basque region

'*So George, my friend, she is, class-wise, one of us. Born, bred and schooled within the confines of working class unemployment and poverty. In her early post-school day she earned a scanty living as a seamstress. Inevitably she moved towards marriage and coupled with a coal miner and spawned six children, but in an era of poverty when young life was often curtailed by malnutrition, only two of her deprived offspring reached adulthood.*

'Her family's financial plight became even more precarious when her husband was sent to prison for leading a miners' strike. In the next few years she became an ardent campaigner to improve conditions for oppressed women in Spain.'

The two International Brigade soldiers refilled their mugs of brandy and lit up their *Lucky Strike* cigarettes before Dai Powell continued his outline of *La Pasionaria's* battle for women's rights in 20th Century Spain.

'She claimed that married women, at the time, were domestic slaves without any human rights,' Dai outlined *La Pasionaria's* poignant plea on behalf of the hardworking female drudge's in Spain. *'Married women, she said sadly, gave up their personality and surrendered themselves to a life of sacrifice. They became enslaved to their children and later baby-sitters for their grandchildren. The one thing I remember about La Pasionaria's impressive invective was when she finally said: "My mother once told me what it was like to be married saying it meant to sew, to give birth and to weep. To weep over a woman's misfortunes, to weep over our powerlessness. To weep over our innocent children, to whom all we could offer was cuddles soaked with our tears. To weep over lives filled with pain, without prospects, with no escape route. It all opened a deluge of bitter tears with a permanent curse in the heart and blasphemy on our tongues."*

'You see, my friend George, that La Pasionaria has all her life fought an unselfish Crusade for all the underprivileged, underpaid, abused or unemployed people around her. That is why she is an

icon for every man and woman who are fighting for the Republicans against the Nationalist insurgents. That is why she is warning the world against the emerging curse of facism from such cruel regimes in totalitarian, dictator dominated cruel regimes in Germany and Italy.

'That is why I will to do everything to support what she is fighting for in this Civil War at risk, like every soldier. I hope what I have told you, my friend, you will stay shoulder to shoulder with me in this battle to provide justice for the working classes throughout the world including of our compatriots in England.'

George Stewart paused for a moment and replied: '*If La Pasionaria's eloquence has influenced you so profoundly Dai pal then I'm with you all the way and sorry for previous doubts.*'

15

Now, as Sergeant Dai Powell's heartfelt lecture wound down, expounding his belief in the importance *La Pasionaria's* inspiring leadership was to the Republican cause, he unveiled a cunning plan for the impending assault on the Nationalist task force embedded on the strategic Corruna Road to his close buddy Acting Corporal George Stewart.

Stewart had been given his promotion to 'Acting Corporal' by Dai following the death of their unit's Lieutenant by enemy fire three days earlier. It left the Welsh Sergeant in command of a battle group of 25 soldiers, of all nationalities, who had volunteered for service with the International Brigade.

Powell had been given orders to make a significant assault to break the Nationalist task force's stranglehold on a seven mile stretch of the Corunna Road-- in an insurgent effort for the second time to capture Madrid.

Sergeant Powell's small group was isolated from the main Republican company encamped 15 kilometres away from the Nationalist deployment. It was a formidable task ahead as he explained to his pal George Stewart, who he had appointed as his assistant on the field of battle.

'*The Nationalists are holding that seven mile stretch of road with 78 men, so before we start we know we will be outnumbered, and outgunned, by a force more than a third larger than ours,*' he told the Acting Corporal from the north east of England. '*So if we are to succeed in what looks like a near impossible task, George, we will have to rely on the element of surprise to even the odds against us.*

'*I intend to use a battle tactic that worked wonders in the war between the Greeks and Trojans more than 3,000 years ago. The Greeks had won many battles against the Trojans but had found it difficult to scale the walls of the enemy's capital city of Troy.*

'*The clever Greek commander, Odysseus, ordered a huge wooden horse to be built, and pulled into the city. It was hollow inside so that a platoon of crack Greek soldiers could hide inside it. Once the statue had been completed the Greek warriors and their leader climbed inside. The citizens of Troy were highly amused with the wooden horse and thought it to be harmless. Simultaneously the Greek Fleet, that was anchored menacingly in the nearby bay, sailed away. The beleagured Trojans were relieved in the belief that the Greeks had withdrawn and retired from the battle.*

'*That night the Trojans spent the night in a drunken orgy. When they lapsed into a hopeless stupor the heavily armed Greek soldiers poured out of the wooden horse and slaughtered the comatose Trojans.*'

The story so intrigued George Stewart that he asked naively: '*But where are we going to get a wooden horse from? Oh I am sorry I said that, Dai, it was a very silly question.*'

Dai Powell laughed uproariously, and then made amends by

trying to save the blushes of his pal: *'Not so silly my friend. Because we are going to use our own version of the Wooden Horse of Troy.'*

Sergeant Powell then unfolded the guileful plan he had devised for the downfall of the Nationalist task force encamped so triumphantly entrenched along the Corunna Road .

'As you know I have had several of our men out scouting the terrain for a couple of days searching for any weakness in the Nationalist's defence,' he explained. *'I think I know the chink in their armour, their Achilles heel and how we can use the Wooden Horse technique.'*

For reasons best known to themselves the Nationalists have decided not to take a field kitchen with them to the Corunna Road deployment instead they send a mobile *"comida carro"* out from their missions main headquarters, several kilometres from the front line, which arrives on the dot of seven o'clock each evening. It carries a hot dinner for every man and enough food for breakfast and the rest of the following day.

'This food wagon is manned by only two men,' said Dai. *'A sergeant cook and a private. We also have discovered these two men stop at a village en route to open a few bottles of beer and munch their own sandwiches at 6-30 every evening in a copse at the edge of the Corunna Road. We will be waiting with our full complement of 25 men to hijack the wagon, capture the two "cookies" or kill them if we have to. That vehicle will be our Wooden Horse. We will clear the vehicle of all the kitchen equipment and our men will all hide inside.*

'Our men, will all be armed with Tommy Guns, that the Republicans have been gifted by supporters in the USA. The Thompson M1928A1 sub machine gun is exactly the right weapon for the close combat with its 100 round drum magazine for this

operation and, if our tactics are successful, our lads will sweep the Nationalists away in just a few salvos.'

The following day Sergeant Powell called all his men together for a briefing on the importance of an action that could be of great significance to the Republican cause.

'It is vital that we go into this action realistically,' he said thumping the tea chest, that served as his make-shift desk. *'We will have the advantage of surprise over the enemy and we must make absolutely certain we do not throw our weapon's superiority away. The Tommy Gun is absolutely the finest weapon in the world at close range.*

'If it was good enough for gangster chief Al Capone's hoodlums when they shot seven of the Dion O'Bannion rival North Street gang in a Chicago garage on 14 February 1929, forever known as the Saint Valentine's Day massacre. It is good enough for us.

'Collectively your Tommy Guns will be primed with 2,500 shells. If that is not enough to send 75 Nationalist pigs to the Devil then you don't deserve to call yourselves soldiers. Our objective is to kill 75 Nationalist insurgents--kill them quickly like a butcher slaughtering pigs in abbatoir.

'I don't want any fucking prisoners--do I make myself fucking clear?'

There was no answer to that query. Sergeant Powell from South Wales had given his orders in concise and brutal fashion. The silence from the 25 men of the British Battalion under his command sat in silent shock at what they had heard. Few of them would sleep soundly that night!

16

Despite a restless night mulling over the gruesome task that Sergeant Dai Powell had set them the 25 men of the International Brigade's British Battalion were keyed up for action.

First came the vital chore of hi-jacking the food wagon and putting the Nationalist army cook-sergeant and his assistant out of action. Jock Ellis, a former out of work riveter, from Clydeside's idle shipyards and unemployed collier Trefor Williams from Amanford were delegated by Sergeant Powell to neutralise the two Nationalist "cookies".

A well aimed throw from Ellis saw his knife fly straight to the Adam's apple of the Nationalist sergeant. As his comrade, shocked with what at happened to his NCO, instinctively reached for his rifle Private Trefor Williams triggered his Tommy Gun with all the aplomb of a Al Capone hit man.

Having been applauded and patted on the back for a slick job Ellis and Williams were chosen by Sergeant Powell to take over the driver's cabin of the food wagon. As it rolled ominously, the rest of their Battallion were squashed inside the vehicle which had been stripped of all it's kitchen equipment and metal containers of steaming food.

Less than 20 minutes later as the food wagon rocked in to the Nationalists' forward base on the Corunna Road to the cheers of men hungering for their evening meal. The double doors at the rear of the wagon were flung open as the British Brigadiers jumped out, their Tommy Guns spraying along the Nationalist lines time and time again. Until an ominous silence bore witness to an overwhelming Republican victory with 75 Nationalist soldiers completely wiped out inside nine minutes without having been given the chance to reach their weapons and retaliate against the deadly chatter of those 25 Republican Tommy Guns.

'*Well done my bonny lads,*' shouted the excited Dai Powell, his adrenalin still surging at the overwhelming success of their mission.

Acting Corporal George Stewart was shaking with the shock of the victory and asked: '*Shall we bury the dead, Sergeant?*'

Dai Powell roared back: '*No we fucking well will do no such thing. Let's get the fuck out of here before those Nationalist bastards send up reserves to see what has happened to their task force.*'

The following day a despatch rider wheeled his motor cycle into the Republican encampment with a message that the Nationalists had withdrawn from from their attack on the Corunna Road. Both sides, with casualties on both sides mounting, considered that the situation on the Corunna Road had become stalemate.

Spain and the rest of the world was shocked and reviled at the butchery that had been carried out during what became known as the Corunna Road massacre.

Yet it was a brilliant piece of military strategy that Sergeant

Dai Powell of the International Brigade's, British Battalion had devised. A marvellous act of leadership which earned him his third promotion in the past. His elevation from the rank of Sergeant to Lieutenant Dai Powell the following day meant he was the first member of the International Brigade to become an officer.

The bloody Battle for the Corunna Road from 13th December 1936 to 15th January 1937 had barely lasted a month leaving 630 dead Nationalists and 200 Republicans dead with scores of wounded on both sides.

Although it had been a bitter conflict it was within the bounds of military discipline. There were several atrocities in this war between Spaniards and Spaniards that were unspeakable and attracted the odium of the civilised world.

In the annals of wartime brutality the world will never forget when Communists in the Andalusian town of Ronda some 500 middle class citizens were herded to the Tajo Gorge and tossed hundreds of metres to their death. Or the horrific day in 1937 when Hitler intervened big-time in the Spanish Civil War a few weeks after the Battle of the Corunna Road. The Nazi dictator sent his flying Condor Legion to the quiet and undefended market town of Guernica, historically the home of Basque liberties. The town was totally without strategic value. The huge German bomber planes dropped wave after wave of bombs on the town a riddled it with machine gun fire. A thousand innocent civilians were slaughtered that awful day.

Nationalist leaders naively claimed they had no prior knowledge of this monstrous attack.

17

With the Nationalists deciding to call off their abortive siege of the Corunna Road the British Battalion unit, under the command of Sergeant Dai Powell, were recalled to link up again with the main force of the International Brigades which was beginning to earn a formidable reputation for their grit, determination and fierceness in battle.

The following morning after their return to the barracks the International Brigade were called on parade when Sergeant Powell, in front of 200 men, was promoted to Lieutenant for his outstanding leadership and bravery in the battle for the Corunna Road. He became the first of the foreign soldiers who had volunteered to fight for the Republican cause to be elevated from the ranks to commissioned officer.

Dai had felt pleased with his conduct in the Corunna Road fracas and in particular how he had burst into the tent and found and summarily despatched the unfortunate commander of the Nationalist task force. Captain Antonio Mesquida had awakened abruptly at the sound of the 25 Republican soldiers' storming the

Nationalist force controlling a seven mile stretch of the Corunna Road. When Sergeant Powell flung back the canvas entrance and fired his Tommy Gun from the hip, blowing the insurgent commander to eternity..

Dai Powell had also noted the behaviour of his close friend George Stewart, who had shrugged off his nervousness 48 hours earlier, to show outstanding valour in the action which was so successful that only five out of a force of 75 Nationalists were given the chance to fire their weapons. Only three of Sergeant Powell's men received injuries--all of them slight flesh wounds.

Immediately the parade, which had featured the ceremony of his promotion from sergeant to lieutenant, had been dismissed by the International Brigade commander, Colonel Felipe Perez, Dai Powell hared across the parade ground for a talk with the base Medical Officer, Captain Alberto Godoy. His object was to find out the whereabouts of the woman he loved, the beautiful Enfermera Pilar Delgado who had been ordered to care for and escort Craig Russell, the unfortunate soldier of the British Battalion who lost his arm during the Nationalist attack on the Republican convoy en route to the Corunna Road battle.

'Congratulations on your promotion to lieutenant,' Captain Godoy cordially greeted Dai at the base medical unit. *'It is no more than you deserve. What can I do for you?'*

Powell replied: *'Thank you for your good wishes Captain Godoy it is very kind of you to congratulate me. But what I have really come to ask you is if and when Nurse Delgado is going to rejoin this unit? As you know she was ordered to escort amputee Private Craig Russell to the French border, the first stage of his unfortunate repatriation to England.'*

Captain Godoy said he regretted that he had to tell Dai that Enfermera Delgado would not be returning to join the International Brigade Medical Unit, at least in the near future.

'After escorting Private Russell to the border near Perpignan Enfermera Delgado reported to Republican Headquarters at Barcelona and was immediately deployed to Malaga where it is expected that the Nationalists will mount their next attack,' the Medical Officer informed him. *'I know you are very close to this nurse Lieutenant Powell. But it might be a long time before you see her again, the way this dreadful war is going. Between you and me the only way you might be able to get together with the lovely nurse is to get you, or your unit, deployed to Málaga where the Republicans are starting to assemble a force to defend the city. It could be one of the most significant actions of the war so far.'*

Dai Powell thanked Captain Godoy for his advice and vowed he would act on it after he had consulted with his close friend George Stewart, whose promotion to the rank of corporal had, that day, been confirmed on his recommendation.

* * *

'I don't want to make a move without consulting you, George,' said the Welshman. *'After all we have been inseperable since we left Jarrow, over a year ago. But I must get together again with Pilar and I have decided to volunteer for service in Málaga, where the next important battle of this war is expected to start soon. That is either to volunteer as a group taking my unit with me, that includes you, or volunteer just personally. After all if you decide to stick with me it means you will be putting your life on the line.'*

Corporal Stewart did not hesitate in giving his reply.

'Look Dai, we started this adventure with the International

Brigades together and I hope we will stay together until we help the Republican's to win this class war and make a contribution for working men and women all over the world,' he said.

The die was cast. Later that day Lieutenant Powell marched into the International Brigades office and asked the Orderly to arrange an interview with the commanding officer, Colonel Felipe Perez.

'*As a matter of fact the Colonel is in now,'* said Private Mateus Gaida, the Colonel's Orderly. '*I am sure he will see you Lieutenant if he is not too busy with other business. Please take a seat and I'll ring Colonel Perez and find out when he will see you.'*

A few minutes later Powell marched smartly into the inner office and snapped off a soldierly salute at his commanding officer, Colonel Felipe Perez.

'*Sit down Lieuntenant,* '* invited the senior officer pointing the comfortable armchair on the opposite side of his imposing desk where a large Republican flag was draped behind. '*No need to stand on ceremony. What can I do for you?'*

Dai Powell, reacted quickly to the Colonel's question: '*Thank you for seeing me so quickly. I have asked to see you so that I can make a special request. I understand on the barrack room grapevine that the next big show in this war is likely to be in Málaga. The Nationalists, I am told, are expected to launch a big onslaught on the Andalusian city.'*

Colonel Perez queried how Powell had heard on the grapevine of the projected Nationalist intentions to send a strong enough force to Southern Spain to capture the ancient city of Málaga.

'*It always bugs me that the barrack room gossipers seem to learn of these things almost as soon my office despite the security smoke screen we try to put up,' said Perez. 'But as it happens this time they haven't got the exact story.'*

The Colonel stretched across his desk and picked up a message from his desk and said: '*This has just arrived by teleprinter from heaquarters ordering me to asssemble a defence force of Brigade strength to protect Málaga. I have already pencilled the British Battalion to take over this task force with Captain Enrique Rotau in charge and you as his second in command.*

'*Oh, and Lieutenant I have already been told of your interest in a rather attractive Spanish army nurse who has already been seconded to Málaga--so the ulterior motive for what you were about to request of me has been revealed. So good luck Lieutenant. I mean that not only in a military sense.*'

18

To borrow a word from the Russian communists, who were trying to mastermind the Republican's war against the threat of fascism taking over Spain, a *troika* of astute minds from the International Brigades formed a think tank to devise tactics on how to defend the little town of Málaga which the Nationalist army had now targeted.

The conference was staged in the office of Colonel Felipe Perez, who would command X1 International Brigade, attended by Captain Enrique Robau who would be in charge of a XIII International Brigade force and Lieutenant Dai Powell who would lead a combined group from the British Battalion and the Dimitrov Battalion which was made up of volunteers from the Balkan countries.

Colonel Perez opened the meeting with a statement: *'For the purpose of this operation only I am promoting Lieutenant Powell to Acting Captain in view of his impressive record since he arrived in Spain. I wondered for some time how a man who had previously earned his living digging coal in a Welsh mine could adapt so well to soldiering and leadership until Dai told me had spent nearly two years at Cardiff University studying military history. Senor Powell if it was up to me I would make your elevation to Captain permanent but the top brass has ruled that non-Spanish officers in the International Brigades should not exceed Spanish officers by more than 50 per cent, and our quota of foreign national Captains is full. But I am sure you and your men will do their duty, as they did so well in the Battle of the Corunna Road.*

'*We must learn the lessons from that success and the part that XI and XII International Brigades, which included Acting Captain Powell's British Battalion, was significant and a decisive factor coupled with the Soviet armoured unit under General Dimitry.*'

The victory at the Corunna Road was just one of many by the Republicans in their defence of Madrid to the delight of the most patriotic woman in Spain-*La Pasionaria!*

'*First I have to warn you that the Nationalist Army has now been reinforced with the arrival of the first Italian volunteers at Cadiz two weeks ago,*' continued Colonel Perez. '*Now I know that we professional soldiers tend to mock the Italian army and call them ice-cream sellers. But the two thousand Italians who have just arrived are supposedly crack troops. We must be ready to use the right tactics to keep the Nationalists at bay in Málaga which has become a strategically important target. Captain Robau's XIII International Brigade force will include two anti-aicraft units because we can expect aerial attacks from the German Condor Legion and Mussolini's Italian fliers. Acting Captain Powell I want you to take the British Battalion's excellent machine gun corps with your task force.*

'*I want your men to take the brunt of any hand to hand fighting for it has been noted how adept they are in the use of the bayonet. My XIII International Brigade force will include six pieces of heavy artillery and the skilled men to operate them. I estimate the total strength of the entire task force under my command, including four field kitchens and two surgically equipped medical units will be 3,000 men.*

'Good luck men! We will set off in 72 hours so use the time to check everything is running smoothly with your men and equipment.'

It was a busy and tense three days of preparation for Acting Captain Dai Powell but every evening, as he wearily climbed into his army cot, he pondered hopefully on the prospect of very soon seeing once again the beautiful Spanish nurse he loved.

19

To unashamedly plagiarise a signal speech made by Winston Churchill, during the turmoil of the Second World War some years later, the battle of Málaga, early in 1937, was neither the beginning or the end of the Spanish Civil War but it was certainly the beginning of the end of that cruel conflagration.

The fighting between the Nationalists, backed by Adolf Hitler's National Socialist Party and Benito Mussolini's Fascists on the one hand in opposition to Russian dictator Josef Stalin's doctrine of worldwide Communism, which supported the Republicans, currently Spain's governing group, had subsided.

But the arrival of black-shirted Italian volunteers spearheaded a humiliating defeat of the Republican held town of Málaga. A victory that prompted horrific reprisals and pillage from the insurgent Nationalists.

Three Nationalist columns had converged on the town. General Gonzalo Quiepo de Llano led the Army of the South advanced from Granada and faced Acting Captain Dai Powell two groups, the British and the Dimitrov Battalions.

Overall Republican commander of the town's defence force was Colonel Felipe Perez who faced the Nationalist forces under the command of Colonel Antonio Munoz, while Republican Captain Enrique's XIII Brigade opposed the black-shirted Italian volunteers led by General Mario Roatta.

Although the Republicans had enough troops on the ground they were poorly organised by their overall commander Colonel Perez, much to Acting Captain Powell's cursing chagrin whose men were the only Republican group who refused to retreat. The Battle of Málaga had started on the 17th January 1937 and by 3rd February the Nationalist attackers had reached the outskirts of the town. Three days later, when the Republicans, tails between their legs, hurriedly retreated northwards to Almeria after sustaining a staggering 1,800 casualties plus another 1,100 men wounded, many of them very seriously, the Nationalist army leader, soon to be Spain's dictator, General Francisco Franco, arrived to congratulate his victorious troops. The Nationalist soldiers ransacked the town of Málaga including its many picturesque churches.

Amongst the plunder they found what was reputedly the severed hand of Saint Teresa of Avila, a Carmelite nun, who died in 1582 at the age of 67, and was canonized by Pope Gregory XV in 1622. A holy relic that Franco kept at his bedside for the rest of his life as a General, then Generalissimo of the Nationalist armed forces during the Civil War followed by his 36 year reign as supreme *Caudillo* of Spain between 1939 and his death in 1975.

Acting Captain Dai Powell's anger at the inept performance of some of the Republican army in the early days of the battle for

Málaga, the lack of leadership in some of the Spanish units resulting eventually in the deaths of 60 percent of the British Battalion was eased a little by the reunion with his beloved nurse Pilar Delgado during this vital action.

20

Acting Captain Dai Powell's two Battalions of International Brigadeers had only served four days of their deployment in the three-week tenure of the fateful Battle of Málaga when they were painfully involved in one of its bloodiest actions.

The warning of what lay ahead came when the Nationalist commander in the west sector of Málaga ordered his mobile artillery units to conduct a three hour non-stop bombardment. Then General Gonzalo Quiepo de Llano sent his crack commando troops over the line under the protection of Powell's men with bayonets fixed.

Dai Powell was personally involved in the action despatching three Nationalist insurgents with his skilfully wielded bayonet and, quite incredibly, four more with his officers' issue Colt.45 pistol. A trusty semi-automatic weapon with a seven-round magazine plus one in chamber, which had once won him a prize of five litres of Spanish brandy in a shooting range competition back at the Republican training base in Albacete.

Acting Captain Powell was initially proud that his unit had

warded off the Nationalists' attack, the only Republican success in this bloody battle, and was then appalled at the count of twenty nine casualities and ten badly wounded men.

At the emergency dressing station attached to his unit Dai Powell found his second in command and best friend, Corporal George Stewart, in charge of sorting some kind of priority for the ten seriously wounded men.

'*How goes it George?*' he queried.

The man from Jarrow in north east England replied: *Well Sir I have had a good look at the ten badly wounded men...*'

Dai Powell interrupted: '*Cut out the Sir's, George pal. There is no need to stand on ceremony when you are talking to me alone. We have always been friends and always will be. My rank in the army will never stand in the way of that! You were saying George...?*'

George Stewart continued his assessment of the seriously injured men: '*Nine of them have sustained bayonet wounds but are stable.*

'*According to our own unit medics they will be able to hold on until an ambulance from our main field hospital, situated on the other side of the town, can get to us some time tomorrow. But the man I am most worried about is a lad from Glasgow, Jock Clelland who sustained a shell wound in his left leg from Nationalist artillery fire at the start of the attack.*

'*He is in a bad way and needs surgery to amputate the leg. Our own medics will attempt to do the operation themselves if there is no other way. But they all stress that a highly qualified surgeon would stand a better chance of saving this man's life. You are the only man with suitable transport and I wonder if you could drive the injured man, with one of our medics to care for him, to the field hospital. It would mean you dodging Nationalist outposts on the way.'*

Captain Dai Powell immediately responded to his friend's request.

'Of course I will do it George,' Powell replied. *'As you know I have only a tiny Ford, but it is nippy and large enough to carry an injured man on a stretcher in the back seat and a medical orderly in the front passenger seat. How long will it take to get Private Jock Clelland ready for the journey?'*

Corporal Stewart immediately replied: *'The medics say they can have him ready inside half an hour and will give him an injection that should make him sleep throughout the journey. The sooner he gets away the better chance he will have of pulling through.'*

Powell agreed to the timing his friend George had mapped out : *'Half an hour it will be then George. I'll get the Ford topped up with gasoline and ready for the off in thirty minutes.'*

21

Although the journey around the perimeters of Málaga town was technically little more than 20 kilometres it became quite an eventful two hour journey when a small Nationalist spotter plane swooped down on the small Ford car being driven at breakneck speed by Captain Dai Powell.

Although it was only a two seater aircraft employed to spot targets for the Nationalist artillery the second seat alongside the pilot was occupied by a soldier who manipulated a specially mounted Maxim Machine Gun from the side window.

Primitive perhaps, awkward, bloody difficult, for the contorted gunner but, nevertheless, a formidable weapon. Air cooled, light, tending to rarely jam compared to rival weapons of its category. It had been widely used by revolutionaries in the Ukraine and Germany in uprisings after World War I. Both sides in the Spanish Civil War used it.

Dai Powell urgently spotting the small Nationalist plane diving down the road towards his car, the Maxim Machine Gun spewing red and yellow ribbons of hate towards him. In a nothing ventured, nothing gained manouvre he swung the steering wheel to the right hurling the car into the thickness of a tree-line verge.

He could hear the Falange pilot zoom the plane down the road making the plane swing round 90 degrees to make another run and second attack. Unable to see Captain Powell's car again, he made two more abortive runs before veering away and heading the plane towards its base and, obviously, for refuelling.

Captain Powell, was desperately worried that the car might have sustained damage serious enough to curtail its mission to get a badly wounded soldier to a military hospital for vital surgery.

His examination of the battered vehicle revealed that the only meaningful harm was a blow-out to the front near side tyre and huge clumps of churned up mud adhering to the underside. Two minor matters, easily remedied by the two innovative Republican soldiers.

By the time the pilot of the Nationalist plane had called up for a couple of fighter planes from his home airfield to take up the search for the car Dai Powell had wheeled the vehicle into the encampment on the south side of Málaga which housed the Republican field hospital.

As two medical orderlys came out from the hospital pushing a stretcher trolley accompanied by a nurse the excited Powell shouted: *'Pilar, Pilar darling at last I've found you at last.'*

Enfermera Delgado looked up and placed the voice with delight: *'Dai, Dai Powell querido. Thank God you are alive. I knew you were here fighting in the defence of Málaga and your unit was involved in a very heavy action two days ago.*

'Oh mi novio it is so wonderful to see you. We will have a talk later, a long talk. But first I must attend to my patient, it is my duty. I will get in touch with you later.'

Captain Dai Powell left the medical orderly who had travelled in the car to care for the seriously wounded Scottish-born soldier at the military hospital. Conscientous in his job the orderly requested that he could watch the amputation of the soldier's left leg to improve his knowledge.

Meanwhile Powell went off to the International Brigade's command office where he requested a billet for the night and a replacement car to take him back to his men, based on the opposite side of Málaga, the following day. He was given a bed in the communal tent reserved for officers of Captain rank and under, also an invitation for dinner in the officer's mess.

Having stowed his toiletry gear and kit bag in the locker adjacent to his bed for the night, Powell repaired to the officers' mess tent where he was regaled with a plate of beef stew and vegetables. The simplicity of the meal sat well with the liberal supply of Rioja Tinto on the tables waiting to sate the palates of fighting men engaged in battle. He was sipping the steaming mug of *café con leche* that followed this excellent repast when he was called to the telephone. It was his beloved Pilar.

'*Hi there Dai amante,*' she said excitely down the line. '*You will be glad to know that private Clelland came through the operation to have his left leg amputated successfully. If he pulls through the night well we should know for sure that he will survive and we can think of him being repatriated to his home in Escocia. But enough of that I am free from duty for the next 24 hours. Let's make the best of our time together querido. If that wreck of a car of yours can hold together I have a girl friend who keeps a small hotel in Torremolinos which is only seven kilometres away well inside the zone controlled by the Republicans. I'll meet you at the base guard room in an hour!*'

22

As Dai Powell was preparing to leave the officer's mess tent, excited at the anticipation of getting some quality time with his beloved Pilar, an orderly brought him a note from his commanding officer, Colonel Felipe Perez, requesting that, after finishing his meal, to call at the base office for a talk.

'*Well done for the fine performance you and your men put up in repelling the Nationalists in your sector,*' said Colonel Perez. '*I understand that you are contemplating rejoining your unit tomorrow. I want you alter that arrangement and delay your departure for another 48 hours in order for me to outline our future strategy. Oh and incidentally I have been given orders from my superior officers to confirm your appointment as full Captain from your present "Acting" rank.* '

The newly elevated Captain thanked his Colonel for the promotion and informed his superior officer that, with his permission, he would be staying off base with his girl friend military nurse Pilar Delgado that night in nearby Torremolinos.

'*That will be perfectly in order,*' grinned Colonel Perez

lasciviosly. *'Torremolinos is under Republican control and the nearest Nationalist forces are more than 10 kilometres away. Oh incidentally I have heard you have a transport problem. I have ordered the Transport pool to issue you with a six cylinder Studebaker, which has been commandeered from a civilian, to replace your battered Ford. You are moving up in the world Captain Powell--a beautiful novia and a big automobile! Let me know your contact telephone in Torremolinos overnight.*

'I'll see you when you return to base tomorrow Captain!'

Pilar Delgado was waiting at the base guard room when Dai drove up in his newly acquired four-door Studebaker limousine. It was the first time he had seen her out of her nurse's uniform. *'Hi there Acting Captain Powell,'* Pilar teased him flirtatiously.

Dai, giving as good as he received, cracked back: *'You need to get your facts right nurse if you want to move up the ladder in your career. I was confirmed as a full Captain by Colonel Felipe Perez less than an hour ago. Who knows? I might make you the General's lady one day.'*

The Hotel Clavel was a neat and clean 20 room establishment situated on the undeveloped sea front at Torremolinos village, which was destined to become one of the largest holiday resorts on Spain's Costa la Sol by the turn of the century.

The hotel owner 45-year-old Senora Mathilde Cristina was a retired school teacher. A lady whose star pupil, four years earlier, had been a poverty stricken Asturian coal miner's daughter Pilar Delgado. She had inherited the hotel after the death of her widowed mother 18 months previously.

'It is lovely to see you again Senora Cristina,' Pilar greeted her former teacher affectionately. *'It is so kind of you to invite us to stay*

in your lovely hotel. Let me introduce you to my novio Captain Dai Powell. He is from England...oh pardon my mistake...from Pais de Gales. Calling a Welshman 'and' Englishman is as bad as calling a Basque a Spaniard.'

Mathilde Cristina thrust out a welcoming hand to Dai and said: *'I see by the insignia on your uniform that you are a member of the International Brigades. We are grateful to all you men from foreign countries who have come to defend Spain from the insidious growth of fascisim which is sweeping Europe. You are welcome to this hotel.*

'Oh Pilar, there is no need to address me as Senora any more. We both left school a long time ago.'

Pilar was quite pleased with what her former teacher said.

'Thank you very much for that but I will have to think carefully before I address you as Mathilde after all I have years of calling you "teacher" or "Senora". What is the latest time you serve desayuno mañana-we don't intend getting up to early?'

Mathilde Cristina was highly amused with the urgency in Pilar's query and answered with her own question: *'Will ten o'clock be late enough for you two lovebirds? If not I can make arrangements to serve you.'*

Dai Powell took over the reins after a silence which indicated his understanding to allow Pilar and Mathilde to sate their female proclivity for prattle.

'Ten o' clock will be fine Senora Cristina,' he said. *'Oh, incidentally I have left the telephone number of this hotel with my unit in case I am needed in an emergency. Please ask your night porter to awaken me at any time in the night if I get a call from the military.'*

Mathilde Cristina had some extra information that delighted Dai.

'*At ten o' clock you will meet another distinguished guest in the breakfast in the dinning room,*' she said whetting the Welshman's curiosity.

Dai Powell risked the chance of being thought rude as he fired the obvious question: '*Oh and who might that be?*'

The hotel owner smiled to show the pride she was feeling in making the announcement: '*She is a famous lady known as Dolores Ibárruri.*'

Dai Powell showed his excitement as he countered: '*You mean the lady better known as…*'

Mathilde Cristina, equally excited with the news she was imparting, interrupted: '*Yes indeed Captain Powell the icon of the Republican movement and a founder of the Spanish Communist Party , La Pasionaria, is staying in this hotel tonight.*'

Dai Powell could not help showing pleasure at the news he had just been given and politely asked Mathilde: '*I think we all deserve a drink at such an honour. Senora would you be kind enough to ask your barman to bring us a bottle of your best champagne in an ice bucket and three glasses?*'

After the hotel owner passed the appropriate order to the hotel barman she confirmed with Dai Powell: '*I am afraid, because of the war, we have no French champagne in stock but you will be served a bottle of Gran Reserva Brut Spanish Cava, which is good enough to satisfy the taste of some of the best judges of fine wines.*'

Dai glanced at Pilar, who nodded her approval, before he

instructed Mathilde Cristina: 'That sounds fine to me. As a matter of fact I happen to prefer Cava to Champagne!'

As befitting three people, who had in earlier years been born, bred and then worked in the pits of the Rhonda Valley and the anthracite mining region of Asturias, they raised their champagne glasses to the underpaid, under privileged workers all across the world who by day, week, month and year, put their lives on the line at the coal face.

As Dai and Pilar wearily wended their way up the hotel staircase to their room they only halted their climb to sensuously kiss each other every three or four steps.

23

Nearly every girl looks back to the magical night when her boy friend revealed his love and for the first time took her to bed with the intent of initiating her into the art of passionate love.

But some one, it seemed, had written a different script for the besotted Enfermera Pilar Delgado and Captain Dai Powell, of the International Brigades on this auspicious night.

The two young people had both been through an exhaustive 24 hours. Pilar, after assisting the surgeon while amputating the left leg of wounded Scottish International Brigades soldier Jock Clelland. Powell because of his efforts in leading two battalions of the International Brigades in an impressive action against the insurgent Nationalists and afterwards driving his car, with the wounded Clelland inside, to the Republican military hospital seven kilometres away despite being strafed by a Nationalist war plane.

Exacerbating their weariness was the bottle of *vino tinto* they consumed with their wholesome dinner of *estofado conejo* and the bottle of *cava* they had shared with hotel owner, Mathilde Cristina, at the end of the night.

'That rabbit stew was as good as my mother used to make for the family,' yawned Pilar as the two sweethearts sat talking on the bedroom sofa.

Dai noted Pilar's agonising yawn and droopy eyes as she fought a losing battle to ward off her lack of sleep. Full of consideration he waited until she collapsed into the arms of *Morpheus,* the god of sleep and dreams, then, caringly, cradling her in his muscular biceps he lifted her to the bed where he pulled the covers around her bestowing a tender goodnight kiss. Within seconds he had crept underneath the quilt alongside her musing, self critically: *'I am not going to go down in history as the world's greatest lover! I hope nobody spreads the news.'*

But, completely fagged out, Dai Powell grinned succumbing to the throes of lassitude with the final thought: *'I can wait. The best is yet to come.'* It was a brilliant prediction as Powell drifted into a torpid middle of the night trance.

His *'best to come'* vision, prophetically, began to materialise as the wintry sun began to rise, edging it's puny rays, four hours later, across the dark horizon of the Costa del Sol. It was 6 am. Dawn was beginning to creep across the slumbering fishing village of Torremolinos as Pilar and Dai awakened simultaneously to a crisp morning they would never forget.

In the agonising preceding minutes, his legs suffered the unspeakable torture of cramp, as, heroically, he tried not to arouse his "*Sleeping Beauty*". But, as if, sensing his torment had released her from the possessive clutches of *Morpheus,* she awakened and circled her arms around his waist reaching for his crown jewels.

Sighing, if he was honest. more relieved at the sublime pleasure of being able to move his cramp-stricken leg, than the romantic overture about to strike its opening notes. But as he felt her cool hand groping to find his speedily engorging member Dai turned inwards towards his captivating lover.

His inquisitive tongue began to find the secret places in the virginal body of a girl who had never experienced intimacy with a man before.

'Oh Dai, mi novio, we seem to have waited for a lifetime for this moment,' she trilled. *'I have been so worried, querido, when I had to escort the wounded soldier to Perpignan, and we were split up for a few weeks, that I would never see you again, or that you would be killed or wounded by the Nationalists .*

'But God has been good and saved you for me. I have never made love with a man before. Let's make the most of the time we have been given together.'

She surrendered her body to him unreservedly. He was insatiable. He could not get enough of her on this wondrous daybreak drama of unbridled sex in a cocktail of tenderness and care for her desires and needs.

After the first orgasm was shared Pilar said: *'Oh my marvellous novio I will always love you. My first and only love.'*

Dai, firmly but gentle, brought her to a crescendo twice more in the next hour before he whispered: *'Pilar, my wonderful sweetheart. I think you agree with me we are now committed to each other. Now we must pull together and find out a way we can forge out a life together while this terrible Civil War rages.'*

Pilar Delgado could not disguise her happiness. *'Love will surely find a way,'* she said emphatically. *'But at the same time neither of us must forget that we have a duty to the Republican cause to fulfill before we can completely devote ourselves to each other. Already I have told you how much I love you, and, for me there will never be another man.'*

24

As the two 'lovebirds' entered the dining room for a late breakfast they were greeted by the hotel proprietor, who was also Pilar Delgado's former school teacher, Mathilde Cristina.

'*Hello you two,*' said Doña Cristina. '*Senora Dolores Ibárruri, would be honoured if both of you would join her for desayuno.*'

Dai and Pilar, still on cloud nine after their romantic dawn assignation, were nevertheless flattered by the invitation.

'*I am so pleased that you are joining me,*' said La Pasionaria. '*It is not often I get the chance to thank two young people who have dedicated themelves to the Republican cause and to free our beloved Spain from the dire threat of world wide facism.*'

After they had all ordered *tortilla españolas, pan tostado y frutas fresco* plus a bottle of vintage *Cava* specially ordered by Donna Ibárruri the icon of leftist Spain.

'*I have the greatest regard for soldiers of the International Brigades like you Captain Powell,*' said *La Pasionaria,* the quality of her oratory was magnetic, which Dai Powell had discovered when he had heard her previously making a public speech in Madrid.

'From all peoples from all races, you have come here like brothers and sisters, like sons and daughters of immortal Spain; and in the hardest days of the Civil War you have already helped save Madrid with your enthusiasm, your heroism and your spirit of sacrifice. For the first time in the history of the peoples ' struggles there is the spectacle, breathtaking in its grandeur, of the formation of the International Brigades to help save a threatened country's freedom and independence of our Spanish land.

'Communists, Socialists, Anarchists, Republicans - men of different colours, differing ideology, antagonistic religions-yet all profoundly loving liberty and justice, you have come and offered yourselves to us unconditionally.'

La Pasionaria then turned and warmly addressed her fellow Spaniard: *'Pilar, I understand you have given your heart to this young International Brigades captain, a Welshman who comes from a coal mining family like ourselves. I understand you plan to marry. When the years pass by and the wounds of war are staunched; when the memory of the sad and bloody days dissipate in a present of liberty, of peace and of well-being; when the rancour has died out and pride in a free country is felt equally by all Spaniards, speak to your children. Tell them of these heroic men of the International Brigades - like the one you plan to wed.'*

Pilar Delgado, the third child of an Asturian coal miner, had come under the spell of Dolores Ibárruri Gómez, the eighth of eleven children, of a collier from the province of Vizcaya in the Basque country-a legend in her own lifetime known by popular acclaim as *La Pasionaria.*

'I respect and agree with everything you have said Doña Ibárrruri,' Pilar exclaimed in a whispered voice that underlined

the admiration she felt for the icon of the Republican cause. *'I particularly concur with what you say about the bravery of the soldiers of the International Brigade who are risking their lives helping to save Spain from the curse of Fascism that is sweeping Europe. But of course I am an enfermera, an enfermera militar, who, like a doctor I am sworn to nurse and save the lives of all soldiers caught up in this awful Civil War.*

'That includes my beloved Dai, who is only different from other soldiers in that I love him and one day we will be married-God sparing us.'

Dai Powell took up the discourse: *'It has been my privilege to twice hear you talk Doña Ibárruri. The first time was at a public meeting when we successfully helped to save the City of Madrid from the invading Nationalists in the Battle for the Corruna Road and the second occasion is this very morning. Can I say with all humility you are an inspiration to the fighters of the Republic whether we hail from Poland, France, Belguim. Scotland, America, Canada, Ireland or, like me, from the coal mining villages of Wales.*

'If, praise be to God that the Republicans prevail in this Civil War you will have made a contribution to the cause as vital as any gun- toting Spaniard or foreigner fighting under the various battle banners of the International Brigades.'

The stimulating breakfast-table talk with *La Pasionaria* put the icing on the precious first night that Pilar and Dai had shared together. It left them in contemplative mood as he tooled the powerful six cylinder *Studebaker* saloon back to their front line base in Malaga.

25

They stopped for coffee at a little bar just four kilometres from the base in Malaga and pledged themselves to each other for the rest of their lives.

'Look Pilar, we both know now how much we love each other,' said Dai Powell, making it clear that he intended not to let his heart rule his head. *'But while we are both involved in this dreadful Civil War it would be irresponsible for us to get married. We would be acting in an absolutely untrustworthy way if we produced, while serving in the front line of the battle against the Nationalists who have ruthlessly killed many young children of Republican supporters. If, God willing, we are both lucky enough to survive this war then we will marry and bring our children up in a world of peace and love.'*

After they kissed each other on arrival at the base guard room Pilar hurried away to her duties at the medical centre while Captain Dai Powell reported to the office of his commanding officer.

Colonel Felipe Perez was in affable mood and said: *'Hola, Captain Powell, I have news for you. You have been invited to* represent the "other ranks" at a strategy meeting of the Republican Army High Command to be held in Madrid in five days time headed by Commander in Chief, General José Miaja Menant and General Enrique Lister, Commander of the Intenational Brigades because of your excellent record as a leader while moving quickly up from the ranks to non-commissioned officer then to Lieutenant and your present rank of full Captain , with the possibility, I hear, of further promotions to come.

'The idea of the meeting will be to form what the Americans call a "think tank" to counter the Nationlista's who, with the help of Hitler and Mussolini, have been able to activate a superior stratagem than us. We are being outgunned by the superiority of the German and, to a much lesser extent, Italian fighter and bomber 'planes' and modern armaments while our soldiers ars still using Great War rifles, grenades and biplanes held together by string.

'You and your unit have been commended for their meritorious effort and victory in your sector during the Battle of Malaga. Before that your skill as a military tactician was noted by the Republican leaders for your brilliant "Wooden Horse" strategy which made a significant part in saving Madrid from the Nationalists during our remarkable victory in the Battle for the Corunna Road. I fully endorse the praise being lavished upon you from the top echelon of the Republican army. My only reservation is that I only wish you were Spanish instead of English.

'I am just afraid Captain Powell is that your nationality will go against you, for the League of Nations are lobbying the rest of the world to adopt a policy of non-intervention in this Civil War which, in all honesty should only concern the people of Spain.

'Although we would lose the support of Josef Stalin's Soviet *fighters we would not have to face the formidable armaments of Nazi Germany and Facist Italy. Your orders Captain Powell is to report to the headquarters of General José Miaja Menant, Commander in Chief of the Republican Army, at 9 am in five days time. Until then you are free to spend the next few days with your novio, the beautiful Enfermera Pilar Delgado. I will speak to the base Medical Officer to give her immediate four days leave. Good luck Captain Powell.'*

Dai was grateful for the announcement that his commanding officer had given him and said: *'Thank you Sir for your support and confidence and I promise that I will not let you down and will try to make a worthwhile contribution to the new Republican 'think thank' dealing with military tactics and strategy.*

'If I may be so bold, Sir, with respect, I would like to ask you for another favour. Under the term of my rank, as a Captain, I believe, I am entitled to an orderly to assist me. I appreciate that this might not be possible but I would like Corporal George Stewart to be seconded as my orderly. I realise this might be possible because the Corporal has been in charge of my unit while I have been here in the last few days.'

Colonel Felipe Perez reassured Captain Powell that he would not stand in the way of Corporal Stewart being appointed as his orderly.

'In fact I can give you some classified information that all Republican forces will be ordered to retreat northwards towards Almeria, to reorganise, and concede the city to the Nationalists. We have to accept that some of our soldiers have been badly organised--your unit being the exception. It is a bad setback for our side to lose a port city like Malaga and it will seriously affect our logistics. It is a defeat and one of the reasons why the "think tank" you are joining has been assembled. But in answer to your request it leaves

Corporal Stewart free to become your orderly. I will send him orders to join you at General Miaja's headquarters in Madrid, five days from now.

'Meanwhile Captain enjoy the next few days with your beautiful nurse. You both deserve the break. Good luck in your new job.'

26

Under normal circumstances the elevation of a foreign volunteer, or a mercenary, in a remarkably short time, from the lowest rank of 'Private', through the system of NCO's to the commissioned rank of Captain with the possibility even of reaching the star rating of General, would suggest a scintillating military career ahead, in his own country, for former South Wales coal miner Dai Powell at the end of the Spanish Civil War.

But in the case of Spanish Civil War veterans, of the Republican persuasion, history was to blow that conjecture to eternity with a force comparable to the 250 kilogram bombs that the ruthless aviators of Hitler's Condor Legion dropped on soldiers, civilians and innocent children of Republican Spain during the horror of the Civil War.

Hermann Goering, Reichsmarshall of the Luftwaffe, after the end of WWII, at his trial during the Nuremburg International Military Tribnual, explained Germany's intrusion into Spain's Civil War: '*Nationalist leader, General Francisco Franco, sent a call to the Third Reich asking for support, particularly in the air. One should never forget that Franco with his troops was stationed in Africa and he could not get his men across as the Spanish fleet was in the charge of the Republicans. The decisive factor was first of all to get all of Franco's troops over to Spain. Hitler thought the matter over . I urged him firstly to support Franco to prevent the spread of communism in that area of the world, and secondly to test my young Luftwaffe airmen at this opportunity.'*

Germany's response to Franco's plea was the supply of:

* One Bomber group of three squadrons of Junkers Ju 52 bombers

* One Fighter group with three squadrons of Heinkel HE51 fighter planes

* One Reconnaissance Group with two squadrons of Heinkel He99 and HE70 reconnaissance bombers and...

* One Seaplane Squadron of Heinkel HE 59 and HE 60 floatplanes.

A total of 100 aircraft and 5,136 men were under the command of General Hugo Sperrie, later promoted to Field Marshall. It involved a total of 19,000 Nazi servicemen. A significant, if not the vital, factor in the Nationalists eventual victory over the Republicans in the three year Civil War.

Many Britons, like Dai Powell, hardened by those three years of gruelling battling on the Iberian flat lands, mountain passes, and deserts were treated like pariahs in their own country when a few months later World War II was declared against Hitler's Nazi Germany and their Axis allies in Fascist Italy led by physco-dictator Benito Musolini.

They were typecast as Reds, Commies, Leftist bastards and politically unwelcome as volunteers in Great Britain's undermanned armed services. Their accusers, from the icon of the Allied powers, British Prime Minister Winston Churchill down to the lowliest back-bench Members of Parliament amazingly ignored the fact that of 2,000 British volunteers who fought with the Republicans, leaving 500 of their comrades in Spanish cemeteries, less than five per cent of them were subscribing members of the Communist Party of Great Britain-a party that through the ages has never been able to challenge the mass support enjoyed by the nation's leading three political parties, Conservatives, Labour and Liberals.

But Dai Powell, as he humorously said, was looking forward to a 'dirty weekend' with his lovely sweetheart Pilar Delgado, and could, as he added, "not give a tosser" about all the political mish-mash that surrounded his prospects of continuing his military career sometime in the future with the British Army.

27

Dai and Pilar, happy as a couple of chirpy parakeets, loaded the Studebaker with enough clothes to last them for the next four days.

Using his soldier's knack of cadging help from comrades Captain Dai Powell persuaded the Sergeant Major in charge of the base cookhouse to pack a large box with picnic food. There was delicious Serrano ham, Manchego cheese, plump local tomatoes and, bless Sergeant Major Ramada's generosity, a couple of bottles of *Rioja Tinto*.

As Dai switched on the Studebaker's powerful engine the beautiful Pilar leant across from the passenger seat and kissed him affectionately on the cheek before asking: *'Where are you taking me querido? I must say I am very excited to be going away with you for a romantic four days. It feels as if you are taking me on honeymoon.'*

The Welshman responded to her fervent mood and said: *'One day, soon I hope, I will really take you on honeymoon. But first we must help to finish off this awful Civil War so that we can get* married. But meanwhile I am taking you to a beautiful little aldea by the Mediterranean called Marbella. The village, is only a few miles away in the province of Málaga, beneath La Concha. It is a tiny village with only 800 inhabitants, but it is estimated that after this Civil War is over it will become one of Europe's most popular holiday resorts. That indicates how picturesque the pueblo is. During Islamic rule of the region the Muslims had built a castle on the outskirts and the name Marbella is derived from the Muslim title of Marbilla. The Spaniards recaptured the village in 1485 and it is one of the most beautiful places along the Mediterranean coast.'*

After a car journey that took little over an hour Dai skilfully tooled the Studebaker into the forecourt of a two hundred year old *finca*. As the big car cruised up the entry road it was easy to understand why it was known as *La Flor de Almendra*. Although it was still only early February many of the almond trees were festooned with blossom varying from white to delicate pinks.

They received a warm reception from the owner of *La Flor de Almendra* who greeted them with the sincere words: '*Señores, bienvenido mi casa tu casa*'.

Paulo Ramirez, was a kindly white-haired retired cattle farmer, who had opened up the six bedroom finca, with his wife Conchita, to paying guests.

Pilar was most impressed when Conchita Ramirez escorted them to their room.

The focal point was an elegant four poster bed, draped in a sky-blue diaphanous material. The bedding was of the finest linen and gave off a faint aroma of lavender. In one corner of the large room, obviously a sign of respect for the chill February wind outside, a small fire gave off the delicate aroma of burning apple wood.

The dressing table and chairs were of a high quality that would have been described in England as Regency style with delicate silk candy striped backs to the chairs and an elegant *chaise longe*--all the woodwork having been crafted from the finest mahogany.

Throughout this tasteful house there was an impressive collection of priceless ceramic figures from the prestigious kilns of the famous Lladro firm. The feature in this refined bedroom was prominently displayed on a carved chest of draws-a line of five nuns heading sedately, one could imagine, for vespers. The expansive sweep of their starched cowls accentuating their piety as they looked downwards at the breviaries they were reading moving at snail's pace towards the chapel.

The line of ceramic saintly sisters, the bedroom lights reflecting from their snowy habits, deeply affected Pilar so much that the young nurse made a reverent sign of the cross. It was if perversely she thought the figurines bestowed a blessing on the bedroom which in the next few nights would provide the backcloth of passionate consummation of her undying love for Dai.

They dined that evening at the finca. A delicious of steaming *cocido,* featuring nutricous cuts of chicken, rabbit, pork and veal still bubbling in the deep bowls placed in front of them with huge wooden *chucharas* to eat it with.

'*These wooden spoons are very sensible,*' laughed Pilar as they broke up chunks of crusty bread to soak up the succulent stew. '*The cocido is so hot that metal spoons would have melted.*'

Captain Dai Powell, casting military form aside, loosened the collar button of his uniform shirt, nodded agreement to her jest, and ravenously consumed his second bowl of the stew.

'*You will not get better grub than this anywhere,*' he mumbled spraying crumbs of crusty bread as he spoke. '*This will put hairs on your chest.*'

Pilar's feminity came to the fore as she fired the final salvo in this culinary chitchat: '*I sincerely hope not Dai, novio. I don't think you would be too happy if I develop hirsute breasts.*'

Dai Powell, having learned a valuable lesson in the art of never arguing with a woman, remained diplomatically dumb!

The two lovers arose early next morning, despite the unbridled passions of the night and after piling into the Studebaker Dai drove them to nearby *La Concha,* where they parked and locked the car and went on a rigorous hike to the mountain of *Juanar.*

They had parked on a ledge and as they got out of the car the wide-eyed Pilar was dumbstruck with the panorama that manifested itself on the skyline. Dai, noting her amazement, quickly thumbed the pages of a guidebook he had borrowed from the owner of their *finca*, Paulo Ramirez.

'*That is just a part of the Sierra Blanca mountain range,*' he explained. '*The peaks that can be seen from the village of Marbella are the mountains of La Concha, Lastonar, Salto del Lobo and finally Juanar where we are heading for today. Juanar is identifiable against the other three mountains, shaped like a pyramid it also has a rounded platform as its peak. Legend says that a fishing boat was lost in a thick coastal fog. As they drifted perilously uncertain which way to swing the boat, the fog cleared for a few seconds and one of the fishermen saw the top of the Juanar mountain. They managed to change course and head to safety. A huge black cross was erected on top of the Juanar mountain in gratitude . A pilgrimage up the mountain takes place every year and a Mass celebrated under the cross to commemorate the amazing escape.'*

The lovers, arms linked, trudged through a pine forest and then a plantation of olive trees as they moved up the Juanar valley. At the top of the mountain they had a wonderful view of the pueblo of Marbella and the Sierra Blanca mountain range and, as it was a clear day, Dai was able to point out the African Coast of Morocco across the Mediterranean Sea.

It was a magical day that both of them would remember for a long time. They stopped for lunch alongside a mountain stream spewing clear water from the peak. Calling on one of the tricks he had learned as a Boy Scout back in South Wales he tied some cord around the neck of a bottle of *vino blanco* he had been given by the Sergeant Major in charge of the base cookhouse.

When they opened up their picnic box, also thanks to the liberal largesse of the base cookhouse *jefe,* Dai retrieved the wine from the stream, pulled the cork and taking a tentative sip, exclaimed: *'That wine is as perfect temperature-wise as if it had been kept in an ice bucket for half an hour or so. Let's hope that the Sergeant Major's Serano ham and Manchego cheese are as good.'*

28

The handsome Captain and his beautiful nurse both agreed their few days holiday in the Marbella area was idyllic and one that both of them would remember for the rest of their lives.

They went for long picnic walks along the trails of the picturesque Sierra Blanca mountain range often resting in a shaded wooded area where they would make passionate love to augment the sexy nights they spent at the finca.

'Have you thought what would happen, what we would do, if I fell pregnant,' Pilar asked him one night as they lay sated after a sex session on the bed bathed in the moonlight arcing through the open bedroom window.

Dai thought carefully before replying to his lover's anxious question.

'Yes my darling, of course I have, all the time,' he said. *'But I am a soldier. A soldier fighting in a foreign country in a Civil War-the worst and most ruthless types of war. We have to face the fact that there is a chance I will be killed. I love you too much to put your whole life in jeopardy by marrying you while this war is on. What*

*would happen to our child if I was killed? There is nothing I want
more than to make you my wife, my love. But we must be strong and
above all patient. Neither of us doubts the other's love. Let us pray
that things work out for us.'*

Pilar could see the sense in what Dai was saying and agreed that
she would have to be patient if she was going to share the rest of
her life with this *guapo* Welshman.

Like all good things their holiday had come to an end and they
had to get up at the crack of dawn on their final morning. After
a quick breakfast and an affectionate farewell to the owners of the
finca, Paulo and Conchita Ramirez, whom they thanked profusely,
Dai nosed the Studebaker to the new base at Almeria where the
Republican's had retreated after surrendering the city of Malaga to
the enemy.

After a sad parting with Pilar, they both were left wondering
when they would meet again. Obeying his orders to the letter,
Dai set off on the gruelling eight hour drive to Madrid where a
new twist to his soaring military career was about to unfold. Dai
had been forewarned that he would have to accept the fact the
headquarters of General José Miaja Menant, Commander in Chief
of the Republican Army, was run on a regime, in soldier-talk, of
bull-shit and red tape.

He was issued with a purple patch for his epaulettes and a band
of the same colour for his cap.

They were purely insignia of the elite group of Republican
military tacticians to which he had been elected.

A couple of hours after he had settled into his new living
quarters the evening before he was to join the Republican military
strategy committee, presided by General José Miaja, Captain Dai

Powell was joined by his close friend Corporal George Stewart, his newly appointed orderly.

'*Hallo, George my old pal,*' he said warmly jumping from his chair to give his mate a Spanish style, arms round their shoulders, *abrazo.* '*It's great to see you again mate. Let's have a drink on our reunion.*'

Powell hustled over to an antique-style sideboard and securing a bottle of *Fundador coñac* with two mega-sized balloon brandy glasses before pouring two generous measures of the amber liquor, which the Corporal described in his gravelly *Geordie* dialect as: '*Large enough to choke a fuckin' pit pony! But cheers Dai and many thanks for arranging for me to be appointed as your new orderly. I am not sure what my new duties will entail but I will try my best not to let you down.*'

The Welshman brushed his buddies thanks aside as he explained about the new Republican tactical think-tank that he was to be a part of and that the Corporal's duties would to act as his orderly and help him with the more mundane tasks.

After they had a long talk about old times, and a few more drinks, the two British soldiers decided to get a good night's after their tiring journeys to Madrid, in readiness for Powell's first appearance at General Miaja's tactical meeting the following morning.

29

Having donned their newly pressed best uniforms and attached special purple insignias to their epaulettes and side caps Captain Dai Powell and his orderly Corporal George Stewart, marching briskly in step, approached the entrance to the imposing headquarters of General José Miaja Menant, the Republican's Commander in Chief.

There they had to produce their ID cards to the two towering sergeants from the *Guardia Civil,* a federal para-military police force which had stayed loyal to the incumbent government during the Civil War under the title of '*Guardia Nacional Republicana*'. They were ushered to the door of a large room where the meeting was to be held with Stewart ordered to take a seat on a row of benches outside while Dai was led inside.

A smartly uniformed officer, his epaulette signifying his rank of four star General, rose from a massive 18th -century military campaign desk of elegant cherry, birch, maple and hardwood construction.

'*Captain Powell, I presume,*' was the hearty greeting from General Miaja. Then indicating another soldier sat in a chair next to the desk the general added: '*May I introduce you to General Enrique Lister, Commander of the International Brigades--I understand that you have not met each other before?*'

General Lister confirmed that he had not met Captain Powell before but reassured the Welshman: '*No I have not had the pleasure, Captain. But I have heard a lot about you and have been very impressed with the success you have had in leading several operations against the Nationalists.*'

General Miaja interrupted and said: '*That's why I have invited you to join us captain. I felt we needed the observations from a man whose escapades and leadership have moved him up from the ranks to captain in such a short time. Although we have not done badly in our early brushes with the enemy I have to admit the defeat in the Battle for Malaga is a big blow particularly the logistics of losing such a strategic shipping port.*

'*But first of all let me lay down some ground rules of this small committee before we get down to real business. The bullshit and spit and polish you saw when you entered this building ends at the door of this room when this committee is in session. Remove your jackets and your ties if you feel more comfortable gentlemen. Forget our different rankings. We will use our first names of Dai, Enrique and José while we are working here.*

'*Dai, I understand you have brought your orderly with you and he is waiting outside? Be kind enough to ask your Corporal to hustle up the kitchen staff and send us two or three pots of coffee and all the accoutrements and a plate of galletas chocolata.*'

Having obeyed the General's order Dai hurried out of the room and passed on the instructions to Corporal George Stewart.

When Dai returned General Miaja addressed him again.

'*I understand you and the Corporal have been togther for some time and joined the International Brigades together?*' queried the General, noting Powell's nod of assent. '*Well this Committee needs someone to take Minutes. If you can gurantee that your man is trustworthy to keep what is decided and discussed between these walls a strict secret we might as well appoint him as our committee clerk rather than bring in another soldier who none of us know.*'

Stewart returned, with a white-coated Mess Steward carrying the coffee tray he was addressed by his pal Captain Dai Powell , who said: '*Corporal while you were out of the room General Miaja suggested that you be seconded to this committee as the official Minute taker. Like all us you will be subject to the top security regulations of the Republican Army and will have to take an oath to that affect.*'

Stewart replied, his formal tone disguising his warm long-standing friendship and camaraderie with Dai Powell: '*I thank General Miaja and, of course, yourself Captain considering me for this important post. Of course you can rely on me to observe the security regulations.*'

General Miaja then produced a huge bible from the drawers of his antique desk and intoned: '*We the assembled committee comprising: General Enrique Lister, Captain Dai Powell and Committee Secretary Corporal George Stewart solemnly swear to strictly observe the security regulations of the Republican Army and under no circumstances divulge the business of the Committee to any other person/s. This oath also applies to myself.*

Signed: General José Miaja Menant
C.I.C. Republican Army.
Dated: 20ᵗʰ February 1937'

The General then turned toward Corporal Stewart and ordered:
'Type three copies of this oath of silence and, to make it binding, we will all sign them and witness each others' signatures, on this Holy Bible.'

The finalities of switching the small Republican Army 'tactical-think-tank' into working mode over General Miaja introduced the serious business of the day.

'Now let us get down to working out how to prevent such a reverse again. As I said earlier we are not standing on protocol in this committee. We will not use our ranks. When we meet, for instance, you will address me as José--not General.

'The latest intelligence I have received is that the Nationalists are planning to deploy some 30,000 troops to the Jarama Valley, to the south-east of Madrid, aiming to seige the Valencia Road in yet another effort to cut off the national capital. I intend to personally take over personal command to see there is no replication of the Malaga fiasco. Now I need help in the form of tactical ideas from this committee to avoid another shambles. '

Then, turning towards General Lister, the commander of the International Brigades, General Miaja asked: *'What are your views on all this Enrique?'*

General Lister didn't mince his words when he replied.

'Although we threw in large numbers of troops in our efforts to defend Malaga, with the exception of the sector under the command of our committee colleague here, Dai Powell, an International Brigades officer, I am proud to say, our Republican force was badly

organised   before ignominiously fleeing northwards   towards Almeria,' stressed Lister. *'Mainly our problem was one of shaky morale as a result of weak leadership in the front line.'*

There was a portentous silence as the Republican Army's highly experienced overall commander, General Miaja, absorbed the International Brigades commander's brutal assessment of the shameful capitulation at Malaga.

'Dai Powell, as a man who has rapidly risen through the ranks of the International Brigade in reward for your bravery and excellent service, what is going wrong at the grass roots of our army,' said Miaja. *'What are your views on the Malaga misadventure? More importantly what can we do to repair the deficiencies amongst lower rank officers?'*

Dai, taking a long swig from the carafe of iced water on the tiny table in front of him, thought carefully before answering General Miaja: *'With due respects José perhaps we are spending too much time looking for reasons why we were defeated at Malaga rather then planning a victory at the impending Battle of Jarama.*

'Nevertheless I have to say that some of the low to middle ranking officers in charge of front line units have shown a disturbing lack of moral fibre. There has been a reluctance by these officers to attack the enemy and a tendency to fall back on defence against foes, who I have to say, generally have better equipment than us.

'What we need to do is to devise a tactical surprise for the Nationalists when they start their offensive to cut the Valencia Road where it runs through the Jarama Valley. We have to persuade them to deploy their strongest units in a position where we can take them by surprise by ambush and do them the most damage. The Nationalists are obsessed with capturing Madrid. Understandably because if

they hope to win this War they know they must take the capital. If we can feed them false intelligence where our strongest units will be then we can take them by surprise and get in a damaging blow against them.

'To do that we must get our mid-ranking officers at unit level to think 'attack' and I suggest we call all officers between and including the ranks of lieutenant to captain for a two day briefing conference at our Republican Army training centre at Albacete in preparation for the battle of Jarama.'

Dai Powell's detailed assessment immediately gained the support of the two Generals--Miaja and Lister. The overall Republican Army commander José Miaja after a nod of approval from the International Brigade chief Enrique Lister said: *'That is a most constructive idea Dai. I am suggesting that you be put in charge of that conference with the substansive rank of Colonel to give you the authority you need to conduct such a briefing.*

'I also command you to liase with Enrique Lister to devise a plan to be executed by the International Brigades that will fool the Nationalist Army into leading their forces into an ambush. Please report that plan to General Sebastian Pozas who will be second in command to me as the overall battle leader, with you two gentlemen in the second tier of command with orders to tour the various front line posts looking for weaknesses

'Thank you gentlemen for your help and input into this meeting. Corporal Stewart you will draw up the Minutes of this meeting in the strictest security and supply typewritten copies to all three of us by 9am tomorrow. Good luck everyone and to our cause in the Battle of Jarama. Long Live the Republic.'

30

The Committee Meeting over, the newly promoted Colonel Dai Powell snapped off a smart salute to the two Generals, Miaja and Lister, and quickly moved into the office that had been made available to him so that he could organise the two-day briefing conference he had been ordered to front for all unit officers between the ranks of lieutenant and captain.

'Get on the phone to the Spanish Communist Party representatives at the Popular Front Government offices and find out where Dña Dolores Ibárruri is located at the moment,' Dai Powell instructed his orderly and close friend Corporal George Stewart. *'I urgently need to talk on the telephone with that wonderful woman known as La Pasionaria.'*

Colonel Powell then busily turned his attention to drafting a signal to unit officers who were to be put under orders to attend the briefing conference to be held at the Republican Army training centre in Albacete in preparation for the critical forthcoming battle of Jarama where, Intelligence Officers forecaste that the Nationalist

Army, commanded by the up and coming General Francisco Franco, would renew their attempt to capture Madrid.

'All Unit commanders between the ranks of lieutenant and captain are ordered to attend a 48 hour briefing conference at nine hundred hours sharp in the main hall of the Albacete training centre on 3rd February 1937. Presiding at the conference, under the direct orders of Commander in Chief, General José Miaja, will be Colonel Dai Powell of the International Brigades' British Battalion, Overnight accomodation and meals will be provided at the Albacete barracks throughout the conference.

From the office of the Commander in Chief, Republican Army 1st February 1937'

Having sent the message to the Sergeant in charge of the headquarters Signal Office for dispatch Dai then turned his attention to George Stewart had just hung up the phone after trying to locate the iconic *La Pasionara*.

'Doña Ibárruri is visiting wounded Republican soldiers at a military hospital,' Corporal Stewart informed his pal. *'After I informed her that you are anxious to talk to her urgently she is waiting at a phone number she gave me for your call. Do you want me to get her on the line now, Dai?'*

Powell was delighted that contact had been made with the legendary *La Pasionara,* and said: *'Yeah, yeah, well done George, get her on the line immediately.'*

Doña Dolores Ibárruri, good as her word, picked up the telephone when it rang.

'Hola, Colonel Powell, I am pleased to talk to you again,' she answered Dai's initial greeting. *'Congratulations on your promotion. Of course I remember enjoying breakfast with you and*

your novia, the lovely Enfermera Pilar Delgado at the fishing village of Torremolinos a few weeks ago. I hope Pilar is well. Now what can I do for you?'

Dai explained that Republican intelligence officers were expecting an assault at Jarama to launch another Nationalist attempt to capture Madrid.

'General José Miaja Menant, Commander in Chief of the Republican Army, is concerned about the defeat of our forces at the recent battle for Malaga,' he said. *'We have examined the causes for that shameful setback and it has been blamed on a lack of moral fibre amongst middle ranking unit leaders. I have been deputed to lecture to all Republican officers between lieutenant and captain ranking, in an effort to persuade them to raise the performance of the men under their command as well as their own calibre as leaders.*

'I have a personal favour to ask you Doña Ibárruri, nay let me rephrase that pompous request. I have a favour to ask you on behalf of the Republican cause for which you have already done so much! Would you be kind enough to address the conference of junior officers to take place at the Republican Army training centre at Albacete with one of your morale-boosting speeches which have done so much already to lift all the supporters of the Popular Front?'

La Pasionara did not dwell long on the proposition that had been placed before her and said: *'Of course I will talk at your conference. It is a duty. Repetition of the overthrow at Malaga is unthinkable. The Republican cause is on the line. For the sake of democracy and the Popular Front we must not let the Fascist murderers succeed.'*

Dai was delighted as he thanked the iconic *La Pasionaria* and added: *'Gracias, gracias Doña Ibárruri. My orderly, Corporal*

George Stewart, will collect you the day after tomorrow and drive you to Albacete where suitable overnight accomdation will be provided for you by the Republican Army.'

Colonel Dai Powell had set the scene for a revival of Republican dreams against the Nationalist Fascists whose war-lords had already unanimously appointed Francisco Franco as Generalisimo-General of Generals-with overall military and civil powers.

Democracy in Spain, as perceived by the Republicans, was in the balance!

31

It was an ironic twist of fate that a lad from the teeming valleys of South Wales, who set to work at the coal face as a 14-year-old boy down the local colliery, assiduously continued his education at night by gaslight and qualified for a place at University, should be elevated to the prestigious rank of Colonel in Spain's Republican Army.

Of course his chosen subject at the University was Military History had filled his mind with tactical ploys of yesteryear that led to impressive victories by lesser armies against stronger enemies. Ploys like the Wooden Horse of Troy he had used to such good effect for the Republican Army in the battle for the Corruna Road. A victory that had brought him to the attention of the Republican's top brass and led to his rapid attention through the ranks.

There was a noisy hubbub from scraping chairs and gossiping 148 officers, many of them cynically suspicious about what they were about to hear, as they waited for Colonel Dai Powell to enter the crowded hall.

'*Best of order for the officer in charge of this conference,*' yelled Corporal George Stewart as Dai Powell briskly paced through the now-silent hall to the empty rostrum where he saluted his audience now stood stiffly at attention.

'*I am here not to lay blame on anyone for our defeat at the Battle of Malaga,* ' said Colonel Powell. '*But I have been ordered by the Commander in Chief of the Republican Army, General José Mija Menant to tell you that it is imperative that a repeat of a setback like Malaga would not only hand over the capital , Madrid, to General Franco and the Nationalists but probably a decisive victory in this Civil War.*

'*General Menant believes that unit leaders, such as yourselves, ranking from lieutenant to captain, must take the responsiblity for following the battle tactics laid down by his headquarters staff, and passed on by senior officers. It is up to you to stir up the men serving under you not to give ground to the Nationalists. To fight to the death against General Franco's murderous fascists and devote their lives and courage to the maintenance of democracy in Republican Spain.*

'*That is the military point of view of the duties that lay in front of you. Now I want you to hear of not only the political morivation but the emotional viewpoint from the Republican civillian population who are depending on you to defend their women, their old people and their children from the barbarian Nationalists--please listen to an icon of the Republican movement --Doña Ibárruri--better known to all of you as the legendary La Pasionaria.*'

The silence around the tiered seating of the lecture hall was profoundly respectful as *La Pasionaria* was ushered towards the stage and assisted to her seat by Colonel Powell who greeted her with an affectionate *abrazo.* Then, with an unmilitary style greeting 148 officers stood and applauded and boisterously cheered the slim, elegant figure dressed in black of the iconic Doña Ibárruri.

From an undisciplined uproar the noise subsided to a poignant silence as *La Pasionaria* rose to make her address:

"Soldiers! Anti-fascists! Spanish Patriots! Confronted with the fascist military uprising, all most rise to their feet, to defend the Republic, to defend peoples' freedoms as well as their achievements towards democracy!

"Through the statements by the government and the parties that comprise the Popular Front, the people understand the gravity of the moment. In Spanish Morroco, as well as in the Canary Islands and the Peninsular, the workers are battling united with the forces still loyal to the Republic, against the uprising militants and fascists.

"Under the battlecry: 'Fascism shall not pass; the Nationalist hangmen shall not pass!' Workers and farmers from all Spanish provinces are joining in the struggle against the enemies of the Republic that have arisen in arms. Communists, Socialists, Anarchists and Republican Democrats, soldiers and other forces remaining loyal to the Republic combined have inflated the first defeats upon the fascist foe , who drag through the mud the very same honourable military tradition that they have boasted to possess so many times.

"The whole country cringes in indignation at these heartless barbarians that would hurl our democratic Spain back down into an abyss of terror and death. However, THEY SHALL NOT PASS! For all of Spain presents itself for battle. In Madrid the people are out in the streets in support of the Government and encouraging its decision and fighting spirit so that it shall reach its conclusion in the smashing of the militant and fascist insurrection.

"Soldiers, sons of the nation! Stay true to the Republican State and fight side by side with the workers, with the forces of the Popular Front, with your parents, your siblings and comrades! Fight for Spain, for the Republic and help them to victory! Workers of all stripes!

"Let no one hesitate! All stand ready for action. All workers, all antifacists must now look upon each other as brothers in arms.'

The standing ovation, led enthusiastically by Colonel Dai Powell from the stage, lasted ten minutes and was climaxed by 148 soldiers lining up for an autograph from the fabulous *La Pasionaria*. Using her pseudonym she signed cigarette packets, identity cards, peseta notes, army pay slips, and the backs of old envelopes. Treasures that the Republican soldiers would keep in the breast pockets of their tunics until their dying day, which, sadly, in many cases, would not be too far away.

32

La Pasionaria, accepted Colonel Dai Powell's cordial invitation to dine with him at the *Restaurante El Callejón, Albacete, that evening.*

'Doña Dolores Ibárruri I feel very honoured that you have accepted my invitation to dinner this evening,' said Dai. *'I hope you wont mind if my orderly Corporal Stewart joins us at the table. You see George is much more than my orderly but my closest pal who started off with me on the Jarrow Hunger March over two years ago, walking the length of England on behalf of our nation's starving workers. Then across to Spain with me to volunteer for service with the International Brigades in support of the Popular Front and the Republican Army.'*

La Pasionaria smiled at the suggestion that she might have some objection to sitting down at a dining table with a humble corporal.

'Colonel Powell I have spent most of my life fighting for the cause of working men and women and the prinicple that all human people

are born equal whatever their status or rank in life is,' said the extraordinary woman who was already a legend in her own lifetime in the minds of the fighting soldiers of the Republican Army.

Dai Powell was not surprised at *La Pasionarias* liberal dissertation.

'Thank you Doña Dolores,' he said. *'Thank you. There is no doubt that your slogan "no pasaran"--they shall not pass- has given the beleagured citizens of Madrid encouragement in the battle against the insurgent Nationalists. '*

La Pasionaria considered Dai's tribute before responding in her typical forthright manner: *'Unfortunately slogans only help to build up morale among the troops. They don't win wars. Remember the Nationalists also have a slogan--*Fe ciega en el Triunfor--Blind faith in victory--*it is just as important to them as "no pasaran" may be to the Republicans.*

'The vital thing is to keep faithful to your own beliefs. I just believe it would be a titanic disaster if my beloved Spain turned towards facism and national socialism. Creeds that practise stringent repression against basic human rights. No political organisation is perfect but at least, as Republicans, we fight for the working classes. People throughout the world who do the hard graft for their entire life with very little reward.'

Dolores, Dai and his pal, George, revelled in the culinary delights of the *Restaurante El Callejón* which was decorated with bullfighting relics and parapemalia and served such typical Spanish food as roast kid, Castllian stew, rice dishes, and snails.

The chatter amongst the three Republican stalwarts was frank, vibrant and entirely centred around the chances that their side had of prevailing against the hated Nationalists.

'Let's be honest it is not disloyal to our Republican Army and those like you two British men who have come to Spain to join the International Brigades to acknowledge the strengths of our enemy,' said *La Pasionaria.* *'Their leader General Francisco Franco is a brilliant soldier and proved his bravery fighting as commander of the Spanish Foreign Legion in Morocco before the outbreak of this Civil War. It earned Franco elevation as the inaugural planner and leader of the new General Military Academy for Army officers at Saragossa in 1928.*

'Within 12 months he had organised the equipping and the curriculum of the Acadamy, which was Spain's simulation of Britain's prestigious military academy for officers at Sandhurst.

'After he had sifted 215 successful candidates, from the 785 candidates who sat the entrance examination, for a place at the Academy he laid down his own version of the ten Commandments for the aspiring officers, as follows.

First Commandment: Love your country.

Second Commandment: Cultivate a great military spirit

Third Commandment: Be chivalrous in spirit

Fourth Commandment: Carry out your duties faithfully and precisely.

Fifth Commandment: Never grumble and do not tolerate the grumble of others.

Sixth Commandment: See to it that you are loved by your inferiors and appreciated by your superiors.

Seventh Commandment: Be ready to volunteer for any sacrifice by asking--and wishing--to be used on occasions when the risks and the fatigue are greatest.

Eighth Commandment: Be a good comrade.

Ninth Commandment: Develop a love of responsibility and decision

Tenth Commandment: Show courage and abnegation.'''

Dai Powell was impressed and said: '*I agree that is a well a thought out summary of the requirements needed by an officer in any Army. It gives me an insight to why the Nationalist Generals jointly elected Franco as their overall leader--the Generalissimo of their Army. Franco is indeed a foe to be reckoned with but that does not mean that he is invincible. We must carefully work out a way to improve our own performance. What do you think George, my friend? You are closest to the other ranks. Where did the blame lay for our failure at the battle for Malaga?*'

George Stewart smiled sardonically as he considered his reply, torn between being brutally honest and answering with a diplomatically soft touch.

'*Barrack rooms are always crawling with criticism against their officers,*' he said. '*Everyone is to blame but themselves. Yet I have to agree that young officers of Lieutenant rank offer the men under their command little inspiration. It is a weak link in our chain of command and one the Nationalists have been able to capitalise on when our junior officers have failed to conform to the plan handed down from the top echelon.*'

Dai Powell thanked *La Pasionaria* and assured her that Corporal Stewart would be at her service to drive her back to Madrid the following morning when he would be addressing 148 of the Republican Army's junior officers on the second day of their briefing conference at the Albacete Training Centre.

33

They had gathered in the assembly hall at the Republican Army training centre in Albacete at 8 am the following morning as Colonel Dai Powell strode in to mount the rostrum for the second day of the briefing conference designed to precede the battle of Jarama.

'I could tell how much you men idolised La Pasionaria when she addressed you in this hall yesterday,' Dai told the assembly. *'As unit commanders you are critical in thwarting the efforts of the Nationalists to cut the Valencia Road where it runs through the Jarama Valley to the South West of the City of Madrid. If the Nationalists succeed and take Madrid it could give them overall victory in this Civil War.*

'Once again La Pasionaria sends us into battle with her famous slogan "no pasaran--they shall not pass" ringing in our ears. To respond to her appeal you must gain the respect of the men serving under you, urge them to show courage, to follow the tactical orders passed down to unit level from the higher command of the Republican Army.

'Repulse the fascists, summon up all your courage and you will

have struck a significant blow towards saving our beloved Spain from the yoke of savage totalitarian dictatorship.

'Good luck to all of you in the battle that faces us!'

With a scraping of chairs on the wooden floor and a thud of army boots the 148 officers, almost as if they were only one man, came to rigid attention and, with sharp symmetry snapped of their smartest salute, when Colonel Dai Powell marched out of the hall, signalling the end of the conference.

34

A 10 foot trestle table was unfolded, its majestic length accentuated by the detailed coloured maps of Madrid and the roads that spiralled towards the Spanish capital strewn across its *madera contrachhapada*-plywood-surface.

The Republican Army think tank comprising General José Miaja Menant, Commander in Chief, General Enrique Lister Commander of the much respected International Brigades, and Colonel Dai Powell, a former Welsh coalminer who in under two years had risen through the ranks on the back of a formidable and growing reputation as a military tactician, and Powell's orderly, Corporal George Stewart, closest pal, official Minute taker and secretary to the think tank.

Powell, who had studied historical military tactics at Cardiff University, had been deputed by General Miaja to produce a plan that would foil the Nationalist Army's third attempt to capture the Spanish capital, Madrid, a plan that would bring victory at the forthcoming Battle of Jarama.

Miaja looked at the other three men present and said: '*Same ground rules as our last meeting gentlemen. No pulling rank from anyone. Just Christian names.'*

Then looking at Powell, the CIC of the Republican Army, said: *'Well Dai are you able to tug another "wooden horse" out of the bag to enable us to deliver a telling blow against the Nationalists at the impending battle of Jarama. But first tell me how your briefing conference for junior officers went at the Albacete training centre. It was a brilliant stroke on your part to persuade La Pasionaria to give the men one of her famous pep talks. '*

The man from the Rhonnda Valley carefully measured his reply and then said: *'No one can stir the blood of fighting men better than Doña Dolores Ibarurri. I could sense as she left the rostrum that 148 officers in the hall would be prepared to fight to the death for her. So much for morale of the junior officers in charge of our units. But morale boosters will not win battles, let alone a fiercely fought patriotic Civil War. What is clear to me if we are to put the Nationalists to the sword and shatter their obsessive ambition to capture Madrid then we must lure the enemy into an ambush. We capitalised on the wiles of the Trojan's when we used their wooden horse trick.*

'Now I want to take a leaf from arguably the most brilliant military tacticians the world has ever known--the Romans, whose theme was: To distress the enemy more by famine than by the sword is the mark of consumate skill.'

Dai Powell knew he had captured the interest of the two Generals who were his think-tank colleagues. The former university graduate in military history explained that when they conquered agricultural territory they commandeered the crops, cattle, sheep and pigs robbing the opposing force facing defeat because of starvation.

The Romans' Plan "B" was the ploy that Powell advised his Republican colleagues to adopt as the most effective way to foil the Nationalists at the forthcoming Battle of Jarama.

'We must intercept the Nationalist Army supplies, arms and ammunition, enroute to the designated battlefield in the Jarama Valley. By cutting their main links of transport we could decimate their supplies to a trickle.

'If we succeed in this plan we could weaken the Nationalists to such a degree they would be unable to offer much resistance to an ambush.

'The bonus is that as the Nationalists weapons, let's face it, are superior than ours because of the help they are getting from the fascist allies Hitler and Mussolini, we would boost our own firepower.'

Generals Miaja and Lister were enthusiastic about the plan Colonel Powell had evolved and which he presented in detail, pointing to parts of the Valencia Road where it ran through the Jarama Valley to the south-east of the City of Madrid.

Dai Powell continued his dissertation: *'I have heard that the overall Nationalist commander General Franco has said, on record, that the International Brigades are showing that they are 'not afraid to die'. I think Franco was being patronising rather than complimentary in that statement. Let's show Franco that Republican soldiers are not afraid to die but also not scared to kill Nationalists in their desire for victory.'*

It was agreed that General Enrique Lister would be in charge of the International Brigade's task force deployed to intercept the Nationalist Army's supplies, arms and ammunition. While Colonel Dai Powell was designated to lead the ambush to trap the seriously weakened Nationalist forces.

Generalissimo Franco appointed General Luis Orgaz to lead

the Nationalist assault, which began on 6th February along the Valencia Road where it bisected the Jarama Valley.

Franco's High Command were delighted that after five days serious hand to hand fighting that General Orgaz's task force seemed to have driven Colonel Dai Powell's Republican's unit eastwards across the River Jarama. But the celebrations were quickly cut short at Franco's headquarters when it was realised that General Orgaz and his men had been sucked into an ambush when Powell called up five thousand reserve troops who had been waiting in reserve in the nearby woods while what the Nationalists believed was his main defending force had steadily given ground during those opening five days.

When Orgaz ordered the Nationalists to retreat across the very ground they had captured only to find that General Enrique Lister had cut off their retreat and hijacked the convoy of lorries carrying all their supplies and desperately needed ammunition.

When the Battle of Jarama ended on 24th February the Nationalists had lost 5,000 men in their latest abortive bid to capture Madrid.

The Republican's also lost nearly 1,400 men, General Lister's International Brigadeers were the worst hit, while Dai Powell had the satisfaction of knowing his tactical plan had worked perfectly despite the loss of more than 400 men under his command.

It was a vital success for the Republicans, a put down once again for Generalissimo Francisco Franco's repeated attempts to clinch Madrid, and yet another boost for Dai Powell 's soaring reputation as one of the outstanding military tacticians involved in the Spanish Civil War.

35

Colonel Dai Powell left his unit on the battlefield and drove to Madrid from the bloody battlefield of Jarama in his official Mercedes saloon car with his orderly corporal George Stewart at the steering wheel.

The other two members of the Republican think-tank committee, General José Miaja Menant, the Commander in Chief, and General Enrique Lister whose International Brigades had fought so valiantly were already waiting for Dai to join them in the debriefing after the Battle of Jarama.

'On behalf of our glorious Republican cause, and of course myself, my heartfelt thanks to both of you,' said General Miaja. *'You Dai Powell have proved to be a brilliant military tactician and absolutely invaluable to our Republican cause. You are a member of the International Brigade who have proved their courage in battle is as staunch as any Spanish soldier in this hard-fought Civil War. It is only right and proper that I should reward your bravery just as I would any Hispanic warrior put their life on the line for the Republic. I therefore promote you to the rank of one star*

General. You will be the first foreign born national to attain such a high rank in the history of the Spanish armed forces--an honour you thoroughly deserve. But I have to be honest with you this elevation can only be at its best for the duration of this Civil War if, as we all hope, the Republic prevail. Also I have to be equally honest that there is a move in the United Nations to persuade both sides of this Civil War to repatriate foreign fighters to their own countries and restrict the conflict only to Spanish citizens.

'As for you Enrique Lister we could not have won the victory at Jarama over the Nationalists without the gallant efforts your men put in hijacking the enemy's supplies and ammunition. To both of you I award the first Republican Spanish Civil War Medals.'

General Miaja then gave Dai and Enrique a warm *abrazo* and a *beso* on each cheek before pinning on the shiny new medals with their Blue, yellow and red vertical shaped ribbons.

'It looks as if we are going to face a few weeks of stalemate while the Nationalists lick their wounds after Jarama,' said General Miaja. *'Let's convene this committee in ten days time. Meanwhile order your unit commanders to sharpen up their men with drills and realistic manouver exercises.'*

36

As Lady Hamilton of Horatio Nelson fame, Lady Marian Fitzwalter of Leaford, better known as Maid Marian, the bonny lass who Robin of Sherwood Forest always had in his longbow sight and regal Clementine Churchill, an aristocratic peeress in her own right, who the doughty Winston adored through five decades of eventful marriage, including two world conflicts, were to discover men of action know how to capture a girl's heart.

Despite not feeling his eager embraces or his keen kisses for several long weeks *Enfermera Militar Pilar* was desperately in love with her soldier boy Dai Powell. As she crept to her tent often enough past midnight, tugging off her rubber boots coated with coagulated blood from the operating table, after sixteen nightmarish hours assisting the surgeon desperately, and sadly often unsuccessfully, striving to save the lives of savagely wounded warriors of both Republican and Nationalist persuasions, she would wearily sink to her knees and say a bedside prayer that her lover would survive the horrors of the Civil War.

Although military security practises prevented him getting in touch with her during the long and heart-aching absences, as much for her sake as for his own while observing the strict protocol of safeguarding military secrets.

Now happily faced with a precious six days of leave before the Commander in Chief, General José Miaja Menant, required the presence of the newly promoted General at the next session of the Republican Army's tactical think-tank committee, Dai Powell set about tracing Pilar amongst the maze of trenchs, fortifications and front line field medical dressing stations. He deputed his orderly and pal, Corporal George Stewart, to trace where Pilar was serving.

After an hour on the line talking to top brass of the Army Medical Corps, Stewart discovered that Pilar was working as the top operating theatre nurse at a field surgical unit in Granada where the Republicans had been strongly entrenched since the reverse in the Battle of Malaga.

'*Well done George,*' said Powell. '*See if you can get the commanding officer of her unit on the line.*'

Less than a hour later Major Rafa Canello sent a medical orderly to *Enfermera Delgado* with his compliments, asking if she would be kind enough to come to his office.

Pilar marched in smartly producing a salute in perfect military style towards her senior officer seated at his desk.

A brilliant surgeon and long-serving Republican Army medic, Major Canello returned the salute less formally and producing a wry smile teased her with a mischievous question: '*Nurse -Delgado do you know a soldier called Powell--Dai Powell?*'

The Major sensed her irritation as she corrected him.

'*I know a Colonel Dai Powell,*' she snapped, determined that her lover should be accorded his correct rank.

'*In that case I either might have been talking to the wrong man or you are not up to date with the latest news,*' said Major Canello still tantalising his operating theatre nurse who he admired for her courage and dedication to duty. '*But seriously, I am sure that I have been talking to the right Dai Powell--a Colonel in the International Brigades, promoted to General two days ago, for his outstanding service to the Republican Army by the Commander in Chief, General José Miaja Menant.*

'*He phoned me just over an hour ago and politely asked me if I would grant you seven days leave to coincide with the six day's furlough he has been given by General Menant. So the head and tail of it is how could I refuse a request from a General? Furthermore Pilar no nurse in the Medical Corps is more deserving of leave than you. Go ahead Pilar enjoy the break with your lover-enjoy the break with your lover! May I wish you both good luck in the future.*

'*General Powell asked me to tell you that he would call to pick you up tomorrow morning.*'

37

At precisely 9 am the following morning General Powell's Mercedes limousine with his orderly, Corporal George Stewart at the steering wheel, rolled into the Republican Army medical facility in Granada and parked outside the office of the commanding surgeon Major Rafa Canello.

Dai Powell received a warm welcome from Major Canello and accepted the offer of coffee and biscuits.

'I want to thank you sincerely Major for releasing Enfermera Delgado for week's leave,' said Dai sincerely. *'With our varying duties taking us in different directions it is extremely difficult for us to get together. A problem that is common to a lot of us involved in this Civil War. A price we have to pay for serving Spain.'*

Major Canello responded in the warmest manner and said: *'First let me thank you for your recent promotion General Powell as those of us serving in the Army, appreciate your dedication to our Republican cause has been invaluable. As for Enfermera Delgado her devotion has been beyond reproach. As matter of fact I am glad to accede to your request. A break will do her good. Her exceptional sense of humanity and compassion to the sick and wounded has led to pleas from me for her to take a recuperative rest.*

'I hope you won't think that I am being presumptious but I would like to offer yourself and Senorita Delgado my family "casa de campo" here in Granada for your week's leave. By explanation my wife is away, with our children, for a month's vacation with her parents in Barcelona. It is more convenient for me to stay here in my quarters at this base while they are away. I will be delighted if you accept my invitation without embarrassment. There is a garage for your car and a separate bedroom, away from the main house, for your orderly.'

Dai Powell was unmistakenly surprised and grateful for the offer.

'I must thank you Major for your generous invitation ,' he said enthusiastically. *'My first reaction is one of embarrassment. But the warmth of your proposal would make it churlish for me to refuse it. I will be indebted and grateful to you.'*

Major Canello did not disguise his pleasure that his invitation had been accepted.

'I am sure you are now impatient to be reunited with your novia,' said the Granada Republican Army Medical Base commander. *'I will send down to the nurses' quarters for her to come here immediately. Meanwhile my clerk Private Oskar Telmo will brief your orderly Corporal Stewart on the directions to find my villa which is only ten kilometres from Granada's city centre.'*

38

Pilar arrived in an attractive sky-blue dress carrying her scarlet lined navy blue nurse's cape in case of inclement weather during their six day vacation.

While Dai's orderly, Corporal George Stewart, politely relieved her of a heavy tooled leather hold-all containing her clothes and toiletry she greeted her beloved Dai. Their kisses were ravenously fervent as if they been separated by years rather than weeks. Nobody watching their ardent body language could possibly be sceptical about their love for each other which erupted into a flurry of eager embraces.

George Stewart gave a perfect demonstration of decorum by concentrating on stacking Pilar's luggage in the trunk of the Mercedes rather than looking directly at his boss General Powell and the attractive nurse he loved in the throes of their *apasionada reunión* .

Nevertheless Stewart was appreciative when Pilar, her excited initial reaction to seeing her beloved Dai sated, turned towards her *novio's* orderly and gave him a meaningful *abrazo*, platonically planting a fond *beso* on his stubbly kiss and chirped: '*It is good to see you again George.*'

The constant Corporal, as devoted as his boss and friend to the bewitchingly beautiful *enfermera* answered with equal enthusiasm: '*No, no Pilar it is my pleasure. It is good to see you looking so good while this cruel Civil War is waging around us.*'

While Dai and Pilar snuggled up, their arms affectionately clasped around each other in the rear of the *Mercedes* limousine, Corporal George Stewart at the steering wheel took 15 minutes to complete the short journey to Major Canello's elegant *finca* just outside the ancient Andalusian city of Granada situated at the foot of the *Sierra Nevada* mountains where the three rivers, *Beiro*, *Darro* and *Genil* met at an elevation of 738 metres.

Pilar was delighted with the symmetry and style of her commanding officer's courtly *campo de casa*. Its verdant olive groves, plump orchards abundant with oranges, lemons and yellow *pomellos* ripe and ready for the *desayuno* table. Dai Powell was equally delighted that his girlfriend was so pleased with the finca where they were to spend a memorable week's furlough from their arduous military duties. Capping the perfection of the finca was the two-roomed granny-flat, with an *en suite* shower room, attached to the garage where George Stewart would sleep away from the main house.

After Corporal Stewart had deposited the lovers' luggage to their spacious luxury bedroom inside the two hundred year old *finca* he was given his orders for the week by his boss General Dai Powell.

'*George, my friend I would be obliged while Pilar and I rest this afternoon if you take the car down to the nearby village and buy enough food from the local* "tienda de comestibles" *to last the three of us for the week,'* said the Welsh born military highflier. *'It would perhaps be a good idea if you consult with Pilar to make a list of what we need. It will mainly be breakfast food because I feel sure we shall be eating our main evening meal out at one of the local Andalusian restaurants. You might ask locally the name of a nearby place they can recommend for dinner tonight when I hope you will join Pilar and myself. Incidentally for the duration of this trip, for security reasons, we will both wear civvies clothes and do not use our ranks when addressing ourselves in public. In short George you will revert to what you have always been--my best pal!'*

The gritty Corporal, born in the hard-working ship building area in the North East of England, was appreciative of Dai's dissertation of devotion: *'Thank you Dai I followed your suggestion before we left Madrid and brought my civvy clothes with me; grey flannel trousers, short sleeve shirt and sports jacket. I checked with our intelligence people in Madrid and they have no knowledge of any Nationalist Army forces in the Andalusian area at all--in fact it is a very staunch Republican area. I'll go and find Pilar and sort out a shopping list and afterwards make a pot of coffee for the two of you before I go off to the local grocery shop.'*

Dai Powell handed Stewart a sizeable wad of Republican issue peseta banknotes and said: *'Thank you George use this money for our expenses during the week and just ask me for more if it runs out!'*

39

Having drawn up a list , the lovely Pilar made it clear what groceries they needed, and even the well-known brands she preferred as George Stewart drove off in the *Mercedes* to complete his shopping trip.

Back in the grand lounge Pilar and Dai did not take long to finish the pot of coffee and demolish the *galletas chocolataa* before, arm-in-arm they climbed up the finca's winding staircase with its elegantly polished wooden handrail. They were both eager to reach the privacy of their bedroom.

An hour later, their honeyed lust between the sheets sated, not once but three times, they lay back on their silk pillow's and sipped glasses of cava from the bottle Dai had opened.

'*I was so proud Dai, my love, when Major Rafa Canello, told me you had been promoted to General,*' said Pilar affectionately. '*The Republican Army should be eternally grateful for what you, and your comrades in the International Brigades are doing for Spain.*'

Dai Powell gratefully accepted the praise his lover lavished on him.

'The cause of the working class has always been near to my heart,' he said. *'Although I am not, and never have been a Communist but quite categorically I could never support a cruel regime such as Facism and Nationalism as practised by ruthless dictators like Mussolini and Hitler in Italy and Germany. That is the reason why Republicans in this country must fight to the death to prevent the Nationalists, led by General Francisco Franco from inflicting a sadistic military dictatorship on our beloved Spain.'*

Pilar replied passionately: *'God knows, Dai darling, you don't have to convince me about fighting for the working class. As the third child of an Asturian coal miner, I see my mother bent, dark-eyed, weary at her life's daily burden cooking, cleaning, washing and mending clothes, struggling to feed a large family. A little wizened woman of 49 who looks 70 years old. I would do anything, anything--do you hear me Dai to ease her torment. Adding to her agony my two brothers are fighting in this war one for the Republicans the other wears the black shirt of the Fascists.*

'Bizarrely both my siblings ardently believe they are fighting for the right cause. My mother will shed the same tears if either one of them is killed in this awful Civil War. Just as a surgical military nurse I quickly noted that the colour of a wounded soldier's blood is the same cloying crimson whether they wear the uniform of the Republican's or the Nationalists.

'Where does that leave us lover boy? You hold the elevated rank of General mi amante Dai and I am proud of that. But to me you are the man I love, the man I want to marry, the man whose children I ache to bear.

'As I have said where does that leave us querido?'

Dai Powell rolled over to Pilar's side of the bed totally shocked at her impassioned outburst. He moved in on her slowly teasing her nipples. She could feel his erection engorge as her hand reached for it. She guided him and he heard her sigh emotionally as he entered her.

Their athletic grinding grew faster as they both reached a climax together. Dai pulled her towards him until they lay face to face.

'Look Pilar both of us know how much we love each other,' he said tenderly. *'I desperately want us to get married as much as you do sweetheart. But because of my duties in the Republican Army I am closer than you about how this Civil War is going. I wouldn't say this to anyone else than you. Not even to my boss, General José Miaja, the Commander in Chief of the Republican Army. But the prospects of us defeating the Nationalists is very much in the balance. For a start our enemy is better equipped than us with modern, guns, ammunition, tanks, aircraft and bombs supplied by Hitler and Mussolini. The military aid we are getting from our Russian allies is nowhere commensurate in quality with what the Nationalists are getting from Germany and Italy.*

'It is true, in all modesty, I have been helping the Republicans to win a few battles by shrewd tactical planning. But in the end the Nationalists' better equipment may well prove to be the facet that gives them ultimate victory. In which case foreigners like myself fighting for the Republicans would either be taken to the frontier and ignominiously kicked out of Spain or, which is more likely, stood up in front of a firing squad. Where do you think that would leave you my love? Pardon me for being vulgar but, as they say in the barrack room, you would be up shit creek without a paddle or, worse, tied up alongside me in front of the firing squad.

I wouldn't chance inflicting that fate on any other person let alone the woman I love with all my heart. That is why I won't marry you Pilar darling until after this war ends. So we will have to take our chances on what our fate will be then. Whatever happens nothing can stop us loving each other and that really is the only thing that matters.'

40

Corporal George Stewart returned from his shopping excursion to the nearby city of Granada having done his homework on behalf of the two lovers in also searching out a suitable restaurant where the three friends would eat that evening.

'As you both know Granada is noted throughout the world for it's ancient Moorish citadel known as Alhambra, which in Arabic literally means the "the red fortress" formerly a palace and fortress of the Muslim rulers of Granada,' he explained. *'So it is not surprising that Arab-influenced food abounds in the city. There are numerous exotically decorated teterias -tea-rooms-who offer couscous and tagine dishes. Also there are a number of kebab-shawarma joints and in particularly one upmarket Moorish restaurant the Arrayanes. There are also many tapas bars, and more authentic Granadine eateries serving fried squash with quail's eggs and great seafood.*

'It is up to you what kind of food you fancy I have a long list of suitable places.'

After a lengthy discussion Dai decided that he would leave it to Pilar to choose what kind of food they should opt for.

'*When I was at college in Bilbao, studying to be a nurse, I shared a room with a Turkish girl or to be more precise, the daughter of a Turkish woman married to a Spanish gas engineer who lived and worked in Istanbul. Soraya Tomello was a beautiful and intelligent girl who taught me lot about how to cook and appreciate Arabic food. I have heard good things about the Restaurante Arrayanes in Granada City and I think it will be an interesting place for us to eat tonight.* '

Dai Powell, tongue in cheek, teased her: '*Hold on old girl--are you advocating we have a teetotal night? Muslims are forbidden to consume alcohol, you know.*'

Pilar Delgado was willing to wage a war of witticism with her lover, and snapped back: '*Oh! I wouldn't dare deprive my "amante guapo" of his daily dose of intoxicant. What about the three of us starting off the night at a typical Granada tapas bar where we can enjoy an aperitivo and a typical Andulasian tapa before we move on to the Restaurante Arrayanes. After our meal we can round off our night with a visit to another bar for our coñacs and cafés--how about that love?*'

Dai smiled, and drawing on the chivalry demanded of a general, commented wryly: '*You win querido! I never argue with a woman. Particularly one as beautiful as my lovely nurse!*'

As for George Stewart, although appreciative that his rapport with his pal the General and the sharp-witted nurse was completely relaxed, said nothing. But he could barely disguise a wry smile as he turned his head away from the bantering sweethearts.

So the scene was set for what would be a wonderful night out for the three bosom pals!.

41

A bottle of chilled *cava,* three over-brimmed champagne *vasos,* and a huge *plato* of highly spiced *tapas* put the two Republican musketeers and one *bella enfermera* into an animated mood for an evening of gaiety and camaraderie.

'*I would pay for the tapas and cava only I have left my monedero at the finca,*' laughed Pilar setting the pattern for some good natured repartee.

'*What's new about that?*' retorted Dai. '*When you remember to bring that nurse's handbag, which you always seem to forget, I expect moths will fly out.*'

George Stewart intervened: '*If you two lovebirds will forgive me. I drew a month's pay when I was in Madrid last week and I have decided I will fork out the pesetas for the tapas.*'

Dai Powell assumed the commanding tones of a one-star general and said emphatically, but with obvious rumour: '*If you two lower ranks will pipe down and listen to a senior officer it is I who will be paying for the whole night which is meant to be a celebration of my recent promotion to the rank of General from Colonel. So that is that! Now let's ask the barman to open another bottle of Cava while we consume this feast of quail's eggs, anchovies, tortillas, Iberico jamon, calamaris and caviar.'*

They were all in a happy mood when an hour later they moved on to the Moorish restaurant known as the Arrayanes for their main meal. George Stewart was glad that they had left the Mercedes back at the finca and had employed a taxi with driver for the evening.

They ordered a large mixed Moorish casserole of cucumbers, aubergine, zucchini, okra, onions and citrus and predominantly the fruit which through the centuries has always been the heraldic symbol of Granada--the Spanish word for pomegranate is in fact *Granada*. From which is made the sweetish non-alcholic liquor Grenadine which accompanied their meal.

Then came a delicious ceramic dish of Moroccan spiced duck with *salsa naranja* and *cous cous*. This was washed down by a typically refreshing Arablic soft drink known as *shineena* or *laban*. Then came a dish of *Mansaf* featuring a large leg of lamb on top of *markook* bread topped by yellow rice. Finally a type of thick dried cheesecloth yoghurt made from goat's milk called *jameed* was poured on top of the lamb and rice giving it a distinct flavour. The dish was garnished with cooked pimentos and almonds.

So having belched, with typical Arabic politeness after a good meal, and tightened their belts, with Dai having donated a couple of pesetas extra to the bill so that a prayer of gratitude could be said for the glory of Allah, the intrepid threesome sallied out into a starry Andalusian night for further adventure.

They strolled across to the taxi they had booked for the night. They were merry after the two bottles of *cava* they had consumed at the *tapas* bar earlier in the evening.

'We would like to see a flamenco show,' Dai told their driver

asking: *'Can you recommend a good one?'* The driver replied immediately: *'Yes I know a cante jondo which is a different and more authentic form of gypsy flamenco than the gaudy rubbish offered to the tourist. It is only a couple of kilometres away in a pobre barrio gitane.'*

Dai, after giving the taxi-driver a nod of approval, looked round at this two friends and said enthusiastically: *'That's it kids pile into the car!'*

Inside quarter of an hour they were speedily transported through narrow cobbled streets to a smoky cave on the edge of Granada. They were greeted by the *dueño* a swarthy, unshaven *gitano,* wisps of ebony hair peeping at the edges of the garish red and green bandana he wore on his head.

Dai and George received a wonderful insight into the culture and origins of flamenco dancing not only from the wondrous performance of the four dancers-three female and one man- and the haunting singing of the cantora and cantor strutting their haunting repertoire of ancient songs on the miniature stage but also from the fluent commentary by Pilar, a diehard *aficionada* of the world's most famous dance ritual.

'Flamenco through the ages has encaptured mysterious beauty, enriched in romance,death and folklore and is accompanied by strange music and heel-tapping dancing,' said the enraptured military nurse.

Pilar explained that Andalucia had always been a land where odd ritual celebrations were staged in the streets during the Holy Week of Easter. Colourful scenes of the Passion parade through the streets, trumpets blaring, drums and cymbals clashing while many of the watching crowds lapsed into uncontrollable tears.

'Andalucia is a land where music and dancing has been an essential part of life for centuries.

'It stretches back to the time when Andalucia was occupied by the Moors for nearly eight hundred years and contributed enormously to its unique music and exotic dancing.'

The Andalucia wine from the *barril* and served at the table in an earthenware *jarras* to top up mega-sized *vasos,* came in a non-stop flow. Dai and George, disciplined soldiers as they were, knew when to call a halt to the "binge" a tad short of paralytic collapse.

Their taxi deposited the weary threesome back at their Granada finca at 4am in the morning.

42

Quite understandably Pilar and Dai slept on late that morning and only awakened when George Stewart wheeled in a trolley with two breakfasts.

'What time is it?' the heavy-eyed General grunted at his orderly.

The Corporal answered promptly saying: *'It is eleven o'clock and an absolutely hot and sunny day.'*

The lovers quickly awakened and were most impressed with their breakfast of grapefruits from the finca's abundant garden and orchard. Fresh pomegranates peeled and the luscious pearls packed in iced yoghurt. There were sardines, butterflyed and sautéed in *mantequilla*. Finally a lovely meal was rounded with two small *tortilla espanolas*.

Half an hour later having demolished and enjoyed a healthy and delicious *desayuno* the two lovers decided that it would be an ideal day to recharge their batteries after the exertions and excitement of their 'night on the town', That is exactly how it turned out to be with Dai and Pilar changing into their swimming gear, parking themselves on two sunbeds, which had been specially made by the local carpenter, at the side of the *finca* pool.

After consultation, George Stewart suggested that if they really wanted to spend the day lounging at the *finca* that he would go to the local market in Granada and buy the ingredients for their main meal of the day. It was agreed. Dai and Pilar then both told George about their likes and dislikes in the matter of food.

Fortunately Granada, in the autonomous region of Andalusia, at this stage, had not been hit as badly as other Spanish areas by the Civil War. It was a region considered in peacetime to be the bread basket of Spain. Rich in agriculture, in fact the biggest producer of the precious olive crops in Spain, the breeding of livestock and in all aspects of the production of food. It was a bastion of the Republican cause and would remain so until the end of the Civil War.

So shopping was not a problem as George Stewart collected the ingredients for a super *cena* that evening. In fact there was no shortage of fresh food in the meat, fruit and vegetable line. He decided on rabbit stew for the main course. For a handful of pesetas he bought three plump *conejo* carcases. To go into the *cocido* pot he also acquired from the *carnicero* a shoulder of prime pork.

Vegetables, covered in dew-drenched Andalucian soil when they were picked from the fields just after dawn were in abundance. Potatoes, their flesh when peeled as yellow as a banana, cabbage as green as an English bowling green and as large and rotund as an inflated Soccer ball, snowy white parsnips as pointed as a spear, and verdant asparagus just begging to be steamed and sprinkled with melted *mantequilla*.

Second crop strawberries sweet and huge, and ripe melons in

two juicy varieties. It would be many years after the ravages caused by Civil War before Andalucia would again be able to revel in such a feast of produce.

Pilar lounged and baked all day in the glory of Granada's morning sunshine before retiring to their bedroom for a siesta after their frugal lunch of country baked bread and Manchego cheese.

No soon as he gently pulled the silky *edredón* around them and nestled up to her Pila could feel Dai's erection. She smiled and said, with all the confidence of a woman deeply in love: '*I knew when you suggested we come up here for a siesta that something else was on your mind other than tiredness, despite our lack of sleep last night. You sexy beast.*'

The Welshman quickly picked up on her mischievous mood and retorted: '*Nurse Pilar Delgado you are a witch. A dirty witch with only one thing on your mind. I suppose it is my duty to please you or else you will cast a wicked witch's evil spell in my direction.*'

Pilar, a gutsy lady who had no intention of letting any man put her down, retaliated: '*I don't know about a witch's spell but you had better defend yourself after being so rude to me hombre.*'

Without warning Pilar pulled the pillow from underneath her head and in one precise movement aimed it, with astonishing accuracy, at Dai's face.

'*Ouch,*' he yelled. '*You could have spoiled my looks! A lot of senoritas have told me that my nose is my most handsome feature.*' In a simultaneous overarm movement he surprised his tormentor by whacking his own pillow on her unsuspecting head.

'*Right,*' she said feigning anger. '*Now you will suffer for that!*'

She flung herself across the bed gripping him around the neck in a feminine version of a half-nelson hold.

Guileful, as only a woman hoplessly infatuated with her man

could be, she knew that in a mock physical battle between them their could only be one victor. As good-naturedly he encircled his muscular biceps around her in a definitive movement designed to tame his teasing Spanish shrew, he felt her relax and surrender to his macho embrace.

She felt his member engorge and erect as for the first time she bent towards him and enraptured him with a passionate session of *fellatio.* Her tongue played a rapid fandango around his penis precipitating a seminal foundation as he came to an unbelievable climax.

He had hardly recovered from the unbelievable experience when he forced her down on her back and with his knees nudged her legs wide open. She breathed heavily with excitement as she sensed what the target for his probing tongue was. She felt an almost electric shock as she felt him search and find her clitoris with his tongue darting in and out like a cobra's.

Within seconds, panting heavily with sheer emotion, she reached her zenith and felt her love juices erupt like a veiled volcano.

'Oh darling,' she gasped. *'Darling I love you so much. Please keep safe in this terrible war. I don't think I could carry on if anything happened to you.'*

43

Dinner that night was another happy occasion for the three friends with Corporal George Stewart's delicious *estofado conejo* highlighting a beautifully planned meal which was washed down with two bottles vintage Malága wine produced from the dark-skinned syrah grapes.

The rabbit stew had been carefully and lovingly constructed by Stewart who had developed an intense interest in food and cooking even to the extent of contemplating a career as a chef when the Spanish Civil War had ended. It contained a generous quantity of sliced red onions, tangy *cebollas*, which had been painstakingly nurtured on terraces dug, a century earlier, by toiling labourers from the hillsides encircling Granada. Long and firm *zanahorias* added a warm orange glow to the *estafado* and more important, in the view of dieticians, the primary source, worldwide, of vitamin A, which helps to strengthen the body's immune system.. Garlic, the lushiest, sharpest garlic in the whole Spanish peninsula was added, as was a cocktail of herbs: basil, sage and parsley.

The whole mouth watering concoction, bubbling fiercly

and emitting an irresistible-appetite-whetting aroma that rose throughout the *finca* and invaded Dai and Pilar's taste-buds to such an extent they hustled to the dining table and grabbed their forks and spoon ready for the gastronomic fray.

The stew was accompanied by a huge bowl of root vegetable mash red-skinned local potatoes, parsnips and Swedes softened with a sprinkle of virgin olive oil and crushed together with young shallots. Chunks of crusty fresh crusty bread were laid out in a basket to mop up the succulent juices.

As General Dai Powell said breathlessly, after each of them had demolished two over brimming dishes of the succulent *estofado*: *'As my deal old grandmother, who lived in Aberdare, used to say when she made a stew of Welsh lamb--that sort of food puts a lining on your stomach and the empty plates tell the tale!'*

Then looking at his lover he said: *'Pilar, I think you and I should raise our glasses in tribute to our "chef" for producing such a wonderful meal!'*

'Chef' George Stewart was only left with the elementary chore of rounding off the marvellous stew with a suitable light dessert. He got it exactly right by placing a large bowl of chilled fruit salad delicate slices of Ogen melons nestled alongside juicy Andalucian *naranjas,* sun-ripened *peras* and the insides of the iconic local *granadas,* known throughout the world as pomegranates.

Over their coffee and brandies the General outlined plans for the following day as he addressed his orderly.

'Tomorrow Pilar and I have decided to take the Mercedes into the country and go for a picnic,' he said. *'You can have a free day George--you deserve a break. But we would be grateful if you could make up a picnic basket in the morning before we leave. Don't worry*

about preparing an evening meal we will find a local bar that sells tapas, or other cooked meals, and grab something to eat.

'But be sure and have a good day yourself and thanks for the fine dinner you prepared for us this evening.'

44

After a hearty breakfast of *Iberico jamon* and poached eggs Dai and Pilar packed the picnic basket made up by George Stewart into the boot of the Mercedes and headed off for the picturesque area of Granada known as the Albaicin.

Located on a hill on the right bank of the river Darro, Albaicin, is the site of the ancient city of Elvira which the Zirid Moors renamed Granada in the 11th Century.

Dai and Pilar marvelled at Albaicin's white-washed *casa's*, chapels, restaurants and bars.

Dai parked the Mercedes and they headed for one of Albaicin's famous *teterias* where they enoyed a pot of herbal tea to accompany a plate of traditional Arabic sweetmeats called *baklava*. For an hour afterwards they walked the old Moorish shopping area viewing market stalls selling slippers, silks and traditional *hookah*-pipes the Moors called *shisha* and other exotic novelties.

They returned to the car and Dai steered the Mercedes up to the *Sacromonte* neighbourhood situated on the extension of the Albaicin hill , along the Darro river.

Sacromonte had become notorious in the 19th Century for its gypsy inhabitants who even a hundred years later still lived in primitive caves on the hillside unloved by Nationalists and Republicans during the Spanish Civil War. This, despite the combatants antipathy towards the *gitanes,* did not alter the fact that the colourful Romany tribes people gave the Sacromonte cave ghetto a reputation as the origin of flamenco, song and dance including the noted Andalucian dance called the *Zambra Gitana* which originated in the Middle East.

Having had the fill of sightseeing Dai wheeled the Mercedes to a quiet hillside grotto where they unpacked the picnic basket prepared by Corporal Stewart. Having finished their tasty *boccadillos* of *Quesos de Leyva,* an Andalucion cheese made with 100% pure sheeps milk, and a local *vino Rosada* the two lovers retired into the grotto from the midday heat for a badly needed *siesta.*

The two devoted *inamoratos* slept soundly for two and half hours. Pilar was the first to stir, as she aroused from her deep slumber, as misted eyes began to focus she was at first shocked, then scared, with the outline of a man standing in the entrance of the grotto.

His image was blurred against the bright sunshine outside. Instinctively she nudged the sleeping Dai unable to raise her voice, her heart beating at a rapid pace, as stark fear took over her quaking body.

Part of a soldier's basic training is to be abruptly awakened from sleep ready to spring immediately into action to deal with any unforeseen emergency. As soon as his eyes Dai spotted the lurking figure in the cave entrance and asked aggressively: *'Who the fucking hell are you?'*

The General, with military shrewdness, noticed that the man was about 5ft 8inches tall, sporting an unkempt salt and pepper beard. He wore a greasy bandana over his head, baggy trousers, and tatty leather sandals. But Dai's closer inspection set alarm bells ringing when he spotted the revolver in the intruder's right hand jerking his aim between both Pilar and himself. Dai could sense real danger and pulled himself to his feet preparing to deal with what was looking like a very nasty situation.

'Not so fast motherfucker,' said the man known as Yossi Canjuro a vicious brigand and the leader of a local cave-dwelling tribe of gypsies. *'If this little toy in my hand goes off the first bullet will spread your brains across this fucking cave which belongs to my tribe who will be very pleased to look after your lovely senorita. We don't see many beautiful women like her in these parts. Put your hands where I can see them, or say a prayer before I send you to meet your Maker!'*

Dai, halted as a true military tactician, weighing up any weaknesses of the gypsy leader. Yossi Canjuro took three paces forward to shorten the range. It gave the Welshman the opportunity to note that the Romany's weapon was a British officer's Great War revolver. It was a Mark VI Webley, named after the Birmingham firearms manufacturers. It was made to fire .455" service cartridges and had a muzzle velocity of 600ft per second.

But on the upside Dai Powell noted that the weapon must be around 20 years old and he thought it did not appear to be in too good a condition. The gypsy did not look too compatible with the ageing handgun and might be easy to attack. So in a bid to gain time, Dai raised his hands.

Yossi Canjuro, over confident, assumed that was a sign of surrender from Dai Powell and venomously yelled at the Welshman:

'*Give me your money motherfucker if you want that puta of yours to live! I mean all the money you've got motherfucker and I'll let your whore go--otherwise you will get a bullet in your head and I'll feed her to my men for the night-- there won't much good left in her after that. Come on motherfucker let's see the colour of your money.*'

Dai Powell, noting the gypsy's twitching finger on that ancient .455", sensed that he had to move quickly if he was to avoid being killed.

'*What a fucking way for a one star general to die,*' he thought. '*Shot by a fucking gypsy cowboy with an antique pistol.*' Dai pulled his wallet from his pocket and hissed at the odious *gitane*: '*You can have all the money we've got as long as you let the girl go!*'

Sure in his mind that the gypsy would kill him in any case whether or not he got the money Dai, pretending his hand was shaking, dropped the wallet as he extended it towards the evil Yossi Canjuro who bent forward greedily grasping for the money. Dai athletically bent his knees and straightened up forcefully flapping his hand at the threatening revolver, as he head butted the gypsy chief whose eyes glazed over.

Dai, drawing on his rugby football skills, then instinctively kicked the *gitane's* wrist sending the pistol flying. Yossi Canjuro, however, showed steel that belied the widely held belief that gypsies were cowardly fighters preferring to administer a knife or a bullet in the back of an enemy. He rebounded off the rocky side of the cave with murderous intent. Dai Powell feinted with his left arm and smashed a crunching right punch into the pit of the Romany's rotund stomach.

Yossi made a nauseous sound as he doubled up retching and threatening to bring up his last meal. Dai grabbed his enemy's tatty shirt and, gripping him under the arms, rammed him, head first, into the rocky side of the cave. Not once but four times mashing the gypsy's face into a strawberry coloured pulp. When Dai let him go the villainous Yossi Canjuro collapsed to the floor like a rag doll. He was in a sorry mess. His front teeth had been smashed from his gums, blood flowing from his misshapen nose.

Dai bent down and frisked his badly beat-up foe. He now turned his attention towards the shell-shocked Pilar who squatted head in hands shivering from the trauma of the previous ten minutes. He put his arms around her to comfort her. Despite that she worked as an operating theatre nurse dealing day-on-day with gory amputations, and worse, she was trembling after the violence that unfolded. Nevertheless she explained: *'I was so frightened he was going to kill you my darling. I just couldn't live without you.'*

Dai gently led back to the Mercedes, which he had parked hidden in a copse, five minutes walk away. When he had gently settled her into the passenger seat he said: *'I have to go back I forgot my wallet in the cave with all our money. I'll be back in a few minutes.'* He departed quickly before the frightened girl could remonstrate with him but he knew what he had to do!

It was important to disable the gypsy and prevent him getting in touch with other members of his tribe. Also he didn't want the traumatised Pilar to know what he had to do!

Yossi Canjuro had managed to get to his feet and had already staggered to the entrance of the cave: *'No, No!,'* he pleaded, assuming that Dai had returned to finish him off particularly as he was brandishing his own revolver.

Dai brought the gypsy down with a kick on the shine and silencing the pistol with the gypsy's torn up shirt, so that Pilar would not hear, he put a round in both Yossi's knees.

'That will keep you quiet bastardo! If I ever see you again scumbag I'll kill you,' he warned. *'I hope you fucking well die before the members of your tribe find you! In fact I would be delighted if you fucking bleed to death before the members of your tribe find you!'*

But General Dai Powell of the Republican Army's International Brigades knew that Pilar and himself had a very lucky escape and he vowed never to venture out during the remainder of their holiday unarmed.

45

Any thoughts of taking the seriously stretched Pilar to a restaurant for dinner that night had gone out of the window as Dai Powell decided to devote his time to consoling the military nurse he adored so much.

As soon as they returned to the finca Dai described to the astonished George Stewart how Pilar and himself had been the victims of what might easily have been a fatal mugging.

'For the rest of our vacation this week the three of us must stick together ,' said Dai. 'From now on, for the sake of security, you and I must not venture out without taking our revolvers. It was a serious incident but it might have been worse. This man was obviously the leader of a group of bandits who prey on innocent people who wander into the Sacromonte district. But we mustn't tar all the gitanes with the same brush because they are instrumental over a hundred years or more of introducing such wonderful art forms as flamenco dance and music to Andalucia.'

George Stewart was most sympathetic with Pilar and Dai after their terrible experience.

'You are absolutely right Dai,' replied Stewart. *'From now on I will be with Pilar and yourself as a rearguard all the time. Now your plans have changed I am not going to let you go without a meal. I have three lovely solomillos-sirloin steaks-and I will rustle up a nice big salad and to go with them patatas brava and salsa mantequilla. Furthermore I have several bottles of Gran Reserva Cava- in fact the very best--that will help Pilar forget her frightening experience today.'*

After an hours rest on the bed followed by a hot bath and a change of clothes Pilar proved she was more resilient than Dai thought she could possibly be when she appeared in the dining room ready to eat.

'Don't fuss Dai ,' she assured her lover. *'It was just too much waking up in the grotto to see that horrible man standing there with a gun in his hand. I was just worried for you--but let me say now how wonderfully brave you were. Splendid. I am so grateful how you defended me and behaved so courageously. But I admit I was shivering with fright thinking you might be killed.'*

Pilar was as good as her word, showing her mettle when, bravely casting thoughts of what happened earlier aside, she kept the dinner party alive joking and teasing the two men throughout the meal.

'What would you like to do tomorrow Pilar?' Dai asked. Her reply was instant and decisive: *'It would be a pity for all three of us that we came to Granada without visiting the wonderful Alhambra.'*

46

It was an inspired idea that prompted military nurse Pilar Delgado to suggest that her lover General Dai Powell, of the Republican Army's International Brigades with his close friend and orderly, Corporal George Stewart, should all spend a precious day of their week's leave viewing the world famous Alhambra which stands imperiously on a hilly terrace on the southeastern edge of Granada.

For fate would decree that the three friends would never again get the chance to visit the famous fortress-palace and its wonderful Islamic architecture interwoven with 16th Century Christian input.

Clutching a garishly coloured guide book detailing the magical qualities of Alhambra-translated into the Arabic language "*Qual at-al Hambra*"-*the red fortress*-was once the residence of Granada's ruling Muslim rulers, Pilar gave the two soldiers a running commentary as if they were ordinary tourists and explained that, like other Christian potentates through the centuries, Charles V,

Holy Roman Emperor, in 1527 added features to Alhambra, and built a palace in his own name.

'Its most westerly aspect is the alcazaba (citadel) will interest you military men as it was designed to be a strongly fortified position,' Pilar trilled excitably. *'The literal translation of the name Alhambra* "red fortress" *derived from the colour of the red clay from which the fort was made by the Moors. The first reference of the fortress was during the battles between the Arabs and the Muladies the resounding victors of that particular war.'*

Dai Powell commended the military logic in the defences designed by the ancient warriors.

Pilar took up her commentary again and said: *'One of the most interesting features of the Palacio Árabe - Moorish Palace is the Harem...'*

Dai teased her by interjecting: *'I am not surprised, that's typical--you sexy minx...'*

Pilar, retaliated humorously: *'I'll disregard that ignorant remark with all the disdain it deserves so I will continue with what I was saying before I was so rudely interrupted.*

'The Harem, which, as you can see, is elaborately decorated, and includes the living quarters for the wives and mistresses of the Arabic monarchs. It contains a communal bathroom with running hot and cold water baths, and pressurized water for showering.

'An interesting point is that the bathrooms were open to the weather to allow in light and air.'

Before the three friends ended their tour of Alhambra, having seen only a fraction of the wondrous sights on view, Pilar finally steered the two men towards the *Salón de los Embajadores (Hall of the Ambassadors).*

'This is the grand reception room where the throne of the reigning

sultan stood. It was there that Christopher Columbus later won the support of rulers , Isabel and Ferdinand, to sail to the New World and earn glory for Spain.'

It had been a very tiring three hour tour and the friends agreed that they could easily spend another day sightseeing if they were going to take in all of the wonders of the *Alahambra Palacio*. But more immediately what they needed was some refreshments and rest as they headed towards a local tapas bar.

Dai paid tribute to his *novia* as the three friends shared a bottle of *Rioja* and sampled the tiny dishes of tapas the *bodega* owner had placed in front of them.

'Thank you Pilar, you made that trip interesting,' he said. *'In the past during my rugby football tours I have visited royal palaces such as Henry VIII's favourite home at Hampton Court and the Palace of Versailles in France and believe me Alhambra palace is well up there with those two marvellous places.'*

47

When the three friends arrived back at their villa there was a Republican motor cycle despatch rider waiting with a message for General Dai Powell from the Commander in Chief's headquarters in Madrid.

It was timed six hours earlier and couched in terse military terms said:

From-General José Miaja Menant CIC Republican Army

To- General Dai Powell, International Brigades, Republican Army

Message-*Terminate your leave immediately. New Intelligence re' Nationalist Army plans requires me to convene an urgent Tactical Committee meeting at my office tomorrow at 9am sharp. Proceed to MADRID as soon as possible and report your arrival at my office. Signed: Jose Miaja Menant (CIC).*

Dai felt it was only fair that he should give Pilar the unfortunate news that he had been ordered back to Madrid immediately. *'I am sorry darling but I have got to cut our vacation short by a couple of days but I have been given orders to return to General Menant's headquarters in the next 24 hours. I don't know when we will be able to meet again but I will be in touch with you as soon as I can. Remember how much I love you darling.'*

Tears welling in her eyes, Pilar bravely controlled herself, and said: *'You are a soldier and like me you have to obey orders. I know that. But every time we get together for a few days it is precious. Look after yourself mi querido!'*

The General then addressed his orderly in an informal way: *'George lay out my uniform for the journey. We are ordered back to Madrid for a meeting of the Tactical Committee. Pack the car with all our luggage and we will leave inside an hour. Don't worry about taking any food we will grab a bite and something to drink at a bar on the road.'*

After affectionately embracing Pilar and giving her a lingering farewell kiss Dai Powell climbed into the passenger seat alongside his friend and orderly George Stewart. The Mercedes rolled northwards at a sedate speed of 80 kilometres an hour because of the poor state of roads that had not been repaired after the damage caused by the procession of heavy military traffic of both Nationalist and Republican persuasions.

'Where do you think the next action in this Civil War will takes us Dai,' queried George Stewart when they stopped for a comfort break and refreshment two hours into the long journey.

Dai Powell considered the question before answering: *'That's a good question my old mate George. I heard before we left Madrid over a week ago that General Emillio Mola, commander of the Nationalists in that sector was starting an offensive in the north. Mola has been steadily building up his force in Vizcayad in preparation for an attack on the Basque capital Bilbao.*

'*This could create a problem for our side because our commander in that area, General Francisco Llano de la Encomiend does not control a very well-armed force which will need urgent reinforcing if they are going to have any chance of repelling a strong Nationalist Army.*'

George Stewart reacted to his friend's assessment of the possible problems that lay ahead and said: '*It looks as if we are heading towards a torrid situation again Dai!*'

Dai Powell seemed remarkably nonchalant as he rejoined: '*Such is the fate of all soldiers throughout the ages. To accomplish the difficult and have a good crack at achieving the impossible.*'

The Nationalists had precipitated their big push in the north when they made the most savage attack in aerial warfare, at that point in history, when they savagely destroyed the sleepy town of

Guernica, historic home of the Basque libertarians. Monday 26 April 1937 would just be another weekly market day thought the good men, women and children of Guernica as soon after dawn they swarmed towards the stalls laden with fruit, vegetables, cheeses, garlic sausages and other produce from the abundant farms and smallholdings that had been carted in from the neighbouring countryside.

It was a rural community, a slumbering *ciudad* with no strategically milititary value whose only armaments were the ageing shot guns hung in every house *cocina* ready for the man to go rabbit shooting after early Mass each Sunday. Without warning, wave after wave of heavy German bomber planes of Hitler's Condor Legion dropped hundreds of ton of high explosive bombs indiscriminately of the fleeing townsfolk. Housewives lay dead, sprawled in bizarrely blood red gutters still clutching the handles of woven baskets over-burdened with fruit and vegetables.

Many of their men folk were sipping their last glass of wine outside one of the town centre bars when all hell descended from the sky. There was the pathetic sight of the distorted tiny arms of dead children still clinging to sugar candy sticks.

It was a day of international infamy that would go down in history alongside the evil treachery of Pearl Harbour, grotesquely, only four years later.

No one was prouder than the ghastly part they had played in this aerial atrocity, which he led, than Colonel Von Richofen of Herman Goering's Luftwaffe, and cousin of Germany's First World War air ace the legendary *Red Baron.*

48

General José Miaja Menant, Commander in Chief of the Republican forces, did not pull any punches when the tactical committee, comprising the two International Brigades generals Dai Powell and Enrique Lister, convened at army headquarters the following morning.

'*Gentlemen our campaign against the Nationalists is at a crossroad,*' he snapped. '*If the enemy succeed in capturing Bilbao it could be the beginning of the end for our Republican cause. The brutal decimation of the small town of Guernica by the German Condor legion's bomber planes emphasises that the Nationalists have been better armed than us by their German and Italian allies. Meanwhile the help we are getting from the Soviet Union is shoddy and second class by comparison.*

'*Our politicians are finding it difficult to persuade other western nations to supply us with arms and ammunition to put up strong opposition against the Nationalists. This is because in the view of the League of Nations we are flaunting the Geneva Convention by using Mercenary soldiers, like the International Brigadeers, from neutral countries.*

'*Exacerbating that view is the statement from Nationalist leader General Franco promising that all foreign personnel fighting for the Republicans will face firing squads in the event of the Nationalists winning the Civil War. So it is imperative at this meeting to come up with tactics to thwart the Nationalist onslaught against the Basque forces defending the Bilbao stronghold.*'

General Dai Powell was the first to respond to the CIC's impassioned dissertation.

'*I have heard that the discipline of the Basque forces, under the command of General Francisco Llano de la Encomienda , is lax. Providing my colleague here, General Enrique Lister, agrees I suggest that a strong supporting force from the International Brigades is despatched to stiffen the support of Bilbao and that he be given overall command for the project.*

'*Meanwhile, with your permission, General Menant, I will leave immediately for the Basque sector to see if I can spot any weakness in the Nationalist force attacking Bilbao. As you have said, Sir, we must pull out everything to thwart the Nationalist effort to capture Bilbao.*'

General Lister responded enthusiastically to General Powell's suggestions and turning towards the Commander in Chief, General Menant, added: '*Although none of us fighting on the Republican side are contemplating defeat in this Civil War we also have a duty to protect the gallant men who have volunteered and risked their lives for the cause. In view of General Franco's barbaric threat to put them in front of firing squads we should be sure to get them across the border and out of Spain if the worst happens.*'

In fact the Republicans were on the back foot from day one of the critical Battle of Bilbao. The poorly armed, morale lacking, Basque defenders gave ground from the outset and the rural towns of Durango and Guernica, after suffering merciless bombing by units of the German Condor Legion, ignominiously surrendered to the Nationalist commander General Emilio Mola's forces.

Even the death of General Mola in an air crash did not deter the relentless advance of the Nationalists who quickly named General Fidel Davila as his replacement. Neither did the sinking of the Nationalist battleship *Espana,* after hitting a mine, lift the depression and the air of defeat that hung over the Republican contingent.

The Basque defenders had cravenly withdrawn behind the 'Ring of Iron' defences around Bilbao by 11th June 1937. General Dai Powell signalled a report to CIC, General Menant in Madrid: *'The Basques are showing the moral fibre of a bunch of scurrying mice being chased by a big cat. The so called Ring of Iron defence is helpless and hopeless under the heavy artillery bombardment put up by the Nationalists. I humbly recommend that the woefully weak General Encomienda be relieved of his post and General Mariano Gamir Ulibarri be appointed successor as commander of the Basque forces and ordered to liaise with our colleague General Enrique Lister and his International Brigades task force. The situation does not look good at all.'*

General Menant acted immediately to Dai Powell's advice withdrawing the out of favour General Encomienda immediately and replacing him with General Ulibarri. It was a positive step but, tragically, a move too late.

Ulibarri's first order having assessed the dire predicament of the Basque defence force was to order the evacuation of the unfortunate civilian inhabitants of the stricken city. The die was cast five days later Ulibarri abandoned Bilbao leaving the triumphant Nationalists to take over the following day. The Republican cause was at its lowest ebb despite the sinking of a Nationalist torpedo boat *Javier Quiroga* off Gibralta. On the political front Spain's Prime Minister, Largo Caballero resigned and Doctor Juan Negrin, a Socialist, formed a new Communist Government.

The politicos' emphasised to General Menant that the Republicans needed a shot in the arm to boost the morale of their followers throughout the war-torn Peninsular.

He called on his tactical committee of General's Dai Powell and Enrique Lister to come up with a plan to produce a badly-needed victory to get the Republican band wagon on the move again.

'The weakest point in the Nationalist defences is around the City of Segovia,' said the studious Powell. *'I believe if we mounted a force of three divisions we could capture the city which would give our Republican cause an immense propaganda and tactical lift considering Segovia's proximity to Madrid.'*

Only the Gudarrama Mountains separated the picturesque Castilian town of Segovia from the Spanish capital which the Nationalists had repeatedly failed to capture. Segovia was in fact Spain and Castile at its best with its twisting alleys and Romanesque churches surrounded by the city's medieval wall.

Generals Menant and Lister after an enthusiastic debate concurred with Powell's judgement of the possibility of Segovia as the next target for an onslaught to boost Republican morale.

49

General Dai Powell's tactical plan for a morale boosting attack on the Castilian town of Segovia was implemented unreservedly by the Republican CIC and General Domingo Moriones was given command over three Divisions deployed for the task.

Powell was driven to the frontline by his orderly George Stewart and was delighted to see the Republican task force break through the Nationalist defence. From a public relations point of view Segovia was a brilliant choice of target by Dai Powell designed to lift the waning spirits of the Republicans,

Within days General Moriones had steered his three Divisions through the fragile Nationalist front line at San Ildefonso where the capture of the historic and prestigious Royal Palace of La Granja was a massive symbol for those who fought under the Republican banner.

Built by the Spanish king Henry IV of Castile as a hunting lodge in the fifteenth century and developed into one of the most luxurious royal palaces in Europe during the centuries it had been a show place for the Iberian nation ever since.

It was a triumphant moment in history but it was only fleeting. Nationalist troops, led by General Jose Varela were quickly deployed from the Madrid front and mounted a counter attack that thwarted any further Republican advance.

In Soccer terms the Battle of Genova was a 1-1 stalemate but nevertheless it did check the run of Republican reverses.

After congratulating General Moriones for pulling the Republicans out of the doldrums General Dai Powell motored back to headquarters in Madrid where he presented the CIC with the happy news.

But on a personal note Dai was perturbed with a letter waiting for him from his beloved Pilar informing him that it had been confirmed that she was pregnant. Obviously as a result of their holiday in Granada two months previously.

He was aware that Pilar would now need to talk to him face to face and hear some reassuring answers to the turmoil of questions that would be disturbing her at this traumatic time.

Fortunately for Dai Powell's peace of mind the month of June 1937 was relatively quiet after the stalemate of the Genova battle. On the 16th of the month the government, on advice from their mentors in Moscow, trying to rationalise the Republican war effort, banned the Trotskyite splinter group known as POUM - the Workers' Party of Marxist Unification.

But Stalin had his own more definitive way of eliminating opposition and five days later sent two ruthless gun-toting agents from Moscow to assassinate Andres Nin in a back alley of Madrid.

Lady Luck was definitely not smiling on the Republicans and there was another devastating blow when their *España-class* 15,700 ton dreadnought battleship *Jaime I* was wrecked off Cartegena by an accidental internal explosion and fire. It was little consolation to the Republicans' top brass that 48 hours later the relatively tiny, by comparison, Nationalist motor torpedo boat was sunk.

The temporary 'All Quiet' on the Spanish Civil War gave Dai Powell the opportunity to turn his attention for a short while to ease the qualms of the woman he loved.

He picked up the phone and rang the Republican Army Centre at Granada.

50

General Dai Powell asked his orderly, George Stewart, to get through to the Republican Army Medical Facility at Granada and ask for the Commanding Surgeon Rafa Canello to be put on the line.

Within five minutes Stewart handed his boss the phone saying: '*I have Major Canello on the line, Dai.*'

The greetings on each side of the telephone were warm.

'*Hi Rafa, it's nice to talk to you again,*' said Dai. '*I am calling you on a private matter....*'

The Republican Army high ranking medic, not intending to be rude, anticipated the reason for the call from General Powell.

'*Likewise Sir, I am pleased to speak with you again. I am pretty sure why you have called me. Enfermera Pilar has confided in me both as her commanding officer and as her personal doctor. I confirmed that she is pregnant. I sympathise if this an event that you didn't plan, or are unhappy about. On the other hand if this what you and Pilar want I share your happiness.*'

Dai, thanked Major Canello for his understanding and, coming immediately to the point, replied: '*I haven't talked to her yet about this matter. I only received her letter yesterday after I returned from the Battle of Segovia. I want immediately get down to Granada for a couple of days to discuss matters with Pilar. Is it possible to get her to the phone.*'

Canello made a comforting reply: '*I repeat the invitation I made on your previous visit a couple of months ago. My finca is again open house for you and Pilar as, because of pressure of work and the mounting numbers of wounded soldiers passing through my operating theatres day by day I am still working, living and sleeping here at the Medical Facility. As for you speaking to Pilar on the telephone I anticipated your request and she is waiting in my outer office. I will get you put through to her immediately.*'

Dai discerned the emotion when Pilar came on the line whispering: '*Hello, novio. I am so sorry querido....*' Dai, with muchas simpático, said: '*Don't, don't, please don't apologise Pilar darling. This is great news. It's not what we had planned. Correction to that statement it is not the timing we had planned.*

'*Both of us have known for some time that our future's are locked together. We have both looked forward to marriage, a life together and, yes, raising a family together in a world at peace.*

'*We must now change our plans readjust to the fact that we are about embark on the wonderful voyage of parenthood. So we have a lot to talk over and I am about to leave in the Mercedes with George Stewart to spend a few days with you in Granada. I will collect you from the Medical Facility early this evening. Please give Major Canello my compliments and make it clear how grateful I am for his offer to again lend us his finca for a few days.*

'So I'll be there in a few hours I am already excited at the prospect of seeing you again so soon!'

Dai could not see the tears coursing down Pilar's cheeks but he sensed the emotive tremor in her voice when she replied: *'Dai, you are mi Señor Maravilloso--en Inglés--Mr Wonderful--I can't wait to see you this evening.'*

51

Pilar came waltzing to the studded door of the Medical Facility, the sequins in her flat evening shoes glittering in the Granada moonlight as George Stewart wheeled the Mercedes smoothly up to the steps.

She tripped down the three flights as George opened the passenger door for her handsome beau, Dai Powell, the gold coloured General's star on his epaulette winking, in the same moonlight.

They met on the level ground. The love and passion overwhelming them both on what was inevitably to be the most eventful and significant assignation in their young lives.

'*Oh, novio,*' she said planting ardent kisses on Dai's swarthy cheeks. '*It is fantástico that you have come so quickly to comfort me. As always I am crazy about you and now I know how much you love me. Perhaps I was stupid but I was worried sick that you would be angry and want to finish with me when you learned that I am pregnant.*'

The Welshman's sun-tanned face visage was a montage of

kindness and the adoration he had always felt for this beautiful Spanish nurse. A love she had never understood fully when he had frequently rejected the suggestion of marriage.

Later, as they lay in the familiar king-size bed at the *finca*, where first their lust, then their passion, and later their love for each other was spent Dai Powell at last found the eloquence to make her comprehend that his rejection of marriage had always been a measure of his devotion for the most wonderful woman he had ever met.

'Please understand darling,' he explained. *'I have only ever thought of your well-being. I have always wanted you to be my wife. But I could see a lot of pain and problems for you while this dreadful Civil War is still going on. This fear was accentuated by the danger for those of us who came to Spain from abroad to fight for the Republicans and are now threatened they will face General Franco's firing squads if the Nationalists win the Civil War . There is an increasing danger that this may in fact happen because, I have to tell you, that the Republican's are not doing well at the moment and could be facing defeat. But now you are with child I must face this problem from a different direction and tomorrow I will go to the city's wonderful Cathedral to see the Archbishop of Granada, and hopefully arrange for us to be married as quickly as possible.*

'I will figure a way to get you and the baby out of Spain and to Britain at a future date. Even if I have to take the risk of staying here to fulfil my duty to the Republican Army until the end of the Spanish Civil War.'

Pilar slept happily and peacefully in her lover's arms that night. She had an ulterior motive for awakening him as dawn broke over a cloudless, puce coloured Andalusian horizon.

He did not complain about losing any sleep!

52

He met His Excellency the Archbishop of Granada, as arranged over the telephone earlier that morning, in the Sacristy of the ancient cathedral which had been founded by Cardinal Pedro González de Mendoza, Archbishop of Toledo, in 1492 under the authority of a papal bull.

It was an historic move in accordance with the Peace Agreement signed by the Spanish kings and the Moorish King Boabdil in January of that year. The present incumbent who greeted General Dai Powell at the Sacristy door, Augustin Parrado y Garcia had been appointed Archbishop of Granada in 1934 succeeding some 30 predecessors appointed by the Vatican over five and half centuries.

A kindly, rubicund, *religioso* tended a flock of more than half a million Catholics, 400 priests and 250 parishes in the troubled times of the Civil War at a time when the Republican government was allied to the atheistic Soviet Union and its God-hating dictator Josef Stalin. The opposing Nationalists were supported by the Roman church who prayed for the destruction of Russia and the Communist cause.

His Excellency Augustin Parrado spelled out how impossible it was for him to actually join the pregnant Pilar Delgado and General Dai Powell in Holy Matrimony.

'*The Republican government, I am sorry to say my son, would like to see a nation completely separate from the Church and follow Russia's march towards a God-less country.*' said the Archbishop. '*They are already under criticism from the League of Nations for allowing foreigners like yourself to intervene in what the rest of the world considers should be purely a Spanish war.*

'*So a Civil authentication for the marriage of a man from Great Britian and a girl from Spain will not be allowed. No Marriage Certificate can be issued to legalise such a partnership.*

'*But I am a Man of God and my vows say that I must minister to all men and women who live in my Diocese whatever their Creed, nationality or beliefs. Although I cannot legalise your marriage the best I can do is Bless Your Union with the Spanish nurse who will mother your child. It will not legitimise your unborn baby or mean that you are married in the eyes of the State. You will make similar vows towards each other as at a wedding ceremony. But at a later date, perhaps in a different country you may be able to put all this behind you and go through an official Civil ceremony.*

'*If you bring Pilar to the Cathedral at 8am tomorrow morning I will hear her confession, as a Catholic, give her Communion so that she is in a State of Grace when I bless your union.*

'*I cannot stress strong enough the importance of keeping all this a secret for the sake of your own and Pilar's safety and even for my own. This could be construed by the Government as breaking the law.*'

Dai Powell was overwhelmed with the kindness that this

benevolent septugenarian Archbiship was showing besides risking his own security to help Pilar and himself.

'I want to humbly thank Your Excellency for what your are doing for us,' he said. *'I could not have had more considerate assistance from a Minister at the Methodist Church in Wales where my family have worshipped for nearly 100 years. It might please you to know that I have already agreed with Pilar that our child, or perhaps children, will be brought up in the Roman Catholic religion. That is only fair for eventually I will be taking her from Spain to live with me in Britain.'*

53

Corporal George Stewart had washed and dillgently polished the official Republican Army Mercedes limousine at dawn that morning to take his boss General Dai Powell and his *novia* Pilar Delgado to Granada's imposing cathedral.

The Archbishop, Augustin Parrado, who was to Bless their Union, met them at the Sacristy door and had paid them the compliment of wearing his full pontifical vestments including mitre, pectoral cross and Episcopal ring.

He welcomed them and invited them to sit down in the elegant Sacristy where the dominant feature was an artistic treasure-- an ancient statue of the highly revered Virgin Mary representing the *Immaculate Conception.*

'After I hear your confession Pilar I will administer Communion to you while I celebrate Mass,' he told Pilar who was beautifully dressed all in white. Not so much a bridal gown as a stylish ivory shift dress bought in Granada the previous evening capped by a simple silver head-band studded with pearls. Her lover stood tall

and immaculate in his best general's uniform with the symbol of his high rank, the gold star, on each epaulette.

'I have decided it is appropiate to conduct the Blessing in the tiny Chapel of the Virgin Pilar which was decorated byFrancisco Aguado between 1782 and 1785 for the burial of one of my

Predecessors, Archbishop Antonio Jorge y Galbán who died in 1787.

After receiving absolution and Confirmation Pilar stood side by side with Dai as they both made the identical vows necessary in an official state-approved marriage.

'Your Excellency with great respect can I ask will God regard us as a married couple?' Pilar politely asked the compassionate prelate.

The Archbishop hesitated before replying, conscious that what he said could be interpreted harshly by anti-religious Republican government officials.

His considered answer was pithy and plucky in its simplicity as he stated: *'Yes my child I am sure in God's eyes you are both married. But when the political climate changes, for your own sakes and that of your unborn child you must legalise your position with a Civil Marriage.*

'Good luck to both of you in your life together. May God go with you always. I am so glad you have both agreed to have your children brought up in the Roman Catholic religion.'

General Dai Powell kissed Pilar affectionately while his orderly George Stewart moved forward from the rear of the Chapel to embrace and congratulate a deliriously happy nurse.

After grateful farewells to the Archbishop they left the Cathedral by the Sacristy door to find George Stewart waiting for them with the Mercedes' engine ticking over smoothly.

'*Where to now?*' asked the orderly.

Dai Powell was definite in reply and said: '*I think some champagne is in order don't you, George? Drive us to a good tapas bar and let's celebrate.*'

That is exactly what the three pals did for the next few hours.

54

George Stewart drove Pilar and Dai back to the finca in mid afternoon engrossed with their love for each other and in a deliriously happy mood having consumed copious amounts of *Cava* and polished off a dozen or so ramekins of the unique *tapas* that the bars and bistros of Granada have always been noted for.

'I think a little siesta is called for before we get ready to go out for our boda banquete *tonight,'* laughed Dai. *'How do you feel about a wedding banquet with oysters, lobsters and ham from Andaluscia's famous black pigs, Mrs Powell?'*

Pilar was amused that he had used the English sobriquet for a married woman rather than *Doña*-the Castilian version and, matching his mood chirped back: *'That will suit me fine marido,*

Remember, earlier this morning, I took a vow to obey you for the rest of our married life.'

So within ten minutes of George Stewart dropping them at the front entrance Dai and Pilar, arms affectionately clutched around each other's waists, climbed the finca's imposing winding staircase.

Although the plan was for a battery-charging Spanish style siesta out of the baking heat of an Andalucian summer day there was an ulterior motive as they discarded their street clothes strewing them across the elegant tiles of the bedroom floor in their haste.

It was an hour later that they breathlessly fell asleep in each other arms having consumated their partnership as committed lovers have done through the ages since Adam and Eve.

Dai was the first to awaken and as he stirred Pilar, her throat dry from the champagne earlier in the day, said she would really love a cup of hot coffee. When, pulling his dressing gown around his muscular torso, Dai padded down the staircase to complete his husbandly chore he was accosted by his orderly.

'Doña Dolores Ibárruri Gómez telephone about half an hour ago,' said George Stewart. *'Our friend Major Rafa Canello, the Chief Medical Officer, told her that you are here. She is also in Granada and would like Pilar and yourself to dine with her at her hotel tonight. She requested that I should ring her back with your answer and left me the number of her hotel.'*

Dai was really pleased with the news and turned to his orderly and said: *'La Pasionaria--she is here in Granada? Oh that's wonderful. In fact it couldn't be better. Get her on the phone please George. I will speak to Doña Ibárruri myself.'*

Five minutes later General Dai Powell was talking to the woman who was the icon of Republican Spain.

'Doña Ibárruri it is wonderful to talk to you again,' the Welsh soldier enthused. *'Of course we will be delighted to meet you tonight. But please don't think me rude but I would like you to dine with us. This is very special night for Pilar and myself -- I will explain later because I don't want to talk about it over the phone because it could implicate another person. I have booked a table at*

the historic Restaurante Sevilla, which is near Granada Cathedral. We will pick you up in our Mercedes from the Hotel Hesperia which is situated in the old city of Granada. At 8 o' clock if that suits you?'

La Pasionaria was noticeably pleased with the suggestion and said she would be ready when the car arrived later.

As Dai returned the telephone to its cradle George Stewart arrived from the kitchen carrying a tray with hot coffee, cream and biscuits which he told his boss he would carry up to the bedroom for the waiting Pilar.

The imminent meeting with the legendary *La Pasionaria* would prove to be another wonderful memory that would stay with Pilar and Dai for as long as they lived.

55

La Pasionaria sat in the rear seat of the Mercedes between the happy couple as George Stewart drove them to the Restaurante Sevilla which was near to the Cathedral.

Dai Powell took the opportunity to explain that Pilar was expecting a baby and that in their abortive effort to get married they had the consolation of having their union blessed at the Cathedral by the Archbishop of Granada that very morning.

'*The government refuses to register a marriage between a Spanish national and a foreigner like me,*' said the disgruntled General. '*Which shows an appalling lack of gratitude towards those of who have come to Spain from other lands to fight for and defend the Republican government.*'

Dolores Ibárruri congratulated Dai and Pilar hugging and kissing both of them as the Mercedes headed towards the restaurant.

'*The problem is politics, world politics,*' explained *La Pasionaria*. '*As you know I was elected as member of the Cortes, the Spanish parliament last year. Or to give my election it's official title I was elected as a deputy of the Partido Comunista de Espana to the Second Republic. The rest of the world are more frightened of Communism rather than the Facist and National Socialist totalitarian regimes of Benito Mussolini in Italy and Germany's Adolf Hitler. It is a fear that the rest of the world will regret in the future. But in accordance with the policy adopted by the League of Nations the world are against working men from England, America and other countries coming to Spain to fight for the Republic of Spain against the Nationalists.*

'Hoping to be able to buy arms and ammunition from the rest of the world's nations the Republic pretend they do not recognise the legal status of the foreign born soldiers fighting for them. In fact there is a move afoot to one day take all International Brigades soldiers to Spain's border and say adios *to them. I do my best to oppose that ridiculous stand with very little success I might add. As you know I am passionately grateful for the devotion and courage you men of the International Brigades have donated to the Republic. In thousands of cases they have given their lives and limbs to our cause.'*

The sombre mood of the party seemed to evaporate into the warm Andalucian evening as George Stewart brought the Mercedes smoothly to a halt outside arguably the most noted eating place in Granada.

'I know this restaurant well,' said *La Pasionaria* when they were seated in the *Restaurante Sevilla's* open air terrace sited in a pedestrian street surrounded by the Cathedral walls while the throbbing from a classical Spanish guitarist added extra enchantment to the ambience.

'Since it opened in 1930 the mouth-watering food of Granada

and Andalucia has attracted hundreds of distinguished visitors from Spain and all over the world. In particular it was the favourite haunt of a very dear friend of mine, the late Federico Garcia Lorca, one of Spain's greatest poets who was an icon of the Andalucian region. .

'Tragically Lorca was summarily executed by the Nationalists at the start of the Spanish Civil War. He was high on the Nationalist hit-list as his sister was married to Granada's Republican mayor and he was known as a follower of Karl Marx. Franco's bastards arrested Lorca at 6 am that fateful morning. Marched him to the local cemetery, lined him up against a wall, and a Falangist firing squad despatched him to a premature eternity.

'When you kindly invited me to join your celebratory party at this, a restaurant full of sentimental memories for me, I decided to bring you both a very special gift.'

La Pasionaria dipped dramatically into the capacious case she had brought with her. From its black bowel she produced an elegantly bound book which she held flamboyantly aloft, proud and triumphant.

'It is a first edition of Federico Garcia Lorca's called "The Gypsy Balladeer"-a collection of poetry which connects with the large numbers of gypsies who reside in the mountains surrounding the city of his birth-- Granada. Lorca, who also travelled all over Spain with a troupe of actors, has signed the book which will be considered as a rare and valuable object of art in years to come.'

La Pasionaria made it clear that she considered Lorca to be a martyr for the Republican cause who fought hard to sever the strong hold the Roman Catholic Church and the bourgeoisie of Spain had over the poor and starving Andalucian peasants.

'I have signed the book to both of you,' she said. *'Treasure it and*

browse through it occasionally to remind you in the future how you both gave your all to Spain.'

The gift was a typically magnanimous gesture from a woman who herself had given her whole adult life to fighting the cause for the working class men and women of Spain.

56

It was a good natured dinner party with Dai Powell, Pilar Delgado and George Stewart making up the quartet dwelling on every word from the wise and dedicated icon of the Republic affectionately known throughout Spain's working class areas as *La Pasionaria*.

'It has been a long haul since I was born into a poor, Carlist, Roman Catholic family in the Basque town of Gallarta,' reminisced the famous Republican leader. *'I'll be 43 years of age come next Christmas but I swear to God so much has happened over the years that I feel as if I am 83.*

'Here as we celebrate your marriage - for I am sure that is what happened today in the eyes of Our Lord, whatever the government says - I wonder if the beautiful Spain I have always loved will

ever be the same after this horrible Civil War. I say that despite the deprivation, poverty and cruelty I witnessed as a child and woman. The General Strike in Spain in 1917, when I was still in my twenties is still vivid in my memory. I had only married Julián Ruiz, a coal miner and political activist the previous year and it was shock when he was imprisoned for participating in the strike.

'He was finally released a bitter man. But he fathered our six children, but four of them died because of the poverty at the time. That was when my fight against injustice began. In 1920 I was elected to the Provincial Committee of the Basque Communist Party. I have never stopped fighting for the same cause ever since.

'I suppose I should not say this in front of a high-ranking soldier such as you, Dai Powell, but I fear that this Civil War is not going well for us Republicans. This is not because we are lacking in spirit but because the Nationalists are being supplied with superior guns, tanks, ammunition, bombs and aircraft by the Facists and National Socialists of Italy and Germany.

'The rest of the Free World chose not to supply us with modern munitions to give us a fair chance. Led by the League of Nations the Free World fear upsetting Hitler and Mussolini by helping us. Time will prove that the Free World have made one of the most catastrophic decisions in the history of mankind.

'Whatever the outcome of this Civil War I wish you General Dai Powell, Corporal George Stewart of the International Brigades and indeed you Military Nurse Pilar luck for the future and thank you from the bottom of my heart for what you have done for the hard-pressed working class people of Spain.'

All that was left to round off an emotional dinner and celebration of Dai and Pilar's Union was an expression of gratitude from the General who had come from coal-bearing Rhonnda Valley to risk his life for Spain's Second Republic.

'Doña Dolores Ibárruri as a soldier I salute the courage you have shown in support of the Republic,' said General Dai Powell. *'The rallying cry you have always shouted, !NO PASARAN!, has been an inspiration to all of us who have fought for the cause. It will go*

down in the annals of your country's history along with the battle cry the Conquistadors yelled during their conquests in South America between the dramatic years of 718 to 1492 AD-- "SANTIAGO y CIERRA, España"--which called for the protection of Spanish troops from St James, the patron Saint of Spain.

'You will be forever known as La Pasionaria the woman who has always fought for the rights of the working men and women of Spain. We will never forget you.'

That summed up the perception that Spain's under classes had of the legendary *La Pasionaria.* It was paradoxical that she should later be accused by her enemies of sanctioning atrocities and murder in the name of the Second Republic.

That dinner at Granada's emblematic *Restaurante Sevilla* with its poignant memories of the brutally martyred poet Federico Garcia Lorca, the impassioned words of the symbolic *La Pasionaria,* and the romantic under-cover 'marriage' of Dai and Pilar in fact marked the end of their all too short honeymoon.

There were affectionate *abrazos* and *besos* of betrothal as they said farewell to each other.

General Dai Powell and his orderly and driver, Corporal George Stewart left Granada at dawn the following morning heading for Madrid and the next meeting of CIC, General Menant's Republican military tactical committee.

The sad and pregnant Pilar Delgado reported back for work at the Republican Army Centre in Granada her troubled thoughts spinning around the safety of her departing lover, the father of her unborn child.

57

General José Miaja Menant, Commander in Chief of the Republican Army, was in positive mood as he addressed the two members of his tactical committee, Generals Enerique Lister and Dai Powell.

'We must find a way to wrest the initiative, to outhink the Nationals, if we are going to prevail. I am relying on you two to come up with a tactical plan that will steer us to a decisive victory and secure the place the Second Republic as the democratically elected government of the people.'

As always, it seemed that Dai Powell was the leading planner of the Tactical Committee with the slower thinking Lister prepared to back his schemes under the ultimate power of General Menant.

'I have heard from our Intelligence people that the Nationalists besieging Madrid are bedding down for a long offensive at the El Escorial- Madrid road towards the town of Brunette,' said the Welshman. *'Let's go for it. Let's attack the Nationalists at this point and move two divisions of our own troops under the commands of Generals Juan Modesto and Enrique Jurado on one side with General*

Lister's International Brigade soldiers creating a pincer movement. I will lead a third Republican force against the enemy rear to entrap the Nationalist.'

The Commander in Chief approved the plan while General Lister agreed that Powell's idea could be a winner.

But war is often unpredictable and sometimes kicks the bravest in ther teeth,

The Republic's initial thrust secured the capture of the town of Brunette driving a five-mile salient into the Nationalist front line. But the Nationalist forces under the command of General Jose Varela rallied and mounted a counter-attack that forced the Republicans back to almost the point where they had began their attack. Meanwhile the Nationalists reformed to capture Bilbao and switched their offensive towards the important city of Santander. They were commanded by General Fidel Davilla who led his force westwards through the Cantabrian Mountains. Despite the large number of troops under the commands of General Marian Gamir and Enrique Lister the Republicans only managed weak resistance

This was due mainly to poor training and a critical shortage of weapons. As bloody August faded away with huge Republican losses and as autumnal September arrived the Republican Army's Basque forces surrendered to Nationalist forces under the command of General Ettore Bastico.

The situation was clear. The Republicans were on the back foot as the Nationalists captured Santander almost without opposition. There was no doubt now that the beleaguered Second Republic was fighting a catch-up war thrusting the multi-national International Brigadeers into an invidious position.

58

In a desperate ploy to divert the Republican trend of reverses General José Miaja Menant, the Commander in Chief, placed General Dai Powell in charge of a mixed task force, including crack Spanish troops and two British battalions of the International Brigades, to reinforce the Republican Army of the East led by General Sebastian Pozas.

General Menant was hungry for a victory to bolster the morale of disillusioned Second Republic supporters.

The joint commanders Pozas and Powell thrust their men into an advance from Catalonia with a view to capturing the city of Saragossa, the capital of Aragon. A beautiful city, also known as Zaragossa, dates back to 14BC when the Romans established a settlement on the banks of the Ebro valley.

Generals Pozas and Powell pushed back the Nationalist forces to the north and south of the River Ebro but were unable to overcome them at Saragossa's most dominating feature *Puente de Piedra*, a stone bridge originally erected by the Romans and rebuilt in 1813 featuring Italian, Basque and French architectural features.

The joint Republican commanders failed to dislodge the

Nationalists from the key areas around Saragossa or to capture the northern outpost of Huesca or Teruel in the south. So September ended with the Republican offensive running out of steam.

Dai, with brutal honesty, was now certain that time was running out for the Republicans however just as their case was against the oppressing Nationalists.

It was time now for him to set in motion personal plans to protect Pilar and the child that he estimated would be arriving around the middle of April the following year--eight months on.

The other threat that might affect his future family had come from the Nationalist's hard-nosed Generalissimo Franco who had stated categorically, if prematurely, that after his facist hordes had taken control of Spain the foreign 'mercenaries' of the International Brigades who had extended the Civil War by fighting for the Republic, would face his firing squads.

'*There will be no mercy,*' said Franco.

'*They came as foreigners to meddle in the political struggle of the Spanish people which was not their concern. Under international law, we believe, they are no better than spies. That is the way they will be treated.*'

To thwart Franco's denouncement the League of Nations advised the political leaders of the Second Republic to repatriate all foreign soldiers fighting with the International Brigades to their own countries and thereby prevent a blood bath sequel to an already savagely cruel Civil War.

That night General Dai Powell put through a telephone call to the beautiful Spanish military nurse who was, what would be considered, in more enlightened future times, his common-law wife.

59

General Dai Powell expounded his theory to the Republican tactical committee in the midst of a deadly silence from his fellow committee members General José Menant, the Commander in Chief, and the International Brigades commander General Enrique Lister.

*'After the set back in Saragossa coinciding with the loss of other battles in Bilbao and Santander the only remaining Republican stronghold in the north of Spain is the city of Gijon and it's environment ,'*said the man from the Rhonda Valley with fearless frankness, looking directly at the CIC. *'With respect I would suggest, Sir, that you recommend Dr Negrin, the Premier of the Second Republic, to move his Government from Valencia to Barcelona, where it is possible we could re-muster and possibly stage a last attempt to upset the Nationalist apple cart. We shall have to put up some kind of token resistance to defend Gijon but we have to be honest and admit that at the moment we are against a Nationalist Army who are armed with better guns, tanks, ships and planes from engineering works of Germany and Italy which are*

working day and night preparing their countries to swallow the rest of Europe in a massive war.

'We have to face the facts that we are fighting on our own while the rest of the world have turned against us believing that Communism, and the Russian dictator Josef Stalin, is to be feared more than the two dictators Hitler and Mussolini.

'Yet Russia continues to send us inferior guns, that jam, ammunition that doesn't explode and aircraft that crashes. They take our national gold in exchange for their trash. Who needs enemies when they have got so-called friends like the Soviets? Even the League of Nations are against us preaching a philosophy of non-intervention to other nations who refuse to sell us arms to match the Nationalist weapons that kill our soldiers, sailors and airmen. Our politicians must plead harder to the rest of the world for arms so that we can make a fist of battling against the Nationalists.'

The Battle of *Gijon* began as Nationalist Generals Antonio Aranda and Jose Solchaga launched an offensive that blasted their forces through the Mountains of Leon following the eastern coastline.. But Aranda's forces were unable to break through all the mountain passes, which were defended by Asturian soldiers trained by the Republican Army.

But General Solchaga rallied his Navarrese force and captured the village of Infiesto. The Asturians were out-flanked and the defenders forced to retreat. Gijon surrendered on 21st October 1937 and the entire northern coast of Spain was now controlled by the Nationalists.

It was little surprise that the Republican forces had two painful set-backs at sea with the scuttling of their submarine C6 after suffering damanage in a Nationalist air attack. This was followed

24 hours later when the Republican destroyer *Ciscar* was sunk also at Gijon by the Nationalist fighters and bombers.

All these worrying facets of the Spanish Civil War crammed his turbulent mind as General Dai Powell picked up his phone to speak to his *novia* , the beautiful military nurse Pilar Delgado.

60

Using the now fragmented national telephone system General Dai Powell finally got through to the Republican Army Medical Centre in Granada and, using his high rank, asked to speak to Military Nurse Pilar Delgado.

Within a few minutes he was pleased to hear the gentle lilt of Pilar's, almost melodic, Castillian tones coming down the line.

'This is strictly between me and you, darling,' he warned. *'The Civil War is not going well for the Republicans although here at headquarters we are working hard on plans to change things round. But as far as you and I are concerned, as we are expecting a child, in a few months or so, we must make contingency plans. There is a rumour that the Nationalist leader Generalissimo Franco will put all members of the International Brigades in front of a firing squad if his side win the war. Meanwhile the League of Nations are putting pressure on the Second Republic government to repatriate all foreign soldiers like myself to avoid such an atrocity. It is a*

worrying situation but I will work out some way of getting you and our unborn baby out of Spain.

'It is a perturbing position with the Nationalists having captured the entire northern coastline and almost all of the northern half of Spain....'

Pilar, unable to disguise her excitement, interrupted, saying: *'I have news for you querido. The Army Medical Centre here in Granada is being deployed to Barcelona. I leave with the unit in a convoy of ambulancias, furgonets and coches tomorrow.'*

The news was welcomed by Dai Powell, who replied: *'Oh that is good news love. Barcelona is the place where the Republican Army will probably make a big stand against the Nationalists. Hopefully it will not be a Last Stand! Well look after yourself, my darling. I am sure I will be reunited with you in Barcelona very soon.'*

As the year 1938 ticked away the Republican Government, no doubt following the advice General Dai Powell had given to General José Menant, the CIC, who gave instructions for the Army Headquarters to be moved forthwith to Barcelona.

At the first meeting of the Republican Army Tactical Committee convened in General Menant's new office in Barcelona Dai Powell was asked what ploy the Republicans should activate in order to pre-empt a Nationalist attack upon Catalonia which was predicted by Army Intelligence.

'We need a victory badly, ' Dai said emphasising his words by hammering his clenched fist on the desk. *'Not only to raise morale although, God Knows, our supporters need that. But we need to send a message to General Franco that there is still plenty of fight left in Republicans. Let us launch an offensive to capture the Aragon city of Teruel from the Nationalists.'*

General Dai Powell came up with an audacious plan that would rock the triumphant Nationalists if it succeeded.

Teruel, a city of 30,000 people is the capital of the province of the same name. Noted for one of the harshest climates in Spain, it's succulent *jamón Serrano-cured ham-cerámicos,* and its two famous *Fiestas-'La vaquilla del ángel'*-during the second weekend of July and *'Bodas de Isabel de Segura'* around the third weekend of February.

What emerged from General Dai Powell's plan-The Battle of Terruel- which ended in February 1938 was the bloodiest confrontation of the Civil War with the two sides suffering more than 100,000 casualties between in the bitter three month struggle.

The Republicans deployed three powerful forces led by Generals Hernandez Sarabia and Leopoldo Menendez and Enrique Lister at the head of an International Brigades division while Dai Powell was at the head of a British battalion in reserve.

The two attack forces commanded by Generals Sarabia and Menendez advanced on Teruel and by nightfall they had completely encircled the city. Colonel Rey d'Harcourt who commanded the Nationalist garrison held out in the south of the city for nearly three weeks until their ammunition and food supplies ran out leaving them no option but surrender.

Generalissimo Franco, incensed with this reverse, ordered Nationalist Generals Jose Varela and Antonio Aranda to rally their troops to counter-attack and relieve Colonel d'Harcourt's hard-pressed defenders but the harsh winter that plagues Teruel closed in and thwarted the move. But in a bloody game of snakes and ladders the Republicans found themselves being blockaded when they were attacked by Franco's cavalry in the north of the city.

This was followed by another Nationalist attack by Moroccan

soldiers under the command of General Juan Yague who had crossed the River Alfambra before making their move. The Nationalists then reoccupied the city as the Republicans unceremoniously retreated along the Valencia Road on the day that the citizens of Teruel should have been praying and celebrating the Fiesta of *Bodas de Isabel Segura* which originated in medieval times.

The Battle of Teruel was one of the most significant engagements of the Spanish Civil War for although it did not signal the end of the Republicans' conflict it was certainly the beginning of the end of the Second Republic.

But there were significant death throes as the Republicans tried to come to terms with the fact that they were facing defeat in the War when two weeks after the Battle of Teruel torpedos from their destroyers sunk the modern Nationalist cruiser *Balears* off *Cartegena* when it was escorting a convoy of merchant vessels laden with arms and ammunition from Nazi Germany.

General Dai Powell knew the end was near when Juan Negrin, the doctor who had become Josef Stalin's puppet, to lead the Second Republic sued for peace.

Franco's response was brutal in its brevity when he sent Dr. Negrin a note which said succinctly: '*Nothing less than unconditional surrender from every Republican fighting man will do!*'

61

The Republicans, understandably fearing fate was closing in on them, were now desperate for a major ploy that could switch their cause into the ascendancy still had faith in their main tactical guru the fighting Welshman General Dai Powell.

At a meeting of Commander in Chief General José Menant's tactical committee Powell unveiled a massive detailed plan how the Republicans could not only relieve the still-beleaguered City of Madrid and divert Nationalist forces from their drive towards Valencia.

'I believe the final and decisive factor of this war will be fought around the River Ebro,' Powell told the Commander in Chief and the other member of the committee, General Enrique Lister of the International Brigades.

'My advice General Menant is that forthwith we should form a Republican Army of the Ebro from the very best troops left under our command. I suggest you put General Juan Modesto, who has an excellent record, in command of this Army of the Ebro with General Lister and myself in reserve with units of the International

Brigades. This, if you pardon the phrase General Menant, must be a shit or bust operation. Win and it is possible we could just possibly turn the tide of the Civil War in our favour. Defeat does not bear thinking about. It could mean Spain living under the yoke and firing squads of a cruel Nationalist dictator.'

In the absence of alternative ideas the CIC, General Menant, had no choice but to give General Dai Powell's plan the go ahead.

Powell threw himself into assembling a force that historians dubbed 'The Republican Army of the Ebro'. Sorting out the best soldiers, NCO's, and officers. Getting hold of the best guns and armaments even utilising the better weapons that had been captured from the Nationalists. Weapons that had been supplied to General Franco's Nationalist Army by Hitler and Mussolini the totalitarian gaffers of warmongering Germany and Italy.

This preparation for, arguably, the most decisive battle of the Spanish Civil War occupied the early days of the summer of 1938. This activity was interrupted early in June when the Republican gunboat *Laya* was sunk by Nationalist aircraft off Valencia-an event marked even more importantly later that day with the exciting news that Pilar had given birth to a baby girl in the Republican Army Medical Centre in Barcelona.

A bonny healthy baby who, according to Pilar's commanding officer and doctor, Major Rafa Canello: *'She weighed in at an average 3.4 kilograms. I am glad to tell you also, General Powell, that Pilar came through it well and stayed the night in a private ward here at the Army Medical Centre here in Barcelona.'*

Dai Powell was, of course, happy with the news and responded warmly: *'As always I thank you for your courtesy Major Canello. With your permission I will be along to see Pilar and the baby in the next few hours. I will be grateful if you would tell her that. Will she still be in the ward at the Medical Centre?'*

Major Canello's reply was encouraging: *'There will be no need for that. We only put her to bed for a few hours because she was tired after the birth. We are discharging her in the next hour and I am re-billeting her in a larger apartment for married couples, suitable for the baby and to accommodate yourself now that Army Headquarters are located in Barcelona.'*

So amongst the carnage and tragic deaths on both sides as, arguably, one of the most cruel Civil Wars in the history of Europe, waged to its horrific conclusion, a brand new life was ushered into the world offering a crumb of hope in the midst of man's inhumanity to mankind.

62

General Dai Powell got his orderly and close pal Corporal George Stewart to drive him across the city of Barcelona to see his lover who had just produced a baby daughter for him less than 24 hours earlier.

'She is just lovely, absolutely wonderful,' cooed the hard-bitten Welsh warrior as he cradled the baby that the proud Pilar had carefully placed in his arms. *'What are we going to call her?'*

Pilar smiled at her lover's impetuosity and cautioned: *'Patience querido, patience. Rome was not built in a day. I was going to talk to you about that because I have given it some thought. I suggest we call her Dolores Megan Powell Delgado--because it is customary that Spanish women keep their surname after marriage--so your lovely little daughter would be called Dolores, not only after my mother but after La Pasoniaria the Republican icon we both admire, Megan after your mother in Wales, Powell your family surname and Delgado the family name I will keep. I understand that such a name would be legal and would be blessed by the sacerdotal at the local Roman Catholic Church told me. There would be legal problems trying to register a British surname in Spain at this time particularly as we are not recognised as legally married by the government..'*

Dai Powell laughed: *'It will be a long signature for young Dolores to write when she is old enough to have her own bank account. But I agree darling with what you have suggested. Both our mothers will be pleased we have perpetuated their names.'*

Pilar was happy with Dai's acquiescence: *'That's good amante. We will leave it a few weeks until little Dolores is a little older and stronger and I will arrange a date with you to have her Christened by the local priest.'*

Dai then produced two surprise gifts as he handed a blue velvet case. Pilar's eyes popped with joy as she opened up the case and saw two pairs of black pearl earrings, one adult size and the other miniature baby size.

'Ooh they are beautiful Mother and child's matching earrings,' she glowed. *'I will have baby's ears pierced when she is old enough. I remember my mother telling me that I was six months old when she had my ears done.'*

Dai Powell then said: *'I have one other surprise to mark this memorable occasion.'*

Just as the Welshman finished the sentence there was a knock at the door as Corporal George Stewart entered accompanied by a mess steward carrying two bottles of iced Cava, glasses and a tray of *tapas*. They were followed into the room to join the party by Major Rafa Canello, the officer commanding the Army Medical Centre in Barcelona.

It was Major Canello who raised his glass to propose the toast: *'Health, Wealth and Happiness to Dai, Pilar and Baby Dolores Delgado.'*

As important as the occasion was an hour later the happy father was heading back in his official Mercedes, driven by Coroporal George Stewart, to the Republican front line at the emerging Battle of the Ebro.

63

General Dai Powell's strategy for the impending Battle of the Ebro held out promise for the beleaguered Republicans when the Army specially formed for this operation, commanded by General Juan Modesto forced the Nationalists to retreat.

The newly dubbed Republican Army of the Ebro in various sectors of the front line caused the adrenalin to flow freely amongst supporters of the Second Republic by advancing 25 miles. But the smiles on General Powell's face was turned to tears when a stray bullet from a Nationalist sniper fatally struck his orderly and bosom pal Corporal George Stewart plumb in the centre of the forehead.

For the first time in a lifetime of hard work and danger as a young coalminer, as a sport-loving university under graduate, as a professional Rugby League footballer, as a participant of the famous Jarrow Hunger March and a soldier of the Republican Army during the bloody Spanish Civil War, Dai Powell from the Rhonda wept unashamedly.

Ross Lewis, a Republican rifleman who hailed from Aberdare, brought his violin to the graveside at the battlefield burial service the following day and played the sad strains of the plaintive British hymn '*Abide with Me*' as the crudely made coffin was lowered into the ground.

But General Powell was not afforded much time to mourn his best friend when the Republican attack began to wane. Powell then changed tactics advising General Modesto to order his Republican Army of the Ebro to dig in and face the inevitable counter attack from a strong Nationalist force under the command of a Franco lackey, General Juan Yague.

In the end superior air power and determined ground attacks by Nationalist troops using modern firearms made in Germany and Italy gradually forced the Republicans to retreat and fall back across the River Ebro.

But General Dai Powell was never destined to witness the significant defeat of the Republican Army at Ebro or their ultimate surrender when hostilities in the gory Spanish Civil War ended four months later.

On 21ˢᵗ September 1938 the Prime Minister of the Second Spanish Republic, Dr Juan Negrin, trying to curry favour in a speech to the League of Nations after failing to broker a peace deal with the merciless General Franco, announced that the International Brigades would be withdrawn from the fighting.

The following day the courageous remnants of the International Brigades were pulled out of the front-line prior to them being repatriated.

64

Anyone who has been made redundant by their employer after giving loyal service to the company will know the feeling of depression that came over General Dai Powell when it sunk in that he was a soldier without a portfolio while the Republican government, he had fought for, was hurtling to ignominious and unconditional surrender against the fascist Nationalist hordes led by General Francisco Franco.

'With respects Sir, may I ask how soon we , of the International Brigades, can expect to be expatriated from Spain and sent to our home countries?' Dai Powell asked his boss General José Menant, Commander-in-Chief of the Republican Army.

Menant, seemed to have the reply at his fingertip, and said: *'After talks with Dr Negrin and government officials who have been consulting with the immigration departments of the various countries involved I have been told that, logistically, it will be at least a month before we can get you all on your way.'*

Powell, was still upset about the unfortunate death of his

former orderly and friend. This was exacerbated with the letter of condolence he had written the previous evening to Mabel and Sam Stewart, of Jarrow, the grieving parents of Corporal George Stewart.

'*Can you tell me Sir, have any plans been made to award pensions to parents whose son has been killed in the cause of the Republic?*' the worried Welshman asked.

General Menant replied: '*Our Republican government had such a plan in mind although nothing has been formulated. But now, we have to face it, with defeat imminent, it is totally unlikely that a future Nationalist government will be so tolerant. In fact General Franco has repeatedly threatened that if his troops prevail in this Civil War that anyone who supported or fought for the Republic stood the chance of facing a firing squad or the hangman. This despite the fact that almost all of the rest of the world recognise the Second Republic as the democratically elected government of Spain.*

'*In fact by expatriating all of you who have fought with the International Brigades we are probably saving you from assassination by Franco's murderous hoodlums.*'

Dai Powell was politically-wise enough to be grateful that General Menant was being so frank in a situation that was extremely sensitive to himself notwithstanding he also faced death by Franco's killing squads.

'*I am sorry to harry you, Sir, at this worrying time,*' said Powell apologetically. '*You have been very considerate to me. But you know I have another problem. The woman I consider to be my wife has just had a baby girl. Do you think, in the event of Franco winning the war, which seems likely, there is any chance I can get Pilar and the baby out of Spain so that we can establish a home in Britain?*'

General Menant was quite informally emotional as he replied:

'I cannot thank you enough for your service to the Republican cause. No Spaniard could have worked harder, been more loyal or braver than you have been. Dai Powell, I would have been proud if you had been my son. Having said all that you know I would do anything for you! I wish I could help with the problem of Pilar and the baby. As it is in the eyes of the Republican government you are not married in the eyes of the law and Pilar remains a Spaniard. So is your baby a Spanish citizen. As such Pilar and the child will not be allowed out of the country at this time.

'If things calm down in the future in the event of the Nationalists prevailing in this Civil War and you two are to go through a civil marriage then Pilar and the child will automatically take your nationality and under international law become British citizens and as such be allowed to leave the country. I am sorry I cannot help you more amigo!

'Finally, although not authorised by the government to issue medals any more, I would like you to accept this Flag of the Second Republic to take back to Britain as a token of the service you have given to Spain. May in years to come, in more peaceful times, you return here and enjoy the sunshine, sea and mountains Spain has to offer.'

That flag, with its blue, yellow and red vertical stripes with the emblem of the Second Republic in the centre would remain one of Dai Powell's proudest possessions for the rest of his life

65

After the emotional farewell with General Menant which ended with affectionate *abrazas* and cheek to cheek *besos,* Spanish style, comrade to comrade, friend to friend, Dai Powell returned to his billet to spend the night with Pilar and their tiny baby daughter.

In Dai it was the worst night in his life as he informed the weeping Pilar that in a few weeks he would be escorted to the Spanish-French border with his International Brigades comrades of many nationalities and repatriated to their own countries. Unable to stem the torrent of tears Pilar pleaded pitifully: *'But why can't I and the baby go with you. I am your wife.'*

Dai's reply was concise: *'Not in the eyes of the law you are not. You are an unmarried Spanish mother and the Republican Government will not let you leave the country and God only knows what stance the Nationalists will take if they win the Civil War which now seems almost certain.*

'I have no option but to leave with the rest of the members of the International Brigades. General Franco has threatened to execute

all of us still in Spain after hostilities cease. I would be no use to you or our lovely baby, Dolores Megan, in a coffin.

'But, darling, I give you my solemn pledge that as soon as the war is over I will come back to Spain legally or illegally and take you and the child back to Britain. I stake my life on that solemn promise.

'Meanwhile we have got possibly a month to live together in Barcelona as man and wife when I have no military duties in the period before the International Brigades are expatriated.'

That is how Dai and Pilar spent the next few weeks before the 15th November 1938-the date etched in the gory chronicle of the Spanish Civil War-when the Welsh warrior marched along with the other surviving members of the International Brigades to the rapturously grateful applause of thousands of Catalan base Republican supporters.

They cast aside the pain of their imminent separation and did the things that all new parents do with their fresh-born bundle of joy. They searched the few stores in Barcelona still open despite the ravages of a savage Civil War. They were rewarded when they found and bought an almost new *cochecito de niño*-a luxury American-built pram that once belonged to the wealthy wife of the USA Consul who left for the States with her newly born baby when the Civil War started.

With Dai pushing the futuristic four wheeler with it pink silk coverlet and pillows they joined the evening *paseo* down the famous Ramblas with other Catalan newly-weds as if the war had never happened. Sometimes Dai would wheel the exotically coach-painted pram to one of the numerous flower stalls and buy her half a dozen long-stemmed roses, whispering in her ear: '*For the most beautiful mother in Barcelona!*'

To which she would coquettishly respond: '*Adularo--I bet you say that to all the senoritas.*'

His reply was just as witty: '*How dare you call me a flatterer? Only the senoritas who places such a bello hija into my arms--that means only you!*'

On other days they would pack a picnic with *Serano* ham, *Mato de Montserrat, a local* cheese, and fresh fruit with a bottle of *Terra Alta* a Catalan wine first produced in the 1920' s at a winery built by César Martinell, a student of Gaudi. They would spread rugs across the golden sands of Barcelona's *Playa de Bogatell* which stretches along the *paseo* to the *San Sebastian Playa* separated in the sea by two stone breakwaters.

Pilar preciously guarding the baby during the fiercest midday sun, nevertheless let baby Dolores build up a golden tan as she rolled in the sand and, cradled in Dai's massive biceps, dip in the warm water of the Mediterranean.

'*Look, look, Pilar,*' said Dai as he cuddled and gently towelled Dolores after a dip in the sea. '*She has got a red mark on her back. It's not a rash is it Pilar? Measles or some other children's ailment, is it darling?*'

Pilar laughed heartily at the anxious concern of the doting father,

'*It is nothing to worry about,*' she grinned anxiously alleviating his worries. '*I asked Major Canello about that at the Republican Army Medical Centre and he assured it is only a birth mark.*'

Relieved at that information Dai Powell still pursued the topic: '*But look Pilar that red mark is in the perfect shape of a three legged star-the emblem that centres the red, yellow and purple flag of the*

International Brigades. It's weird, almost as if it was an omen. A lucky omen I hope.'

The identical flag held proudly aloft in front of thousands of Catalan supporters of the Republic cheering as 13,000 volunteers of the International Brigades staged a farewell parade in Barcelona before repatriation to their own countfries

The sombre final reckoning in the annals of the Spanish Civil War estimated of the 59,380 volunteers of the International Brigades 9,934 (16.7 percent) died and 7,686 (12.9 percent) were seriously wounded.

The final farewell to the International Brigades was eloquently made by Dolores Ibárruri, the iconic *La Pasionaria.*

From a specially erected rostrum in Barcelona she said:

It is very difficult to say a few words in farewell to the heroes of the International Brigades, because of what they are and what they represent. A feeling of sorrow, an infinite grief catches our throat - sorrow for those going away, for the soldiers of the highest ideal of human redemption, exiles from their countries persecuted by the tyrants of all peoples - grief for those who will stay here forever mingled with the Spanish soil, in the very depth of our heart, hallowed by our feeling of eternal gratitude.

From all peoples, from all races, you came to us like brothers like sons of immortal Spain; And in the hardest days of the war, when the capital of the Spanish Republic was threatened, it was you, gallant comrades of the Internationals, who helped save the city with your fighting enthusiasm, your heroism and your spirit of sacrifice - and Jarama and Guadalajara, Brunete and Belchite, Levante and the Ebro, in immortal verses sign of the courage, the sacrifice, the daring, the discipline of the men of the International Brigades.

For the first time in the history of the people's struggles, there was the spectacle, breathtaking in its grandeur, of the formation of International Brigades to help save a threatened country's freedom And independence - the freedom and independence of our Spanish land.

Communists, Socialists, Anarchists, Republicans - men of different colours, different ideology, antagonistic religions - yet all profoundly loving liberty and justice, they came and offered themselves to us unconditionally .

They gave us everything - their youth or their maturity; their science or their experience, their blood and their lives; their hopes and aspirations - and they asked us for nothing. But yes, it must be said, they did want a post in battle, they aspired to the honour of dying for us.

Banners of Spain! Salute these many heroes! Be lowered to honour so many martyrs!

Mothers! Women! When the years pass by and the wounds of war are staunched; when the memory of the sad and bloody days dissipates in a present of liberty, of peace and of wellbeing; when the rancours have died out and pride in a free country is felt equally by all Spaniards, speak to your children. Tell them of these men of the International Brigades.

Recount for them, coming over seas and mountains, crossing frontiers bristling with bayonets, sought by raving dogs thirsting to tear their flesh, these men reached our country as crusaders for freedom to fight and die for Spain's liberty and independence threatened by German and Italian fascism. They gave us everything

- their loves, their countries, home and fortune, fathers, mothers, wives, brothers, sisters and children - and they came and said to us; "We are here. Your cause, Spain's cause is ours. It is the cause of all advanced and progressive mankind."

After listening to that passionate discourse there was hardly a dry eye amongst an audience of Republican supporters heavy in heart in the knowledge that defeat faced their side. The cheers rang round as, heads high, the proud gladiators of the International Brigades took a well deserved acclaim n from the emotional citizens of Barcelona.

No one was prouder than General Dai Powell who was signalled out with several other outstanding International Brigade heroes to have a special medal for meritorious service pinned to his tunic breast pocket by the Second Republic's President Manuel Azaña

Behind the chain-smoking Azaña, as special guests of *La Pasionaria*, baby Dolores Megan Powell Delgado cooed in her mother's arms happily unaware that her *papá* was one of the stars of a memorable day.

66

After the emotional and historic farewell march-past, the final salute to the *Brigadas Internacionales* the iconic Dolores Ibárruri whispered to her friend Republican General Dai Powell on the VIP rostrum.

'I would be very pleased if you and your wife, Pilar, would do me the honour tonight of dining with me at the famous Casa Bofarull Restaurante, better known worldwide as "Los Caracoles",' said the enigmatic *La Pasionaria* enthusiastically. *'I will reserve a private room so that we can dine and talk in peace for I have many important things to say to you. Tell Pilar to bring little Dolores with her. I will arrange with the Bofarull family who have owned the restaurant since it was opened in 1835 to have a child's cot to be erected in our private dining room. I am just dying to cuddle my tiny namesake. I love niños, I have had six children, including three girls born as triplets in 1923, you know, unfortunately four died before adulthood mainly because of malnutrition as a result of extreme poverty. One of the many jobs I did for the cause was to organise a crèche to enable Republican mothers to do war work.'*

So the scene was set for a memorable dinner at the charismatic one hundred and three year old *Los Caracoles Restaurante* set in the emblematic Gothic District of Barcelona and owned and run by the third generation of the founder Bofarull family.

As usual Dolores Ibárruri was dressed all in black. Ebony tresses, streaked with grey bearing witness to the hard life she had led, slicked back tightly to form a bun. As soon as Dai and Pilar joined her in the private dining room she picked up the 12 week old Dolores Megan, clasping the baby to her breasts indicating the internal pain she still felt for her own four children who had died so prematurely.

Eventually baby Dolores Megan was placed gently into the elegant cot which had once been used by the latest offspring of the prolific restaurant owning Bofarull clan.

'Apart from the pleasure of dining with two of my closest friends who in their different ways I was anxious to have an important talk with you about the future,' said *La Pasionaria. 'I can understand how anxious you both are about being separated after Dai is repatriated to England.*

'That particularly applies to you Pilar querido with the extra responsibility that goes with it of caring and supporting a niña. While for you Dai the task of smuggling yourself back into Spain and spiriting Pilar and the baby out of the country illegally will be formidable. You can, of course, play the waiting game and hope the next government, after a Nationalist victory, will act humanely.

'But I doubt that. There have already been terrible atrocities committed by both Nationalists and, I am sorry to say, also by the Republicans. But the Nationalists have already asserted that men, and yes women, who have fought or helped the Republicans can expect reprisals. There will be firing squads waiting for many prisioners.

'Now, without giving you information that would endanger your lives any further, I can tell you that I am part of a clandestine organisation setting up a resistance movement to fight a guerrila battle against the Nationalist after they take over our lovely country.

'Among other things, which it is better for you not to know, will be an escape route to smuggle persecuted Republicans out of Spain so they can continue the fight against the Nationalist hoodlums.

'This information will be particularly of interest to you if ever you have to arrange a stealthy escape from Nationalist Spain. I will be one of the leaders of that resistance movement even although it looks as if I myself will have to flee Spain to seek safety and sanctuary in another country. I will keep you informed Dai of my contact details so that I can put you in touch with our Republican resistance movement so that when the time comes they will help you to covertly travel to Spain and help Pilar and little Dolores Megan to escape.

'As for you Pilar it will be better for you to know as little as possible about what I have just told you or, indeed, about Dai's plans to rescue you, which knowing his resilience, I am sure he will do some time. Meanwhile I will help Dai to keep in touch with our undercover organisation which will still be working after the Nationalists take over.

'Good luck in the future to both of you and thank you what you have done for the Republican cause. Now let's enjoy our dinner and for an hour or so forget our problems.'

The meal was superb, fresh salmon, followed by suckling pig, which one would expect from a restaurant renowned as *Los Caracoles*. The only one who did not appreciate the good food for was three month old Dolores Megan who slept soundly in her borrowed cot throughout the whole affair.

67

It was only a few days until the end of the eventful year of 1938 when more than one hundred men of the International Brigades, British Battalion, were taken in a cavalcade of motor coaches, chartered by the Republican Army, to transport them across the Spanish border to the massive rail terminus at Perpignan on the French side of the frontier,

Dai Powell had said an emotional and tearful farewell to Pilar and baby, Dolores Megan, spiced with repeated assurances that he would be back to take them to England as soon as possible.

He had secured a comfortable one-bed roomed apartment in Barcelona for them where the elderly woman who lived in an apartment on the lower floor had agreed to look after the baby while Pilar, temporarily, continued her career as a military nurse. There were no problems from either the Republican immigration officials on the Spanish side of the border while the officers on the French control were '*muy simpático*' to the brave Britons who had risked life and limb to fight against the hated Nationalists.

Dai's British passport was in good order and, although he was still sad at the parting from Pilar and the baby, he was paradoxically quite elated that he was again in the free world and liberated from the constraints, cruelty and bloodshed of a savage Civil War.

While the rest of his former International Brigades' comrades entrained at Perpignan for the long overnight rail journey to Paris, the first leg of their long trek to the Calais and Dover ferry terminal, Dai Powell decided to spend a few days in the French border commune of Perpignan.

There was a method in what many people would consider as Powell's madness in not returning posthaste to Britain which he had left some three traumatic years back. His plan was to study the Perpignan - frontier areas looking for a suitable place and for a person who might help him when he returned to smuggle Pilar out of Spain.

Using his penchant for planning that had seen him soar up the ranks of the Republican Army from private to the higher echelons of command as a general, Dai Powell had done some astute mental homework in the weeks leading up to his repatriation.

He figured out a shrewd strategy how to organise an escape for his lover and child.

'*Who are the most experienced men in the world at slipping across frontiers surreptitiously?'* he asked himself. He came up with several answers none of which really rang the bell - long distance truck drivers, commercial travellers, sheep farmers whose flocks graze across border-lines? No! No! None of those types fitted the kind of man he was looking for. That night, having kissed Pilar and turning over on his pillow and dropping off to sleep, as so many deep thinkers have discovered, the answer came to him.

'*Cigarette smugglers, they flit across frontiers as many times as they sit down to a hot dinners,'* he thought joyously. '*Because of* their own security they cross from country to country by secret routes avoiding Customs and Immigration check points.   They probably have to bribe certain police and border officials but that's a small business cost.   The mark-up for the world's most popular cigarette brands at a price that avoids tax is huge.   It is one of the most lucrative crimes in the world which most law enforcing officers shut a blind eye to when their palms are crossed with silver.

'That is the kind of guy I am looking for and he must be found in a border town.'

Dai Powell, checked into a tiny hotel in Perpignan, a town bizarrely that was once the continental capital of the Kingdom of Mallorca in the 13ᵗʰ and 14ᵗʰ centuries but was now part of Southern France. He was wise enough to guess that the kind of man he was looking for would be found in one of the bars or taverns of this town of some 50,000 people at the foot of the snow-covered Pyrénées.

So Dai sprang from the starting blocks the following morning, in his quest for help in extricating Pilar and their baby from war-torn Spain, by going on a pub crawl around the bars and bistros of the ancient *commune* of Perpignan.

He drew a blank in the first three bars he called on, limiting himself to one small glass of *bier,* and one pertinent question to each innkeeper.

'*Where can I buy some American cigarettes?*' he asked.   *No, not a pack but I want to buy ten cartons--2,000 cigarettes--to take back to England?*'

At the fourth bar, *The Pink Parrot,* the boss was extremely helpful. *If you really want to buy that quantity of cigarettes,*' said the bar-keeper. '*The guy you want is at the table over there. He is Jean Pierre Perez, a French Catalan, and the most successful tobacco smuggler this side of the Pyrénées. Take him over a glass of his favourite anís he'll not only supply you with any brand of cigarette in the world but he will be your friend for life.'*

Dai Powell was not stupid enough to ignore knowledgeable advice. Ordering and paying for a large glass of anís he carried the potent drink across to the reputed cigarette smuggler.

'*Bonjour Monsieur Jean-Pierre,*' he said warmly, placing the drink in front of the Frenchman.

'*Bonjour Monsieur, I see you have been talking to the innkeeper, Henri Paul,*' replied Jean-Pierre nodding gratefully towards the anís. '*How can I help you?*'

Dai Powell responded: '*Well, Jean-Pierre my initial request which led me to you enquired whether you could supply me with ten cartons of Camels, the American brand--in other words 2,000 cigarettes?*'

Jean-Pierre replied enthusiastically: '*No sweat, I have thousands of American cigarillos both Camels and Lucky Strike. I also stock Ducados, from Spain which are made from the blackest of black Turkish tobacco, and Players, Gold Flake and Capstan Full Strength from England. All at prices minus the tax added by various countries.*'

The Welshman, delighted with what Jean-Pierre had told him, retorted: '*Consider that order for two thousand Camels confirmed and I will pay you up front before I leave for England in three days time. But Jean-Pierre there is another matter that you might be able to help me with and which would be of benefit to you. However I would be reluctant to discuss it in a public place like this. Is there anywhere we can meet privately without any danger of being overheard?*'

Jean-Pierre, never a man to scorn the chance of clinching a

business deal, replied: '*Oui Monsieur you would do me the honour if you dined with my wife and I at my modest home at the other end of Perpignan town. We will be able to talk in private there. Shall we say eight o'clock this evening?*' Then producing a stub of a grubby pencil and a piece of tatty paper Jean-Pierre wrote down his address and instructions how to get there and handed it to Dai.

The Welsh warrior was about to set off on a learning curve under the street-wise know-how of one the shrewdest petty crooks on the French-Spanish frontier, the astute doyen of the Pyrénéan cigarette smugglers, Jean-Pierre Perez a chain-smoker of the evil smelling *Gauloises* cigarettes. Ever the man for the niceties of protocol, Dai went on safari to Perpignan's best florist to buy a tribute for his dinner hostess, the obese but jolly, Madam Lauren Perez. He did not forget to buy a litre of anís from the local wine shop for Jean Pierre.

68

The meal that was set in front of him by Jean-Pierre Perez's homely wife Madame Lauren was a typically delicious fusion of Catalan-French cuisine.

Suckling lamb reared on the lush grass, enriched by the Spring snow that carpet the lower midi-Pyrénées slopes, roasted on a base of freshly gathered garlic cloves. New potatoes satuteed in *beurre di Andorra* and dew fresh *petite pois,* followed by *Cremé Brulee* oozing with clotted cream freshly churned and whipped at nearby *Los Escaldes.*

The red wine was a rich *Gran Reserva* illegally imported across the border from a vineyard a few kilometres from Barcelona by Jean-Pierre in barter for a few cartons contraband *Lucky Strike.*

'Don't remember ever enjoying a better meal than that Madame Perez,' said Dai Powell, who had already won the heart of the generously bosomed Lauren with his arrival gift of flowers. *'As for that vino tinto it is awesome Jean-Pierre.'*

The cigarette smuggler was pleased with the compliment to his knowledge of wine retorted: *'Now Senor Powell let you and I adjourn to the porch, armed with another bottle of the wine you like so much, and then you can tell me how I can be of service tlo you.'*

Dai Powell paused for a moment or two deciding, diplomatically, how to make a pitch to this likeable French-Catalan petty-crook.

'Jean-Pierre,' Dai queried metaphorically putting his toe in the water. *'How do you stand on the controversial topic of the Spanish Civil War?'*

Jean-Pierre Perez laughed at Dai Powell's directness.

'Don't worry I have been expecting you to ask me that,' laughed the Frenchman. *'Before you explain anything else let me tell you that you were one of the several thousand Brits, Americanos and other nationalities, men of the Brigadas Internacionales who were escorted to the French frontier a few days ago and repatriated. Furthermore I know you were an outstanding soldier the only one of two members of the International Brigades, with Enrique Lister, to attain the exalted rank of General in the Republican Army.*

'Now let me assure you, before you say anything else, I hate the Nationalists. I repeat I hate the fucking Nationalist Socialists--and every cock-sucking Kraut who supports that megalomaniac former house painter, Adolf Hitler. Why? Because I am half gitane--my mother was a gypsy from Romania. The world is appalled about what Hitler is doing to the Jews but he is persecuting and murdering just as many Romany gypsies and homsexuals in his evil plan to producing a pure blooded Germanic Aryan race.

'He is already killing Jews, Gypsies, Slavs and queers by the thousands in factories of torture. When Hitler finally sends out his sadistic storm troopers to conquer the whole of Europe, which is his target the world will take notice. I have dedicated myself to join those who will fight a gueriila war against the Nazis and I allied

myself with Dolores Ibárruri-La Pasionaria-who is organising a resistance movement for the Republicans at the end of the Spanish Civil War which is now certain to end with overwhelming victory for the Nationalists. Now tell me exactly what I can do for you.'

Dai Powell was absolutely flabbergasted with the vicious diatribe that had gushed like a broken fire hydrant from Jean-Pierre.

'I have to leave the woman I love, Pilar, and our 13-week-old daughter, Dorlores Megan back in Barcelona,' Dai explained. 'Because of red-tape the Second Spanish Republican government refuse to recognise that Pilar and I are married because they refused to allow to us to go through a civil ceremony. Yet our union was blessed by the Archbishop of Granada. So in the eyes of the Republican politicians Pilar is still Spanish, not British as it would be if our marriage was legalised....'

Jean-Pierre interrupted saying: 'Now you seek my help to surreptitiously get your wife and child out of Spain when the war is over. The Nationalist government will refuse to sanction their departure from Spain. I know this because La Pasionaria told me and asked if I would help.

'The answer to that request is short and simple--Dai Powell let me give you a solemn pledge now.

When the time comes I will help to smuggle your loved ones out of Spain. The Republican cause owe you that for your outstanding courage and devotion in the fight for the world's working classes.'

A pledge Dai Powell carried in his troubled thoughts as he began the tedious train and ferry journey to Britain the following day from Perpignan via Paris, Calais and Dover where he had another hard decision to make.

69

As Dai Powell envisaged the trip back to the UK was tortuous, uncomfortable, freezing cold at times and basically memorable for many hours of hunger and insufficient liquid refreshment.

At Perpignan station he managed to purchase a one-way ticket to Paris on the 9pm train to Paris. The first blow was that there were no sleeping berths available so he found himself jammed in carriage for eight people with eleven other persons. On the platform before the train departed he found that all the bars and cafés were closed for the night. The only food outlet was a woman wielding a catering trolley who was preparing to shut down because she had nearly sold out of food. Dai managed to purchase her last small *fromage baguette* and a tiny bottle of lukewarm drinking water.

The carriage was small and dirty creating an obnoxious stench as the ancient French train slowly rattled north through the night towards Paris. There was never a queue of less than ten people all through the night as a result the archaic toilet flush gave up the ghost after four hours to add to the inconvenience of the toilet paper running out. The demand throughout the train for old newspaper and periodicals, not for reading, was acute.

Dirty, unshaven, damp with overnight perspiration, heavy eyed for lack of sleep Dai Powell felt like a wreck as the old train huffed and puffed its way into the Paris terminal where, with two hours to spare before catching his connection to Calais, he hastened towards the station's marble-floored toilet to clean up before going to the buffet for a substantial breakfast of ham and eggs. The journey from Paris to Calais was certainly a lot more comfortable. The train cleaner and more modern. The view from the windows as the train ate up the kilometres was lush green and brown of rich French farm land. Of grazing cattle and sheep, of prolific crops of wheat, barley potatoes, cabbage and carrots.

The ferry crossing from Calais was also pleasant enough on a freshly painted French vessel where Dai sat on a row of seats along each side of the prow with the refreshing wind blowing in his face.

It was 8pm before the ferry slowly edged into the landing pier at Dover and Dai Powell had already decided that he needed a good night's sleep before deciding the following morning what he should do.

His burning problem was to chose the following morning whether to travel posthaste to Wales to see his mother and father who he had not spoken with for over three and half years. He just hoped they had received his regular letters from war-torn Spain. If they had replied their letters had never reached him on the Republican front line. But his father was a month short of his 90th birthday having spent 44 years at the coalface before retiring at 60, while his mother was six years younger. He just prayed to God they were still alive and in good health.

But he had another pressing duty nagging at him to go and see old Sam and Mabel Stewart the parents of his late orderly and best friend George Stewart to explain to them how their loving son had died a heroe.

He found a cheap hotel oposite the Dover ferry terminal and decided to search for a café where he would order a substantial meal and then get early to bed before deciding what to do about his nagging problem the following morning.

70

He found a café in a nearby street that mainly catered for the seamen and other crew who manned the daily and nightly ferries across the English Channel.

After years of garlic dominated Spanish meals it was a nostalgic return to good old British grub. He regaled in the steak and kidney pudding, onion gravy, mashed potatoes, carrots and peas followed by rhubarb and thick Birds custard. The mug of tea that completed this gastronomic repast was strong, the darkest brown, and needed its lacing of three spoons of Tate & Lyle's.

He rolled into bed back at the hotel. Nodded off immediately his head hit the pillow and obliviously settled down to a badly needed nine-hour sleep.

At the table the following morning, after tucking in to a hearty English breakfast of bacon, eggs, pork sausage, black pudding, fried bread and tomatoes, he wiped his mouth with the paper serviette and made his mind up what he was goingto do.

'I don't think my Mum and Dad are going to mind me delaying my return home by a few more days,' he mused. *'In fact I am sure*

that, my Mum in particular, will approve me going up to Jarrow to comfort Mr and Mrs Stewart on the loss of their son. In fact they both knew and liked my pal George and will be sad that he was killed in action in the Spanish Civil War.'

Dai then figured out that it was going to cost him a small fortune to travel by train all the way to Jarrow in the Northeast of England and afterwards all the way across country again to his parents' home in South Wales. The answer was simple. Now that he was back in "Civvy Street" he would need to find a job, and the search for employment would be accelerated if he had a car. So it would be sensible if he bought a second hand vehicle in Dover and use it for his long journey from Kent to Jarrow and then on to South Wales.

His next port of call was to the tiny local branch of the renowned Yorkshire Bank where he still had an account which held the balance of the money he earned as a professional Rugby League footballer with one of the top clubs for which he played at Wembley.

The bank teller, having checked his passport, then referred him to the branch manager in answer to his request for a balance to his account.

The 56-year-old manager, Derek Allbright, fortuitously was a Rugby football supporter and remembered watching Dai play as an amateur, under the Union code, for Llanelli against London Wasps and for Wales against England at Cardiff before transferring to the professional code.

'You have been abroad, I believe ' asked Allbright curiously. Dai had nothing to hide and immediately replied: *'Yes I have spent more than two years in Spain.'* The bank manager continued the good natured inquisition, and said: *'Fighting*

for the Republicans, I heard. Well that was a big loss to rugby football. I say that although I am a die-hard supporter of the 15-a-side Union version of the game. But I will never forget the two Union games I saw you play as an amateur for Llanelli against Wasps. and for Wales against England at Cardiff where you scored one of the most brilliant tries I have ever seen. Now let's get down to business. You have asked for details of the balance of your account with this bank.

'Well I can tell you, that with the interest accrued during the past two years, you have five thousand six hundred and fifty seven pounds in your favour. Now how can I help you?'

Dai Powell came straight to the point. *'I only got in on the cross-channel ferry from Calais last night and I need to buy a car today so that I can take up life as a civilian again. I need a new cheque book and the assurance from you that my cheque to a car dealer will be honoured.*

Allbright interrupted Dai with a constructive question: *'There will be no problem about the cheque. Maybe I can help you with an introduction to a local car dealer and get you a good price. What make of car do you fancy?'*

Dai answered: *'Oh, a Ford would do. You get a lot of car with a Ford and I need a reliable vehicle as I am going up to the Northeast of England from here and then down to South Wales.'*

The bank chief smiled as he countered: *'God is about to smile on you. The owner of the Ford Franchise in this town is Ben George--he's as Welsh as you and a rugby football fanatic. He'll be overboard to meet you and delighted to give you a good deal!'*

71

The meeting with the car dealer was elongated in the oval shape of a rugby football, for Ben George from Aberdare knew almost as much about the rugger star as Dai knew about himself.

The preamble about past games took all of 40 minutes and another 20 minutes was soaked up with Mr Ben George's recollections of the games he had seen Dai Powell play for Llanelli and Wales and on one occasion for Great Britain against France in a Rugby League international match.

'I went to the match wearing a wig and false moustache that day,' laughed the car dealer. *'Just in case my neighbours saw me-you know how much Welsh fans hate the 13-a-side game of rugby league? Perhaps that will change one day.*

'I am sorry I am running away with myself in my excitement at meeting you I am forgetting what you came here for. My friend Derek Allbright says you need a car. Take a good look around the sales room and see if there is anything you fancy .'

Dai Powell cast his eyes around the show room and finally his eyes rested on a 1936 version of a Ford V8 convertible de luxe tudor sedan parked near the up-and-under showroom doors. He looked towards Ben George and said enviously: *'I have always fancied that model since Ford introduced it in 1932. Now, seven years later, it has improved immensely.'*

Ben George laughed heartily and guffawed: *'You've got a good eye. That's the car I am using myself at the moment...'* Dai Powell interrupted abruptly: *'Oh I didn't mean to....'* Ben George held up his hand and assured Dai: *'Oh don't worry boyho I don't get sentimental over cars. My job is to sell 'em. When that car rolls out of the showroom I will drive another model until that one is sold. The only person who complains is my missus who would prefer I drove my top of the range Rolls Royce Phantom III all the time--well she would, wouldn't she?*

'If the Ford V8 convertible is the car you like then that is the one I will sell you. Be assured I will quote you a price you cannot refuse. Here's the keys, take it down the road for a spin and when you return tell me what you think and I'll take you to the excellent pub next door for lunch and we'll cement the deal.'

The car purred like a cat when he switched on the engine and roared like a tiger when he put his foot on the acelerator on a long stretch of open road.

He was delighted as he tooled the Ford V8 convertible back to the showroom in the knowledge that the only thing remaining was to complete the deal. *'I am not surprised that you are impressed,'* glowed Ben George, the owner of the Ford Concession for the Kent area. *'Ford have been way ahead of the rest of the car industry since they introduced the V8 open models and station wagons seven years ago. The range from the outset gave motorists tremendous value for* money. *The original model with it's cast-iron flat-head produced al least 78mph.*

'*Streamlining began in 1933 with much swoopier models with a longer wheelbase. Now today the car body's are all steel. The car you have just test-driven was put on the market for $900 US just over a year ago and now, because of my respect for you as a great rugby player, I am offering it to you for a knockdown £200. Do you want to shake hands on the deal.*'

Dai Powell held out his hand and sealed the deal and sitting at Ben George's showroom desk and wrote out his cheque before repairing to the *Kent Cob* pub next door to lunch with the car salesman.

Before leaving the showroom Ben George shouted towards his assistant, Tim Phillips: '*Get the Ford V8 convertible cleaned and polished Tim, please, and ask our mechanic to fill it up with petrol and check the oil while we are at lunch. Thank you!*'

After an excellent meal Dai said a fond farewell to Ben George before thanking him for his generosity. Then it was back to the hotel for a goodnight's sleep before setting off at 8am the next morning in his new car on the 300 odd mile journey to the northeast of England.

Although, as a ranking General in the Republican Army, Dai had enjoyed the privileged use of an Mercedes Benz limousine, albeit an ageing 15-year-old commandeered model, he was almost as excited as schoolboy at finally *owning* his very first new car. He drove the Ford V8 convertible, hood down, the slip wind blowing his tousled hair at a fast, if not hair-raising, pace maintaining a reasonable 35 miles an hour average on the busy trunk roads overtaking lorries laden with goods from the Continent, motor coaches filled with tourists, and a variety of private cars.

He made half a dozen comfort stops along the route north occasionally pulling up at truck-drivers' cafés for refreshments. It was 7-15pm on a crispy fine evening when he rolled into the outskirts of the industrial town of Jarrow from which he had joined two hundred unemployed Geordie shipyard workers on the famous Hunger March nearly three years previously.

Ten minutes later he wheeled the Ford V8 convertible up to the front door of Number 28 Victoria Street the home of the grieving Sam and Mabel Stewart, the ageing parents of his late International Brigades orderly and best pal Corporal George Stewart. It was Mabel who opened the door a chink and, peering out to see who it was, said nervously:

'*Who's that?*' Then, as the watery eyes slowly focussed , she recogn ised the caller and, almost joyously, said: '*Dai? Dai hinnie--is it really you? Come in love. Come in--don't stand out there on the doorstep!*'

He was ushered into the cosy lounge where a coalfire gave a hospitable glow. Dai kissedMabel on both cheeks and shook Sam's hand firmly.

'*I have come here straight from Dover where I landed two days ago having been repatriated from Spain with the other volunteers of the International Brigades who have been fighting for the Republicans,* ' explained Dai. Then, without more ado, he immediately stated the things he had travelled so many miles to explain to these bereaved parents.

'*Your George died a hero. Have no doubt about that. He gave his life fighting for the cause of underpaid, unemployed workers of Europe against the totalitarian masters who abuse them.*'

He then dug deep into his leather holdall to retrieve the pitifully personal belongings of their late son. There was a brand newMeerschaum pipe, which he had bought at an up-market tobacconist s in Granada for Sam's 70th birthday, three month's earlier. For Mabel, also garishly gift-wrapped at a large Barcelona store, the late George Stewart, had bought an elegant triangular mantilla in a stylish mixture of rose and ivory tulle, which he thought she could wear across her shoulders on the evenings she spent playing whist at the Mothers' Institute.

But the item that prompted a torrent of tears from his mother was a battered old cigarette tin which had a ragged edged photograph of herself pasted inside the lid.

'Oh my baby,' she sobbed. *'My bonny lad. He never forgot his old Mum.'*

Dai then personally gifted Sam with two cartons of *Lucky Strike* American cigarettes that he had bought from tobacco smuggler Jean-Pierre Perez. As he made it clear he was about to leave Sam Stewart asked: *'Where are you staying tonight lad'*

Dai replied: *'I have to leave first thing tomorrow to motor to South Wales. I haven't seen my own Mum and Dad for nearly two years. I thought of booking in for the night at that little bed and breakfast place near the Jarrow railway station.'*

'Oh no you wont Son,' stormed Sam faking his anger. *'Just go and fetch your case from the car and take it upstairs you will be staying in George's old room. Your old mate would never forgive me if I let you stay in a hotel. And when you have put your case in the bedroom I am going to take you down to the Shipwrights' Welfare Club and treat you to a pint of good old northeast ale which you haven't tasted for a long time. When we get back Mabel will have some bread cheese and pickles for our supper!'*

And that's the way it was. Only they drank four pints of the *"good old"* between them. As they merrily strolled back to 28 Victoria Street Dai said humorously: *'I couldn't refuse your invitation to stay the night when I thought of the wonderful fry-ups your Mabel used to put in front of George and myself.'*

Dai laughed heartily and then impishly added: *'Sam do you think she'll have some black pudding for breakfast tomorrow?'*

72

It was a tearful farewell on the doorstep of number 28 Victoria Street, Jarrow, as Dai Powell prepared to set off on in his long car journey to South Wales.

After thanking Mr and Mrs Stewart for their hospitality Dai was lovingly embraced by the ageing couple. Sam Stewart summed up the emotion as Dai's pilgrimage, to comfort them about the death of their soldier son, George, in the Spanish Civil War, came to an end.

'*Look after yourself Dai hinnie,*' said the unemployed shipyard riveter. '*As far as Mabel and myself are concerned you are our delegate son now our own lad has gone. I know you have your own Mum and Dad in Wales, and please give them our regards, but we feel that a little bit of you belongs to us as you were our George's best mate. Keep in touch with us. You have our phone number. Remember you will always be a welcome guest.*'

Tears ran down Mabel Stewart's face as she said: '*Take care lad. Remember we both love you very much. You know I sometimes look into your face and see my little Georgie smiling back. Oh, Dai here are some ham sandwiches I have made for your long journey. Goodbye love.'*

As Dai turned the Ford V8 convertible down Victoria Street towards the southward bound trunk road a damp mist clouded his eyes.

He stopped for tea and to refuel the Ford V convertible with petrol near Leeds where he ate some of Mabel's ham sandwiches. At Birmingham he chose a truck-drivers' café for lunch and regaled himself royally on plump pork sausages, mashed potates, mushy peas and two slices of thick doorsteps of crusty bread liberally spread with Stork.

As Dai Powell wheeled into the coal-rich Rhondda Valleys he heard the chapel bell at Tylorstown ringing for some obscure reason. Now as he headed the Ford convertible along the scenic route he had a nostalgic revisit to his childhood, the rich memories of teenage, and past battles on the rugby field against other villages.

The car rolled past Porth, Trebanog, Penycraig and past the colliery at Tonypandy where he first began work, as a pit boy, at 13-years-of-age. Then he caught a glimpse of the rugger pitch, at Llwynpia where he ran 20-yards to score his first try-a feat that attracted the Lanelli club to sign him. Now he really was on home territory.

Treorchy was the nearest town to his home village of Ynswen, little more than a mile away, where he was looking forward to reunite with his beloved mother and father after his three years absence from the Rhonnda Valleys.

But he could not resist a whimsical recall of boyhood memories when he would cycle to the Treorchy childrens' cinema where he would chew bubble-gum and yell along with a hundred local kids at the exploits of cowboy Tom Mix, Chinese detective Charlie Chan and Tarzan the hero of the jungle.

As the Ford V8 convertible rolled into Ynswen, Dai noticed the village was still as sleepy as ever, he pulled up outside the miner's cottage where his father and mother had lived for 25 years.

Ignoring the front door he shinned over a low fence into the backyard, past the freebie ton of coal delivered every month to pensioners by the local pit. Through the tiled scullery and into the cosy kitchen-lounge.

His mother looked from an easy chair strategically placed near the black-leaded stove where a large kettle gave out a gentle stream of vapour. She looked up to adjust her "specs", slowly focussed as her hands, gnarled with rheumatics, grasped the arms of the chair and, painfully, levered herself to her feet.

She struggled to find the words but managed to stutter: *'Dai, Dai my lovely boy--is it really you, after all those years? Come on over here and give your old Mam a hug.'*

Dai Powell, always a man of action did more than that that, his strong arms encircled her waist as effortlessly he lifted the old lady round as he kissed her with all the pent-up love he had saved up for the past eventful years.

'Mam, Mam, you haven't altered a bit,' he teased her. *'You are still the best looking lass in the Rhonnda!'*

It was then that Dai noticed another elderly lady sat in the easy chair on the other side of the kitchen-lounge. He recognised her as his mother's younger sister, who he remembered lived in the next village in the valley, Treherbert. *'Gwyneth, Aunt Gwyneth--God its is ages since I last saw you,'* he said and went over and gave his auntie a kiss on the cheek. But now with the excitement of being reunited with his mother calming down Dai fired a question at his mother: *'But Mam where is my Dad? He's not gone down the Miners' Welfare for a pint has he? If so I'll go down to join him and buy him another pint!'*

His mother said sadly: *'I'm sorry Dai boyho but your da' is in Cardiff Infirmary. Dr Aneurin Jenkins sent him three days ago. Mainly as a precaution said the doctor because of your da's age--he'll be 90 later this year you know. Gwyneth and I went on the bus to Cardiff and visited him this afternoon.'*

Dai immediately said: *'I'll take the car and go and see him straight away...'*

Mrs Powell interrupted: *'No son there is no rush. Visiting hours at the hospital are over today. You can take me to Cardiff at visiting time tomorrow afternoon. If that's alright with you?'*

Dai concurred and said: *'If you say so Mam--you are the boss, as always.'*

73

Dai Powell tucked into the breakfast fry-up his mother placed on the gingham table cloth in front of him the following morning.

They were both dog-tired having sat up until 2-00am talking. A close son to mother chat when Dai told her about Pilar, the girl he called his wife, and their 14 week old baby girl Dolores Megan.

'*I could not sleep,*' said Mrs Powell. '*Thinking that I now have a beautiful Spanish daughter-in-law and a little darling of a grandaughter who has been named Megan, after me.*'

Dai was delighted with his mother's approval of the extended family he had presented her with.

'*Now I have to work a way to smuggle Pilar and Dolores Megan out of Spain,*' he said, adding. '*Perhaps you will be kind enough to give Pilar the recipe for these delicious traditional potato cakes--I forget the Welsh name for them?*'

Megan rebuked her big son: '*Shame on you forgetting the Welsh language lessons you were given at the village school twenty years ago. The Welsh name for potato cake is: Teisen Datws Pob--now don't forget again!*'

Dai snapped a mock military salute at his mother saying: '*Yes madam, no madam I won't forget. But, seriously there is a constituent in those potato cakes that I can't identify the taste--all I know is accompanied by Welsh ham and eggs your Teisen Datws Pob complete one of the tastiest breakfasts I have ever enjoyed.*'

Megan Powell was obviously flattered by her son's compliments about her cooking and she added: '*The ingredient you mentioned is probably the ¼ tsp ground cinnamon I add, tell Pilar, to the 450g potatos, peeled, boiled, drained and cooled; 3 tbs plain flour, 2tbs brown sugar, and 1 tbs baking powder. Mash and beat the potatoes until smooth, then add all the remaining ingredients and mix thoroughly. Turn the mixture into a well-greased loaf tin transferring it to an oven pre-heated to 200 degrees Centigrade. Bake for ten minutes then turn down the oven temperature to 160 degrees C and bake for80 minutes longer. Allow the cake to cool in its tin for 10 minutes and then turn on to a wire rack and allow to cool before slicing, spreading with butter and serving.*

'*Tell Pilar to please send me the recipe for a Spanish potato omelette you have mentioned a couple of times....*'

There was goodnatured mischief in Dai's eyes as he turned to his mother and intervened: '*I can tell you Mam that one of the ingredients of a Tortilla Espanola are eggs...*'

Megan showed her Welsh spirit as she threw a wet tea towel, which landed on her son's nose: '*Listen Dai bach--don't cheek your old mother--when you were eight I used to put you across my knee and spank your bottom--so watch it boyho.*'

They both roared with laughter. Somehow they had rolled back the years.

Dai then set out the plans for the day.

'*Mam, you said last night that with Dad in hospital you haven't had a chance to have your hair done as usual,'* he said. *'Well get dressed and I'll take you to the hairdresser in Treorchy you used to like and I'll treat you to a cut, shampoo and set. After that we'll have lunch, like the old days, at Morgan's Café, and then drive on afterwards to the Cardiff Infirmary to see Dad when visiting starts as 2-00pm. How's that suit you Duchess?'*

Megan Powell was ecstatic that her big son was being so considerate: *'That will be absolutely terrific Dai bach,'* she glowed as she went off to put on her best dress.

Half an hour later Megan sat, like the Queen in her best dress and hat, in the passenger seat of her son Dai's posh new Ford convertible. She felt even more special when he pulled up outside her favourite hairdressers in the tiny town of Treorchy. Inside he handed her over to the owner Kathy Lewis and gave her the money she asked for her mother's cut, shampoo and set and asked how long before he could collect Megan.

'Oh, make it 45 minutes and your Mam's hair-do should be finished by then,' said the hairdresser.

So it was 11-45am when Dai collected his mother.

'You look wonderful Mam,' he glowed. *'Really sexy.'*

Megan Powell, pretending to be angry, snapped: *'You are a cheeky monkey Dai bach. However did I manage to spawn a saucy devil like you?'*

After slipping Kathy Lewis a pound as a tip and thanking the hairdresser for her service Dai helped his mother into the passenger seat of the Ford V8 convertible.

When the Powell's, mother and son, entered the café the dark-suited proprietor, Michael Morgan, came forward to greet them and immediately recognised Dai, his old school pal.

'Dai, Dai Powell it must be a month of Sundays since I last saw

you Dai bach,' said Morgan. *'I heard you were in Spain fighting the good fight for the working classes. In fact the article I read in the South Wales Echo claimed that you were a high-flying General in the Republican Army-good for you boyho.'*

Then turning towards Megan he said warmly: *'Lovely to see you again after all these years. In fact the last time I met you was one Sunday after your Dai and I had been playing rugby in the park. You sent us to wash off our mud in the tin tub in the yard filled with hot water. Then you sat us down to a slap-up roast beef dinner.'*

Michael Morgan then escorted them to a discreet table in the corner of the restaurant. They ordered roast chicken with all the trimmings, followed by apple pie and custard. When Dai asked for the bill the restaurant boss said: *'It's on the house it's my way of saying thanks for that roast beef dinner at your house all those years ago Mrs Powell.'*

Dai and Michael shook hands with the promise they would soon ring each other and arrange to go out for a drink.

74

Dai and Megan had arrived at the regal looking building of the 116-year-old Cardiff Royal Infirmary five minutes before the afternoon visiting hours were about to start.

At the end of the corridor, leading to the ward where her husband was bedded down, Megan Powell excused herself.

'You go on and have a few minutes alone with your father,' she said diplomatically. *'I need to go to the bathroom after that big lunch. I will join you both in a few minutes after I have had a quick wash and brush up. Oh, Dai while you are in the hospital you had better ask to see your Da's doctor and see what he has to say about his condition.'*

The ward was long. Thirty six beds. Two serried ranks of beds on each side of the ward. In some beds patients were propped up reading, in others the incumbents lay quietly moaning beneath the starched sheets. A fair number of the patients looked anxiously towards the door of the ward to see if they were going to have any visitors that day.

Dai's eyes searched desperately as he walked slowly across the polished lino flooring which reeked of carbolic disinfectant that had been slopped around the perimeter on the cleaner's mops earlier that morning. Finally he spotted the old man, despite the oxygen mask that almost effectively disguised the wrinkled face streaked with coal marks.

'*How are you Dad?*' he said picking up his father's right hand and felt the calluses thickened by 40 years of wielding a pickaxe at the coalface. The old eyes, that really required these days the use of the steel-rimmed spectacles that lay in his locker, nevertheless focussed and recognised his visitor. With a sweep of his left hand the old man pulled away the oxygen face mask and in a trembling voice said; '*Dai, Dai bach--is it really you boy?*'

Then, turning towards the man in the next bed with whom he had obviously formed a friendly relationship, said: '*William this is my son Dai come to see me all the way from Spain He is a General in the Republican Army fighting for the rights of the unemployed Spanish coal miners, you know. Did you read the piece about him in the South Wales Echo a few weeks ago?*'

Dai Powell laughed heartily at the old man's excitable diatribe and said: '*Yes Da' it's me. Now stop boasting about my exploits or I'll get a big head.*'

At that moment Megan Powell joined her son at her husband's bedside anxiously querying him: '*How are you love? Are you feeling any better today? Have you been eating your food?*'

Dai and Powell Senior laughed at Megan's impetuosity and the old man cautioned her: '*Now hold on a bit old girl. Not so many questions. Let's talk about the return of our lad. How did you get here today not on that old rattling bus again surely?*'

Megan Powell assured her spouse that she had travelled to the Royal Infirmary in style.

'*In Dai's shiny new Ford,* 'she said tremulously. '*He treated me to a hairdo in Treorchy and we went to Morgan's for lunch.*'

All the excitement seemed to have got to Dai's father and the frail old man began to cough uncontrollably. A nurse flounced briskly down the ward when she heard the coughing and, gently chiding the elderly patient said: '*You naughty boy! Put that oxygen mask on. Do you think you are Clark Gable trying to show your face to the lassies?*'

A few gasps of the life-essential atmospheric gas regulated the patient's breathing and he said to the nurse: '*If I wasn't a happily married man I'd take you out for a fling nurse.*'

Which prompted a pithy comment from Dai's mother: '*You cheeky old goat, you can't manage one woman let alone two.*'

Whereupon the old man pretended to hide his face, complete with mask, under the sheet.

Meanwhile Dai had strolled to the desk at the end of the ward to speak to the Sister in charge. '*I have just returned from Spain to see my father,*' he said. '*I would like to see the doctor or consultant in charge of my dad's case. I need to know details of his condition. Our family homeis at the village of Ynswen in the Rhonnda so it is not that easy for my elderly mother to get here to the hospital.*'

The Sister Iris Williams, after excusing herself, turned away and picked up the internal phone.

A few minutes later she turned round and said: '*Dr Emlyn Evans happens to be doing his rounds in the next ward and says he will be happy to talk to you in ten minutes time. He will see you in the little visitors' room to the right in the corridor at the entrance to this ward. I hope this helps you Mr Powell.*'

After returning to his father's bedside to inform his mother he would be absent for perhaps half an hour or so to talk to the doctor Dai went to the visitors'room to keep the assignation with the medico.

As he whiled away quarter of an hour waiting for the hard-working Dr Evans the ever-curious Dai Powell picked up the European Edition of a new compact magazine called *Reader's Digest* which he was fascinated to learn was conceived in a hayfield bunkhouse in Montana by a former US soldier, Sergeant DeWitt Wallace, a disenchanted "preacher's kid" and college drop-out. Prophetically, he was sure the magazine would be a huge success in the future.

He had hardly noticed the time go by when Dr Evans, a tall greying man with a pair of pince-nez spectacles perched on top of a nose which bore a blue tint as testimony to his bent for Scotch whisky.

He was a man of medicine who didn't beat about the bush when delivering a prognosis and said: '*Your father is suffering from acute coal dust pneumoconiosos and silcosis, which at nearly 90 years of age, must be considered terminal. A habit of 40 Woodbines a day for 40 working years exacerbated his condition. We have done as much as we can for him here, and I am prepared to discharge him from this Infirmary tomorrow in the care of yourself and your mother. He will need a wheelchair, which we are prepared to loan you, and arrange with your local GP, Dr.Aneurin Jenkins, for the medication and oxygen he will need at home, including the visiting services of a District Nurse. That is the top and bottom of the situation as far as your father is concerned Mr Powell.*

'*May I say finally, as a rugby supporter and the Honorary Medical Officer of Cardiff Rugby Club, I was proud to see you once play for the Principality when you beat England 7-3 at*

Twickenham and was sorry when you changed over to the Rugby League code. Although I can understand that many young men today cannot afford to play as amateurs. Perhaps the enlightened day will come when the Rugby Union accept professionalism.'

Dai Powell had one final question for the straight-talking Dr Evans, and asked plaintively:

'How long has my father got?'

The answer came almost as decisive as a rifle shot: *'If I was a betting man, instead of being an Elder of my Baptist chapel I would wager on less than six months!'*

75

Megan Powell was happy, the following morning, that her husband was being discharged from Cardiff Royal Infirmary and agreed that, logistically, it was best that Dai collected his father on his own, plus the wheelchair the hospital had agreed to lend them.

Dai pulled the Ford V8 convertible up to the nearest entrance to the ward where his father had been incumbent for ten days. With the help of a hospital porter he wheeled the old man down to the hospital entrance and gently edged him out of the wheelchair, and guiding his father's bottom into the passenger seat he lifted his dad's legs into the well of the car. The porter folded the wheelchair flat, and with Dai holding one side, manoeuvred it flat into the boot of the Ford V8 convertible. There was no problem unloading his father at the miner's cottage and installing the old man on the Victorian sofa in the front lounge tenderly covered him up to his neck with a fleecy blanket. Dai then hoisted from the backyard a loaded scuttle of the local pit's free monthly ton of coal to their pensioners, and soon had a fire blazing.

Now his dad was safely home Dai felt he knew the direction he must go for the time being and that was to be alongside his mother for the next few months which he planned to make as happy as possible for his father. But his plan had to be altered even before they had even been implemented. The local postman arrived at ten o'clock with his daily delivery.

It was startling news, via letter, from *La Pasionaria,* in Russia, who under the threat of elimination, execution or assassination, whatever General Francisco Franco's bloodthirsty hit-men liked to call it, had been given sanctuary in Moscow. The feisty Republican icon described the final theatre of, arguably, one of the most horrific Civil Wars in the historical saga of man's inhumanity to man, had unfolded in Madrid when the Nationalist forces, posted on the outskirts of the Spanish capital, were approached by a weakling Republican Colonel called Segismundo Casado who tried to stage a coup among the defenders hoping to get more humane surrender terms from Nationalist leader Franco.

But merciless Franco refused anything less than unconditional surrender from the beleagured Republicans. On March 28th 1939 Franco's army marched into Madrid and on the 1st April the Spanish Civil War was declared officially over. Many Republicans fled across the border to France, but many of the remaining survivors were either imprisoned or executed. More than half a million Spaniards had lost their lives in the three year civil conflict.

La Pasionaria's cryptic message from Red Square was brief and brutally to the point: GET PILAR AND BABY OUT OF SPAIN AS SOON AS POSSIBLE. Dolores Ibárruri.

The ever-alert Dai Powell knew that meant he not only had to change his tactics and return to Spain immediately but he had to give his father a serious explanation about his new daughter in law and the little grandaughter who were marooned in perilous war-torn Spain.

But nothing seemed to faze the old man.

'Dolores Ibárurri-there is not a collier in the Rhonnda Valley who has not heard of that wonderful lady who is the grandaughter, daughter, sister and wife of miners,' said Powell senior.

'She has fought all her life for underprivileged coal miners. Those of us in Wales, who have toiled at the coal face idolise. I feel honoured that La Pasionaria is a friend and adviser to my son.'

Dai Powell drew his chair up to the sofa where his father lay and told the old man how he had come to be friendly with the renowned *La Pasionaria* and had come under the spell of the magnetic Republican icon.

Dai also explained how he had met and fell in love with Republican Army nurse Pilar Delgado and added: *'She's really a wonderful girl and you'll love her Dad. She comes from Asturias and her father and two elder brothers all work in the anthracite mines.'*

The old man was quite excited about the news that his daughter in law also came from mining stock. *'I once went on a weekend coach trip run by the Miners' Union to Asturias. Those anthracite miners were wonderful hosts and looked after us royally, I have to say they are really tough men and have to work in terrible conditions and have always been underpaid.'*

Dai Powell then shocked his father when he detailed how the Republican Government refused to legalise the blessing of his union with Pilar at Granada Cathedral as a civil marriage, which meant that Pilar was deemed to be a Spanish citizen and not entitled to a British passport. It would mean he would to have to run the gauntlet of the Spanish legal system if he was going to be able to smuggle Pilar and the baby out of Spain.

'Look Dai bach I know why you were planning to stay here in Ynswen for a few months' said the old man. *'I am not a fool you know. I have accepted for some time that my number is nearly up.*

No, don't argue boy its only a matter of a short time now. But we are now talking of your Mam and mine's new extended family. I want to see my lovely daughter-in-law Pilar and beautiful granddaughter Dolores Megan. Now I am asking you to leave tomorrow and head for Spain and bring Pilar and the baby back here so that I can see them before I pass on.

'Before you leave tomorrow I will give you a cheque for five thousand pounds which you can cash at the Co-op Bank in Treorchy. Give Harry Bruce, the bank manager, my regards. If you want to know where I got the cash from it is part of the insurance compensation I received after breaking my hip when I was injured and nearly died after an accident at the coal face thirty years ago.

'No arguments boy. We are talking about rescuing your mother and I's daughter in-law, and Grandchild and probably saving their lives.'

The die was cast and Dai knew that there was no use in arguing with his teak-hard dad when he was in that kind of hard mood. A hardness created by four decades of back-breaking work down the pit.

76

Dai Powell realised the tone of the dramatically phrased letter with the Moscow postmark from the legendary 44-year-old Dolores Ibárruri, the Republican icon known as *La Pasionaria* meant, plagiarising a term beloved of contract lawyers, that *"time was of the essence"*.

He had to move quickly if he was to rescue Pilar and tiny Dolores Megan. Dai never gave a second thought that the task ahead was formidable if not practically impossible to smuggle out an adult and toddler from Spain. A country cowed under the guns, whips and vicious hoodlums of the totalitarian Nationalist Government now ruled by General Franco, who was destined to live 30 years longer than his infamous Nazi and Fascist allies Hitler and Mussolini,

He had only a few hours sleep that night as he prepared to leave on what he figured would be approximately a gruelling 1,300 kilometre journey to Barcelona, although he did not expect to take the Austin V8 convertible any further than the French-Spanish border town of Perpignan.

There were was a hustle and bustle throughout the evening as

Mrs Megan Powell denied her 80 odd years preparing a huge hamper for the journey. It was if she was a yesteryear mother watching her soldier son go off to the Crusades with the gritty message: *'Return from your mission victorious boy, or on your shield with honour if you are defeated.'*

There were plump pies of both the meat and the fruit varieties, Welsh cakes baked on the black-leaded oven, sandwiches, of the doorstep sort, obese with crumbly Caerphilly cheese and half a dozen bottles of miners' ale brewed by S.A.Brain of Cardiff since 1882.

'My grandfather used to walk into the pub after his shift at the pit and down two pints of Brains one after the other,' recalled Megan. *'That is because to this day miners' beer is low gravity and sweetish and can be consumed by the pint to clear the throat of coal dust. Grandfather would go straight to the counter, wait for the barmaid to pull the two pints, and shout in a loud Welsh voice "Iechyd da" or as the English pronounce it "yacky da-meaning good health"-sink the two pints in ten seconds, then walk sedately back to the cottage where my mother would have the tin tub in the yard filled with hot water for his bath. Those were the days boyo. No money but a lot of laughs!"*

Dai laughed at his mother's anecdote and said: *'My Great Grandpa must have been quite a guy--I would love to have met him. Well I am certainly not going to starve on my long car journey to Spain, thanks to you mother.'* Megan Powell had a pithy reply to that: *'I hope you never starve for the rest of your life, son!'*

Dai was up at the crack of dawn the next morning on schedule to leave in the Ford V8 convertible at 8-45am so that he could call in at the Co-op Bank in Treorchy to cash the cheque for £5,000 that his father had given him to fund his mission to smuggle his 'wife' Pilar and their toddler daughter out of war-torn Spain.

He would follow the route, in reverse, that he had taken three months earlier when the Republican Government decided to repatriate the International Brigades in a failed attempt to curry favour with the League of Nations in their battle against General Franco's Nationalists.

A route that would take him out of Wales, across the south of England to Dover where, with the car on board, he would take the cross Channel ferry to Calais. Then came the long road journey down the spine of France, skirting Paris, past the opulent Palace of Versailles the brain child of the exotic King Louis XIV, who reigned over France for a record 72 years, three months and eighteen days.

Then over the spectacular road across the midi-Pyrenees to the border town of Perpignan where he would enlist the help of his friend, the likeable rogue and cigarette smuggler, Jean-Pierre Perez.

The long journey went as planned. After an overnight stay in Dover, and tedious car trip through France, it was nine o'clock in the evening when he pulled the Ford V8 cabriolet up outside Jean-Pierre's house.

77

Dai was upset about the emotional farewell with his parents, particularly in view of his father's advanced age and his failing health, plus the dreaded thought that he might never see his dad again.

But, in the knowledge that he was going to Spain with both his parent's blessing and whole hearted support for his perilous mission, he put aside any misgivings to concentrate on getting to Perpignan as quickly as possible to liaise with his pal Jean-Pierre Perez.

It was in fact Jean-Pierre who came to the door of his house as the Ford V8 pulled up in the outskirts of Perpignan-a strangely sombre Jean-Pierre, totally different to his normally jovial demeanour.

'Dai, mon ami,' said Jean-Pierre. *'I sent you a letter yesterday but obviously you had left Angleterre before it had arrived. Come inside boy. I have a lot to tell you.'*

Dai, curious about Jean-Pierre's down-beat mood, replied: *'I hope it is good news mon ami.'*

Significantly Jean-Pierre did not make any comment as he ushered his Welsh friend into the house.

After Dai had greeted Madame Lauren Perez with a kiss on each cheek he was left alone with Jean-Pierre.

' *I have got bad news for you,*' said the cigarette smuggler. '*Terrible news in fact Dai, mon ami. Your Pilar is dead, murdered in cold blood by Franco's hoodlums two days ago.*'

Dai Powell was aghast . Dumbstruck with shock which quickly flared into rage.

'*Fucking murdered?*' he roared. '*Who would do such a thing? I'll cut their sodding hearts out if you tell me who did it.*'

Then, as if in his anguish he had forgotten his little child, he poignantly asked: '*What about the niña? What about my tiny querido Dolores Megan?*'

Jean-Pierre then began a long dissertation about the dire circumstances in immediate post-Civil War Spain.

'*I am not saying that General Franco, personally put his signature to Pilar's execution but he has obviously ordered his officers to kill die-hard Republican supporters all across Spain, civilians, soldiers and even women sympathisers,*' he explained. '*Shooting on the streets and firing squads are an every day occurrence. Children are taken away from their mothers and placed in care of Nationalist families if they are too young to go to the special orphanages being set-up.*

'*Your Dolores Megan is alive and fostered out for the time being with the wife of a former Nationalist Army sergeant and now a Civil Administrator for Franco. Don't worry members of the Republican Resistance movement, organised and set up by La Pasionaria before she fled to Russia, are keeping their eye on your daughter.*

'*Now, as far as you seeking out revenge for your wife Pilar's murder is concerned, Spain under the new totalitarian Nationalist government is like one big concentration camp. You must now think only of the problem of getting the child across the border with help from the Republican Resistance Movement and myself, of course.*

'The chink in the Nationalists' armour at the moment is the appalling weakness in the country's infrastructure. There is a serious shortage of food because of the ravages of war to the crops and livestock. Shortage of oil for cooking, for manufacturing, for producing electricity, for fuel for vehicles in fact a shortage of fucking everything at the moment.

'That is why Franco's minions are allowing people like me from the border regions of Perpignan and Andorra to take goods and food to help sustain a starving country. As usual I am peddling cigarettes to Franco's soldiers, also wine because many of Spain's vineyards have been badly damaged by the war. I have a friend here in Perpignan, a baker, who carries a lorry load of bread across the frontier. He takes his freshly baked bread to Barcelona's 100-year-old Boqueria Market, the most emblematic market in the whole of Spain where, pathetically, 90 per cent of the stalls are empty because impoverished traders have nothing to sell.

'That has opened a way for us to get across the border and back to rescue little Dolores Megan.

'To complete the sad story of Pilar's death she was dragged from her bed at 3am one morning, the baby savagely tugged away from her. Pilar, with four men and one other women were taken to a wood and lined up at the edge of a trench, which was to be their grave and shot by a firing squad. The denouncement against Pilar was that of spying for the Republic, that she had given succour to political agitator Dolores Ibárruri, known as La Pasionaria, and to yourself a

mercenary soldier an enemy of the Nationalist cause. Trumped up charges which would never stand up in a Court of Law. Forget revenging Pilar's assassination-for that is what it is like for thousands of others at this terrible time. Giving your life in order to revenge Pilar would be pointless. Far better rescue the young life which you helped to bring into the world.

'So that is the parlous state of Spain in May 1939 under the rule of conquering General Francisco Franco. It will take months, if not years, to get the country on its feet again. To fill the empty stomachs of its people. To get the citizens back to work on the land and in the factories and dismiss the bitter memories of one of the worst Civil Wars in history.

'Meanwhile you have to do what any decent father would do and rescue your lovely little girl. Never forget Pilar but don't allow grief to stand in the way of your duty. Tomorrow when you have a good sleep to recover from your long journey we will both get down to planning a winning strategy how to get your Dolores Megan from the hell that , at the moment, is Spain.'

Dai Powell, struggling to control his naturally aggressive instincts, accepted that his tobacco-smuggling pal was absolutely right and that a formidable task lay ahead of him.

78

Jean-Pierre Perez did not waste any time before convening a meeting, the next day, between various people who wanted to help Dai Powell, the former General in the disbanded International Brigades who had allied themselves so gallantly with the Republican Army, to smuggle his motherless ten month old baby girl out of war-ravaged Spain.

There was Marcel Leblanc, whose family had been baking bread for the townsfolk of the border-town Perpignan for the past 100 years, and nowadays was allowed to enter Spain on three days a week with his van loaded with freshly baked baguettes, loaves and rolls to sell to the starving people of Barcelona at the famous Boqueria Market.

Perpignan butcher Martin Groverre was another Perpignan trader welcomed across the Spanish border three times a week with a full lorry of beef, lamb and pork carcases as well as several hundred slaughtered chickens.

Border farmer Tomas Giron crossed the border twice a week heading for the market with his tractor towing a trailer over-laden with badly needed, freshly picked, potatoes, carrots and cabbage which were always sold out at the Boqueria Market. While Jean-Pierre Perez's 15-year-old Mercedes van was packed to the roof with contraband cigarettes and wine for which there were always eager customers. Commodities in short supply on the Spanish side of the border.

Phillipé Jiminez was a member of the outlawed Republican Resistance, based on the French side his duty was to liaise with the movement operating in the now Nationalist controlled Spain.

They faced hardly any red-tape from the frontier guards of a country in which its infrastructure and economic system was creaking after three years of debilitating civil war. Death by hunger was rife to add to the mountains of cadavers being piled up by General Franco's bloodthirsty killing squads hell-bent on ridding Spain of as many former Republican military and civilian supporters as possible. All of these people were only too willing to help Dai Powell, in the quest to smuggle ten-month-old Dolores Megan out of Spain, out of respect to the courage and dedication he had given to the Republican cause in the previous three years.

'*Let's see what we can do to get this innocent child across the border,*' said Jean-Pierre, calling the meeting to order.

The cigarette smuggler had arranged things with style. There were six chairs arranged around the dining table.

Two bottles of high quality, uncorked, *Chateauneuf-de-Pape*, stood breathing, in the centre of the table, with a *balón* wine glass in front of each chair. As might have been expected at the home of a notorious tobacco smuggler, several packets of cigarettes were strewn around with little plates of almonds, tiny silver onions, *pimientos padron* and minute hard-boiled quails' eggs.

'*I will take the responsibility for chairing this meeting as I have supplied the wine and smokes,'* said Jean-Pierre, tongue in cheek, who received a round of laughter from the other five men. *'We are all here to help Dai Powell rescue his little girl. Not because we are all Communists but because everyone around this table hates Facism, National Socialism-call it what you like.*

'First thing we need is to settle how to get Dai and the child across the border from Spain to France. Anyone got any ideas how that can be done?'

The Perpignan baker and owner of the famous local *pasteleria* which made mouth-watering cakes and sugary fancies, Marcel Leblanc, was the first man at the meeting to volunteer his services.

'My family have been taking the bread we bake and the sweetmeats, we are famous for making, to Barcelona's renowned Boqueria Market for a century,' explained Leblanc. *'We are trusted by most of the public even if not by Franco's followers. This trust over 100 years takes in the period when my late grandfather, Emille and father, Josef, manned our own stall in the market. Nowadays I cross the border with my van loaded with bread and cakes accompanied by my wife Emily and daughter Therése who is the same age as Monsieur Powell's little girl. We make the crossing three times a week at 6am in the morning with little Therése, nearly always fast asleep, in the special cot which I have fitted into the back of the van. My suggestion is that we go out on the outward journey with a rolled up blanket in the cot to fool the border guards that it is our child. The border guards are more interested in the half a dozen loaves and bag of cakes we give them each trip. On the return journey, which is usually around 9 pm in the evening, from Barcelona we could bring little Dolores Megan Powell back with us, hopefully, sleeping in the cot--it is unlikely to cause much curiosity with the border guards. I am sure the ploy will work.'*

There was concord amongst those present that the plan mooted by Marcel Leblanc would work.

'*Good,*' said Leblanc. '*That's it then, all we have to do is fine-tune that plan. All that my wife Emily has to do is to find, what the Americans' call, a baby-sitter for our little daughter Thérése that day.*'

A statement that was quickly picked up by Jean-Pierre's wife, Lauren, who was not at the table but perched on a stool on the periphery wall. She intervened in a loud voice: '*That will be me-I'll be the baby-sitter. I'll look after little Thérése for the day. It's been a long time since I've been able to cuddle a toddler!*'

Jean-Pierre brought the meeting to order again with the next facet of the plan to rescue toddler Dolores Megan Powell.

'*Now we are agreed on how to get the child Dolores Megan Powell out of Spain, we have to decide the safest way of getting her father Dai Powell into the country.*' he said. '*Dai will, obviously, want to personally activate her rescue from the Nationalist household who have been given the responsibility of fostering and brain washing her and two more unfortunate children* whose *Republican parents have been murdered by Franco's thugs. Remember if Dai is captured, as a former General in the Republican Army, he will certainly face a firing squad.*

'*The owner of the house where these little children are incarcerated, if that is the right word, is now a high ranking member of the Falange a die-hard Fascist and a torturer who works for Franco. No one is going to be too sorry if he is eliminated during this exercise.*'

Jean-Pierre did not have to explain to the group that the *Falange* was the official name for the Spanish Fascist Party. Founded in 1933 by José Antonio Primo de Rivera, son of the former Spanish dictator General Primo de Rivera. The Falange emphasised the national traditions of Spain and combined these with fascist ideology. His adoption of classic fascist ideals brought the Falange into direct conflict with the Republicans who were viewed by the Falange as bringing non-Spanish beliefs into a Roman Catholic Society- primarily communism, a belief that rejected religion as *"the opium of the people"*, according to Karl Marx.

Phillipé Jiminez informed those present that he was under orders from *La Pasionaria,* the icon of the defeated Republicans, from her new base in Russia to liaise with the newly formed, under cover Republican Resistance Movement and former General Dai Powell and help him to smuggle his little daughter out of war-torn Spain.

'While doing that the Resistance Movement will also rescue the other two children who are in the custody of the Falangist married couple ordered by Franco's administrators to foster and brain-wash these toddlers with facist propaganda,' said Jiminez. *'The Resistance Movement will be responsible for getting the other two orphaned children to France where they have blood relatives to take over their care after their parents were executed by Franco's firing squads. On a need to know basis we will not give this meeting any details how we will rescue these other two children.'*

'Neither, on a need to know basis, will we disclose how we will get Dai Powell out of Spain after the rescue of these three unfortunate children has been completed. Capture of any one of the rescuers by Franco's hoodlums will certainly mean execution and horrific torture. That is why security and discretion by the people in this room is imperative for everyone's sake.

Border farmer Tomas Giron, whose fertile holding was situated on the slopes outside Perpignan took up the point that Jean-Pierre had raised a few minutes earlier said: *'Given average luck I am sure that I can get General Powell across the border safely. My high-topped trailer, which I pull by tractor has a secret compartment at the front. When I load up the trailer with potatoes, carrots and cabbages they completely cover the secret compartment which is large enough to hide a man. I have installed a breathing tube so there is no problem for the person secreted into the compartment. But I will need back-up from the Resistance once we cross the frontier to transfer Monsieur Powell into a faster vehicle to carry him on to Barcelona.*

'My Deutz F2M tractor - is only three years old with two gear transmission via a roller chain produces 14 horse power-but pulling a loaded covered trailer can only manage a speed of 16.09 kilometres an hours.'

So the well-thought-out plan for the rescue of little Dolores Megan Powell from the insidious clutches of General Franco's thugs had been rolled out. Those who had committed themselves with the daunting task of implementing it, could only pray for success.

79

"Operation Dolores Megan" - that is what Jean-Pierre and the rest of the planners decided to call a project that threatened perils, even violent death, to those sworn to make it succeed.

It took 48 hours to organise the preparation for the dangerous operation. Because of the snail-pace progress of the unwieldy Deutz F2M tractor, driven by border-farmer Tomas Giron, the intrepid Dai Powell was the first of the principals to start off on the hazardous journey to Barcelona.

The adrenalin was pumping wildly as Dai climbed into the cavernous secret compartment in the covered trailer. He placed the large tube into his mouth and answered in the affirmative when farmer Giron asked him if he was breathing satisfactorily. Giron, using a huge hay fork, tossed in as many freshly picked potatoes, carrots and cabbages to fill the trailer to the brim. Through the tube Dai confirmed again that he was still able to breathe comfortably.

Dai Powell, anecdotally recalled for many years afterwards that the next hour and half was the most nightmarish journey he had ever made, the worst moment came when he felt the tractor brake and the lumbering trailer shudder to a halt at the Spanish frontier control. But Tomas Giron was confidently in control as he exchanged pleasantries with the border guards who were delighted with the two sacks of potatoes and vegetables to take back home to their wives suffering from the food shortages caused by the Civil War.

The odd conveyance began to move slowly away and rumbled on for another half an hour, before jerking to a halt again which, to Dai's relief, was the rendezvous point pre-arranged with *La Pasionaria's* newly formed Resistance Movement member who was sworn to harass the ruling Nationalist party as much as possible.

Dai knew everything was OK when Tomas Giron slid open the hatch to the secret compartment of the trailer and pulled him out. Already waiting was the Republican Resistance fighter Alfonso Prada who said: *'Senor Powell, I have been sent to collect you. I am to take you on the back of my motorbike, as quickly as possible, to a safe house on the outskirts of Barcelona where you will meet my colleagues. May I say it is my privilege to help you in return for the courageous service you gave to our cause as an officer in the International Brigades during the recent Civil War.'*

Dai Powell thanked the Resistance fighter and added: *'Thank you Alfonso it has been one of the privileges in my life to have fought for the Republicans. We must never give up the fight until the insidious ogre of fascism is wiped off the world map.'*

They said farewell to border-farmer Tomas Giron as he wheeled his lumbering load on its three hour crawl to the Boqueria Market where the starving people had been queuing since dawn to buy his precious load. He would not get back to his own bed in Perpignan until after midnight, rising at daylight, to help his wife to pick potatoes, cabbage and carrots for another tortuous 16 kilometres journey to Barcelona.

Dai Powell straddled the padded pillion of the dusty red La Mondiale 1931 confident in the knowledge that the 350cc machine would carry him, Alfonso Prada at the handlebars, to the safe house in Barcelona at four times the speed of Tomas Giron's creaking tractor. Nevertheless he bestowed a Spanish-style *abrazo* with a *beso* to each of the border farmer's stubbly cheeks as the motorbike wheeled away on a different route.

The remainder of the team that had taken part in the planning session for the rescue of little Dolores Megan at the meeting in Jean-Pierre's house made their own way across the frontier by different routes to Barcelona's renowned Boqueria Market.

Jean-Pierre himself breezed past the Control point having cheered up the border guards with several cartons of contraband cigarettes and half a dozen bottles of wine from the huge load in his van which he would sell-out within in two hours of his arrival at the market.

Butcher, Martin Groverre, took a different route and used an alternative border control to cross over with his lorry load of beef, lamb and pork carcases collected from the Perpignan abattoir the previous evening. While Marcel, the current owner of the 100-year-old Perpignan Family Le Blank bakery firm also had little trouble at the frontier after sweetening the Spanish customs officers with a sack of baguettes and loaves baked fresh that very night.

"Operation Dolores Megan", the rescue of Dai Powell's little daughter, would take place the following day, the fine-tuning, the final planning of the escapade, would be finalised by those involved in the actual rescue at the safe house that evening when the local Resistance fighters would reveal the latest intelligence about the house where Dolores Megan was being kept.

80

José Vacca, a former sergeant in the Republican Army, had successfully remained under cover since General Franco's Nationalists had prevailed after three years of vicious Civil War.

But unlike the main core of the Republican movement he refused to bow before ignominy of unconditional surrender and was a willing recruit to the Resistance Fighters set up by *La Pasionaria* before she departed to sanctuary from Franco's hit-men in Moscow where she would continue to lead the opposition to the fascist dictator.

Vacca presided at the final briefing hours before *"Operation Dolores Megan"* got under way.

'*The house where General Dai Powell's eleven months old daughter is held belongs to Daniel Clari and his wife Rosita,'* explained Vacca. '*Clari is the Nationalist's highest ranking government administrator in Barcelona. There is no doubt that he is Franco's top representative in Catalunya and, again, no doubt signs the authority, on behalf of Franco, for all the executions of Republicans by firing squad in the area in the weeks since the end of the Civil War. Perhaps its by way of a perquisite from Franco that his wife, Rosita has been given the job of fostering young children, like Dolores Megan, whose mothers and both parents in some cases have been executed, until they are old enough to go to Nationalist orphanages where they will be brainwashed into fascist beliefs. Senora Rosita Clari has three children under her care at the moment Dolores Megan and two other orphaned children who we will also rescue as they have relatives in France where they fled after the Civil War.*

'We have kept a close watch on the Clari household for the past two weeks through binoculars and have found that the best time to snatch these three unfortunate kids would be at midday. At 11 am each day Senora puts the three children in their cots on the garden terrace for a siesta. By midday they are all sound asleep. Daniel Clari leaves for his work at the Nationalist Administration offices at 8 am each day and rarely comes home until evening.'

Vacca then handed Dai Powell a bulky parcel wrapped in waxed paper and explained: *Senora Dolores Ibárruri - La Pasionaria-has left you a regalo with her warmest regards and a message for all of us in this operation which said: No Pasarán! - her old battle cry. Here open your parcel.'*

Dai Powell, curiously ripped the waxed wrapping from the package which his friend and mentor *La Pasionaria* **had sent all the way from Moscow, which, turned out to be a pistol.**

Vacca, with a touch of envy in his voice, said: *'It is a Russian Tokarev TT pistol mod. 1933 said to be the finest handgun in the world at this point of time. You are a lucky man to own it Senor Powell. It is a formidable weapon, with good penetration, using 7.63mm cartridges, with an effective range. The only down-point is the absence of a safety catch. The only way to carry it in your holster or pocket is to leave one of its eight cartridge chambers empty while carrying this weapon. You* *will find the factory in the USSR have the fixed sight zeroed for 25 meters. Good luck with your new pistol Senor.'*

Vacca then finalised the rescue plan for *"Operation Dolores Megan"* which would move into action at noon the following day.

'We will move in precisely at 12 o'clock,' he explained. *'General Powell will command the operation and I will act as his deputy. We will temporarily incapacitate Senora Rosita Clari by administering chloroform on a folded towel.*

'General Powell will make his own arrangements to get his daughter across the French border while I will organise the movement to reunite the other two orphaned children with their relatives in France. The least we know about each other's plan to flee from Spain the better, in case we are captured some time in the future and are tortured by Franco's thugs.'

Dai had no reason to query the plans and proceeded that evening to complete his personal arrangements for evacuating little Dolores Megan from Nationalist controlled Spain. He had already agreed that his daughter would be surreptitiously carried across the Spanish-French border control installed in the cot fitted into the van of Perpignan baker Marcel le Blanc and normally occupied by his own little girl who was the same age as Dolores Megan.

From Perpignan Dai planned to speed his daughter to Paris in his Ford V8 convertible where, on arrival at the British Embassy he would ask for a temporary passport in the name of 11 month old Doris Megan Powell. He would travel from there to Calais and on to England via the cross channel ferry to Dover.

But he was under no illusions there was a lot that could go wrong before he placed Dolores Megan into the safe and eager arms of her grandmother on arrival at her new home in the Rhonnda Valley where he was sure she would be cherished for the rest of her life.

81

When Dai Powell woke up at sunrise the following morning he knew that this day in 1939 would not rank historically alongside milestones such as 1215 when King John signed Magna Carta at Runnymede, or, 1492 when Columbus discovered the New World, or, 1815 when the Battle of Waterloo was won ending Napoleon's dream to rule Europe.

But it was the day he would wreak retribution against General Franco's harsh totalitarian regime for the evil and totally unjust execution of his beloved Pilar by rescuing their adorable baby daughter from the cruel clutch of Spain's ruthless Nationalist Party.

He gathered his team of four undercover members of the newly formed Republican Resistance Movement, dedicated to fight to the death, until Spain was freed from the fascist yoke. A struggle that continued for nigh on four decades until General Francisco Franco died at the age of 82 in 1975.

Dai turned to José Vacca, the senior of the four Resistance fighters, who would act as his deputy. *'José you will take two of* the men and enter the house through the front door,' he said. 'Most probably you will encounter the lady of the house, Rosita Clari, first. In which case render her harmless with the chloroform and tie her up.

'I will take your other man with me and we will get access to the back garden terrace by scaling the wooden fence. In the hope that Rosita Clari will have been put out of action to. We will snatch the three toddlers from their cots on the terrace. I will carry my Dolores Megan away in the motor cycle and side car I will have parked outside while you José will transfer the other two children to the van you will be using. For neither of us know how the other will transport the child or children out of Spain. It is better that way, for security reasons, in case either or both of us are captured and tortured by Franco's thugs. We will not be able to disclose what we don't know!'

The plan worked perfectly-or it seemed to. As Dai Powell and José Vacca learned as leaders in the Republican Army the unexpected often turns up to spike the best laid plans.

What Powell and Vacca did not expect or know was that, completely out of the norm the man of the house had not gone to his office that morning.. It was a serious misjudgement. Sadistic Nationalist administrator, Daniel Clari, was in an upstairs bedroom sleeping off a hang-over when the Resistance fighters burst in.

Clari was disturbed by a noise from downstairs when José Vacca, the former Republican Army sergeant and his Resistance fighters went in through the front door, overcame and chloroformed Rosita Clari. Shaking his head to clear the effects of his alcoholic haze Daniel Clari stumbled to the bedroom window and saw Dai Powell and the other Resistance fighter scaling the perimeter fence surrounding his back garden.

In that brief moment Daniel Clari's pulsing headache. cleared in remarkably quick time as he pulled on a pair of trousers and withdrew from the nearby wardrobe a valuable 20 gauge Stevens Model 311A side-by-side-double barrel shotgun the Generalissimo had gifted him when they went out shooting game in the woods near Madrid.

Oddly this ancient sports gun was the only weapon owned by the gory man who had signed the death warrants of 138 Republican men and women who had died in front of Franco's firing squads during the few weeks since the end of the Civil War. Those massacred under his vile authority included, Pilar Delgado. Dai Powell would never forget it!

Daniel Clari crept slowly down the staircase, the shotgun cocked and ready to fire. But at the trigger Clari was no trained warrior. This puffy Nationalist Government civil servant who sent people, men and women to execution before Franco's daily firing squads never lost an hour's sleep as he penned his flourishing signature to the death warrants.

Looking at a man's back through the shotgun sights rather than a deer, wild boar, fox or even a rabbit was a different situation. It required a certain amount of courage. A quality that the wobbly Clari was short of. As he tip-toed round the first bend at the top of the staircase he spotted one of José Vacca's Resistance fighters squatted on the lowest stair step watching his two colleagues administering chloroform and tieing up Rosita Clari.

Faced with the target of a man's back the shaking Clari unhesitatingly, with a twitching finger, pulled the trigger and in a frantic avalanche of flying blood and bone despatched the unfortunate Republican Resistance fighter to eternity.

As one man prematurely joined his Maker another appeared

on the staircase wielding a hand gun his eyes frantically searching upwards for a target. In an instinctive moment of self-preservation, often prevalent in cowards, without a further thought the trembling Clari fired the ancient gun again and blew the man's head away to turn the mess at the bottom of the staircase into a bloody morass.

José Vacca, as a superbly trained former NCO in the Republican Army, sensing the dire position he was in having lost his two men, withdrew to the garden leaving Rosita Clari still drugged and bound in the house.

He immediately connected with Dai Powell, who had already lifted the three toddlers from their cots leaving them in the charge of the third Resistance Fighter and explained what the situation was.

'*It is Daniel Clari, he must have been in the house upstairs in bed instead of going to work as usual,*' said the frantic Vacca. '*He's already killed my two men with, what I am sure is a shotgun. He's got the high ground. We cannot proceed with the operation of rescuing the three ninas while dealing with him otherwise we'll have the whole of Franco's Army out looking for us.*'

Dai Powell, went beserk as he pulled his new Tokarev TT pistol from his holster and rolled the barrel to bring a cartridge in line with the hammer. He affectionately patted the wooden stock and said: '*Thank you La Pasionaria--I know you will not fail me at this crucial time!*'

It was not strictly true to say that Dai Powell had lost his cool which would have been most unprofessional for a trained soldier. But the adrenalin was gushing as he began the most perilous combat of his career with the two fold aim of avenging the savage execution of his beloved Pilar and the rescue of their little child Dolores Megan.

'*This is my job,*' he told the worried Vacca. '*I have a vested interest in eliminating that ghoulish butcher Daniel Clari. You get the three children into the car you have outside. Start the engine and keep it running until I join you after dealing with Clari.*'

Not overly pleased that he was being eliminated from the action José Vacca, as a good soldier, acknowledged that Dai Powell was in command and his tactics, in a crisis, were sound.

Scanning the back of the house he noticed a curtain move slightly. He knew then that the murderous Daniel Clari, his deadly shotgun at the ready, was sizing up his strategy against what he assumed were a bunch of renegade Republicans. He was unaware at this stage that his wife, Rosita, was laying trussed up downstairs still unconscious from the effects of the chloroform that had been administered to her.

Dai Powell decided to attack from the front of the house as Clari seemed to be concentrating on the rear of the building.

Powell was desperately looking for an element of surprise against a heavily armed opponent who had the advantage of familiarity with the battle-terrain. Creeping on all fours around the perimeter of the grounds Dai was delighted that José Vacca and his two unfortunate Resistance fighters had left the front door off the latch when earlier they had entered the house.

The Welshman crouched, as still as the proverbial mouse, as he tried to locate out where his adversary was lurking with his lethal shotgun at the ready. Then he heard a faint scuffle from above and realised that the depraved Daniel Clari was carefully creeping downstairs. Rather than let Franco's insidious execution-fixer have the advantage of the high ground Powell slid into a dark corner of the hallway letting Clari creep to the kitchen where his chloroforn comatose wife lay trussed like a chicken ready for the oven.

Powell stealthily crept after him to the kitchen door, where he saw Clari bending over his inert wife. Now Powell knew he had the upper hand.

'Don't move Clari,' he shouted forcefully. *'Don't even bat a fuckin' eyelid or you are a dead man.'*

Clari, startled out of his mind by the authorative command from his rear, nevertheless turned with the shotgun drooping from his right arm. *'Who the fuck are you?'* he yelled screwing up his eyes in an effort to recognise his assailant.

Powell, his finger twitching in readiness on the trigger of the Tokaret TT pistol used his military rank for effect: *'I am General Dai Powell formerly of the Republican Army. But you probably remenber the name of my wife better ? She was Pilar Delgado the woman you sent to the firing squad on Franco's orders recently…'*

Clari was a quivering jelly but nevertheless tried to talk his way out of trouble, and countered: *'Pilar Delgado, the spy who gave succour to that enemy of the Nationalist cause known as La Pasionaria?….'*

Powell's fiery Gallic temper turned into a red mist as he countered: *'No you fuckin' asshole. Just think about it when you go to hell in a minute or so--not a spy but a devoted nurse who tended wounded and dying Republican and Nationalist soldiers alike with loving and tender care….'*

Then spotting a slight movement from Clari as he tried to raise the Stevens shotgun Powell, with all the skill of a master marksman, fired the Tokarev TT pistol from the hip.

It was an uncannily brilliant shot the 7.63mm Mauser cartridge transferring Clari's shattered right knee to a glutionous gory mess on the kitchen's tiled wall. Clari was in no doubt now that only a desperate action could save him as he crawled pathetically across the kitchen floor, amazingly still clutching the shotgun. He tried to raise the ancient weapon at which point the merciless Powel fired again. It was another shining shot that reduced the Nationalist civil servant's left knee to an ensanguined stump.

Amazingly, writhing in his death throes, Clari managed to pull the trigger of the thunderous double-barrelled 20 gauge shot gun. Instead of hurtling towards Dai Powell the two cartridge, plunged into a metal container of Calor gas. This was a brand new fuel developed in England two years previously for kitchen ovens. In Spain, where the infrastructure had been destroyed by artillery fire and bombs, mains gas was unavailable, it was an amazing development for harassed Spanish housewives and cooks. But it was highly inflamable.

In a split second one side of the kitchen was transformed into a blazing inferno. After lone final token movement Powell sent a final shot into Clari's temple which sent the Franco side-kick to eternity. Within minutes Rosita, his wife, mercifully oblivious to what had occurred, also died from smoke inhalation.

'*I'd better get the fuck out of here,*' said Powell to himself as he scampered from the burning house via the back door.

82

José Vacca was at the wheel of the 1929 Morris Cowley, which had been stolen in Valencia by the Resistance Movement the week before, and, with no police record system in place after the cessation of hostilities in the Civil War, was considered to be a 'safe' vehicle.

Dai Powell looked into the rear of the vehicle and saw at a glance that Dolores Megan and the other two Spanish toddlers were asleep, tucked up in blankets.. *'Shove over José,'* said the Welshman breathing hard after the high-octane action of the past half an hour or. *'I'll drive--I know a way to get across the French border without going through a Spanish frontier post. All hell is going to break loose here in a few minutes. The kitchen inside the house is ablaze and soon the place will be inundated with fire engines, police cars and ambulances. I'll tell you all about it as we go.'* Slipping the old Morris Cowley into gear and double declutching, Dai pressed the acelerator and at a furious pace made a skidding turn at the corner of the street and sped northwards.

'The police will call out Franco's militia if they can quickly fathom what has happened inside the house,' said the former Republican

general gunning the Morris with breathtaking aplomb that would have been approved by Henry Birkin, who, in 1930, set up the fastest lap-time in the seven year old Le Mans 24 hour motor race. Birkin had hurtled his 4.4 litre Bentley around the tight circuit in a time of 6 hours 48 minutes, an average speed of 144.362 kilometres an hour.

'*We are heading towards Andorra,*' explained Powell sweating profusely under the strain of keeping four wheels of the Morris Cowley on the road. '*There is a farm on the Andorra side in which the border slices across one of their wheat fields. Once across that border line and we're safe without going through any frontier control. The farmer is a friend of mine, a friend and Republican supporter, we should have no problems.*'

Within an hour Powell had gunned the car to the Spanish edge of the farm where he spotted his farmer friend Jacques Leboef driving a tractor. '*Franco's men may be chasing us,*' explained Dai. '*We must get across the frontier line as soon as possible.*' Leboef, delighted to see his old friend, was only too happy to help said: '*Keep your car on this track for five minutes until you come to a hedge with a gap in it. Once through that gap, you are in France and the Spanish police or soldiers will not dare to cross the line.*

'*Park your car in the barn adjoining the farm house and I will go ahead and arrange for my missus to have a meal ready for you.*'

It all worked perfectly and half an hour later Dai and José were sat down at the mega-sized wooden kitchen table attacking a nourishing feast of lamb stew thickened with home grown potatoes, carrots and onions. Large chunks of crusty rustic bread on the side and a bottle of robust *Beaujolais*.

As they stuffed themselves with the wholesome fare Madame Leboef repaired to the bathroom where, to the sounds of happy gurgles and giggles she bathed the three toddlers and swathed them in luxuriously thick white bath towels. Then after a deep search in a linen cupboard she produced a pile of toddler clothes, used 18-years-previously by her twin daughters who were now attending the prestigious *Sorbonne Universtity,* Paris.

As Dai prepared to steer the old Morris Cowley out of the farmyard, heading for Perpignan, he profusely thanked Madame Leboef and surreptitiously slipped a wad of *franc* notes into her husband's hand.

83

There was a merry reunion of the Republican supporters at the house of Jean-Pierre Perez in Perpignan when they met that evening after a momentous and harassing day.

They arrived at various times governed by the business they had done at Barcelona's famous Boqueria Market and the capability of their varying forms of transport. The last to arrive was farmer Tomas Giron at 9pm after delivering and selling his load of potatoes, cabbages and carrots at the Boqueria Market and then setting off back to Perpignan in his snail-paced tractor-trailer to complete a six-hour return journey.

'I was fucking glad you had to change your plans and that I wasn't called on to bring you back Senor Powell,' said Giron. *'By the time I set off the balloon had gone up and Franco's murdering bastards, the police and the Guardia Civil examined every nook and cranny of my tractor rig. They poked their bayonets through every crevice and I got really worried they were going to ram one up my arse!'*

Jean-Pierre Perez brought the meeting to order and looking,

at Dai, said with a little humour, under the circumstances: '*You certainly know to organise a party. It seemed as if every soldier in Franco's army was searching for you during the day. With the help of the national and local policia and the Guardia Civil. I would not be surprised if he didn't call out the Marines and the Navy as well. But the downside is that Franco's civil administrators ordered that 20 Barcelona citizens, indiscriminately accused of being Republican supporters, were shot as reprisals by firing squad in Plaza Catalunya this afternoon as a reprisal for the killing of that evil bastard Daniel Clari. Even the thousands of pigeons who live in the square seemed to be weeping at the brutality!*

'*Before we continue I think we should all stand and observe a minute's silence in memory also of the two Resistance fighters who gave their lives in today's operation for the release of the three children as bravely as if they had died as soldiers in action for the Republic in the 11 Civil War.*'

Someone asked what had happened to the third Resistance Fighter who took part in the operation to rescue the children. Dai Powell immediately answered that query.

'*He disappeared into the street as José Vacca and I drove away with the three children in the Morris Cowley,*' said Powell. '*The plan was always for him to stay in Spain and we can only pray that Franco's hoodlums do not capture him.*

'*José and I will stay in Perpignan tonight thanks to the hospitality of our friend Jean-Pierre Perez. Tomorrow we will both leave Perpignan--José will take the two Republican kids to their relatives in France and then face the dangerous task of getting himself back into Spain. I will leave with my daughter Dolores-Megan for the United Kingdom. Thank you all for your help. Long live the Republic or, as Pasionaria would say: !NO PASARÁN!--THE FACISTS SHALL NOT PASS!'*

They split up with emotional farewell having sealed their association by polishing off two bottles of *Fundador* brandy courtesy again of cigarette smuggler Jean-Pierre.

84

For Dai Jones, former coal miner, university graduate, professional rugby footballer, political protester, and distinguished soldier, it was the last lap on a long and testing marathon from the South Wales coalfields, Jarrow, London, Spain and back to the Rhonnda to unite his motherless child, Dolores Megan, to her Welsh heritage.

There was much activity during the night at the Perez household as Jean-Pierre and his wife prepared the way for the journeys that José Vacca and Dai would have to make to get the children they had rescued into the safe arms of the caring relatives that would love and nurture them for the rest of their lives.

Piles of sandwiches, ham, cheese, sausage were made and packed into paper bags in the boots of José's Moris Cowley and Dai's Ford V8 convertible, along with bottles of water and milk for the children.

After breakfast José Vacca put the two children, in his care into their home-made carry-cots in the rear of the Morris and said farewell to Dai and the Perez family without, for security reasons, disclosing to which region of France he would be heading.

It was then Dai's turn to say goodbye. Thanking Madame Perez for washing, ironing and packing a large bundle of toddler's clothes for little Dolores Megan. Jean-Pierre was pleased with the two thousand pounds in English banknotes that were pressed into hand in gratitude for his help.

By early afternoon Dai pulled the Ford V8 up to the British Embassy in Paris and parked the car in the courtyard. Wrapping a blanket around Dolores Megan he entered the embassy where he requested an interview with the Ambassador.

Sir Eric Parsons welcomed the Welshman and patiently listened to the story he had to tell and the request for the issue of a temporary passport that would admit Dolores Megan through the British Immigation officals when they disembarked from the ferry at Dover.

Sir Eric was sympathetic and said: *'Your reputation precedes you Mr Powell all of us regaled over the past three years with stories of your exploits as a general in the International Brigades. There will be no problem in supplying you with a temporary passport for Dolores Megan using your surname as her father.*

'The day is getting late for you to continue your long journey. We will put you up in one of our guest rooms here at the embassy. You will do me the honour of dining with Lady Parsons and myself. Meanwhile our Embassy nurse, Sister Gregory, will look after Dolores Megan for the night, feeding her, bathing her and putting her to bed.

'I will also ask my secretary to book you both and your car on the midday Calais to Dover ferry.'

Dinner with Sir Eric and Lady Parsons was a delightful affair and spiced with interesting conversation.

'*Disturbing reports are coming through to our intelligence people of terrible atrocities being done in post civil-war Spain on the orders of General Francisco Franco,*' said Sir Eric.

Dai Powell, knew he was being invited to comment and said: '*I am sorry to say, Sir, that only yesterday afternoon that Franco's Nationalist troops indiscriminately shot 20 innocent citizens by firing squad in Barcelona's largest square, Plaza Catalunya. I will have to live with that atrocity on my conscience for the rest of my life because that was a horribly cruel reprisal to punish us for rescuing three children and smuggling them out of Spain. The parents of two of the children had been killed by Franco's thugs while my partner Pilar, a nurse and the mother of my daughter, was shot by firing squad and ridiculously indicted for spying on behalf of the Republicans.*'

Sir Eric, a kindly thoughtful man, then spoke of other problems: '*It is all similar, we hear, to the terrible things being committed in Germany under Hitler . Jews and gypsies are being massacred by the Nazis. Soon we will have to face those problems squarely because a Second World War is imminent if we are going to preserve democracy across Europe. I personally believe that the threat from Fascism and National Socialism is far worse than that from Communism!*

'*In the Diplomatic Servce we are asked, and trained, not to dabble in politics. But between you and me and these four walls Prime Minister Neville Chamberlain is living in a fool's paradise in thinking that his policy of appeasing Germany, when he signed the Munich Agreement last year, will dampen Hitler's ambition to conquer and rule Europe. History will prove me right!*'

Wise words that became prophetically true three months later when the Second World War was declared.

85

Grateful and impressed with the courtesy and efficiency of the British Embassy staff in Paris Dai Powell pointed the nose of the Ford 8 convertible towards the ferry port of Calais with little Dolores Megan gurgling happily in her cot on the small rear seat. Appreciative of the fertile French countryside flourishing in the warm Spring sunshine he hummed a few Welsh songs as he wheeled the Ford 8 convertible northwards so much ahead of schedule that he could afford to stop at a tavern for a mid-morning glass of beer and a baguette filled with garlic sausage with a cup of warm milk for Dolores who was the centre of attraction for the buxom lady who ran the bar.

On arrival and disembarking from the ferry at Dover and tendering the child's temporary passport to Immigration officials without problems he decided to drive straight on to South Wales without another overnight stop.

It was 7pm when Dai pulled the Ford V8 convertible up in front of his mother and father's cottage at the mining village of Ynswen in the Rhonnda valley. Cradling Dolores Megan he went round to the back yard and into the kitchen where he placed the child in his mother's arms with the emotive words: *'Ma-this is your granddaughter little Dolores Megan. I have to tell you that I promised Pilar that the child will be brought up as a Catholic'*

Megan Senior sprang from her armchair showering the little girl with kisses and cooed: *'I have no problem with that as long as she believes in God. Oh you little darling you are really lovely. We will take you into Treorchy tomorrow and buy you a doll. One of those pretty dollies that open and shut their eyes.'*

But then, gathering her thoughts, Megan Powell turned to Dai and asked: *'But Dai where is my daughter in law . Where is Pilar?'*

Dai could only reply in a hoarse voice with emotion almost overcoming him. *'It breaks my heart to tell you Ma but my lovely Pilar is dead--murdered by General Franco's soldiers…..'*

Megan Powell, equally as emotional as her son, could only sob: *'Oh my poor baby Dolores Megan, you sad, sad child to be left without a mother at such an early age! Don't worry Angel I will be your mother from now on…'* Then looking at her son Megan Powell said: *'As for the daughter in law I will never meet, my heart goes out to in your loss my son. Your Dad and I share your grief.*

'By the way you had better go and see your father. He is on the sofa in the front room.' Dai carried Dolores Megan in to meet her grandfather and gently laid her down beside the old man who was breathing heavily and had deteriorated since the last time he had seen him.

He told his Dad the sad story about Pilar and promised him that he would always care for his mother if anything happened to him. The old man let the child grasp his bony first finger and responded by tickling her tummy which produced a giggle from little Dolores Megan.

'*If you look in that locker you'll find a bag please pass it to me Dai bach,*' said Powell Senior. A request Dai immediately acknowledged prompting his father to grope into the bag and produce a pull-string purse made of chamois leather. He opened the purse and tipped one hundred golden sovereigns on to the counterpane that was covering him. '*I know I haven't got long to go now son. These sovereigns were going to be my legacy to Pilar the daughter in law I never met. Now she has gone they will my legacy to my little grandaughter. It may not seem much at the moment but in a few years they could be quite valuable. May they bring her happiness.*'

Dai's father died two weeks later another victim amongst the thousands of South Wales coal miners who succumbed to the dreaded miners' disease of sillicosis.

So, to end our story on a happy note, Dolores Megan thrived on the love care and attention lavished on her by her doting grandmother until the old lady's death.

Dai Powell was typical of talented men misdirected by recruiting officers when WWII was declared three months later. Ignoring the military talent he had shown by remarkably rising from the ranks to General in the Republican Army they decided to send him back to the coal mines -the job he had done after leaving school. He didn't complain just donned his moleskin working trousers and flannel shirt and did his shift in the local pit. Trudged back black-faced to his mother's cottage each evening and bathed in the tin-tub which also hung in the backyard. On Sundays he would take Dolores Megan for a walk in the park where he would buy her an icecream.

But in 1941, when England were being badly mauled by Hitler life took on another twist. A smartly uniformed British Army captain arrived at the cottage in Ynswen and

Introduced himself to Dai and said: '*Mr Powell I believe you are a man who can help us.*

'*If I am not mistaken I believe you can serve Britain better by joining the Army than hewing coal down the pit as important as that job is. I have been appointed by, lets say, someone in Downing Street who smokes cigars, to form a special regiment. It will be called the SAS, short for Special Air Services, and will be an elite force capable of completing seemingly impossible tasks. Answer me a question Mr Powell - are you still a paid-up member of the Communist Party?*'

Dai smiled at the question and answered: '*No I chucked that in when I saw how the Russians behaved in the Spanish Civil War and how substandard some of their equipment was.*'

Dai's visitor was satisfied with that remark and replied: '*Well come and join us. You will start like everyone else in the new regiment in the ranks. But I would guess with your record and experience you will soon be offered a commission.*'

That is how things worked out for Dai Powell and by the end of the war he had risen to the rank of Major in the SAS with many top secret missions to his credit plus a Military Cross for gallantry. He stayed with the SAS after the war when the regiment became a potent force against terrorism.

In 1944 he married a beautiful nurse from Swansea, who became a third arm to Dai's mother in the nurturing of Dolores Megan. Two years later she presented Dai with twin sisters who Dolores Megan cuddled and kissed and generally bossed taking advantage of her six years seniority.

Following the death of his mother in 1946 Dai moved his family to a beautiful house on the picturesque Gower Coast.

The old fairy tales always used to end: *"They all lived happily for ever afterwards!"*

But for Dai Powell it could be said that he always lived up to the motto of the elite SAS Regiment: WHO DARES WINS.

SPANISH CIVIL WAR THE OTHER SIDE OF THE COIN

By John Davies (Author)

After researching and writing the novel *LA PASIONARIA I knew, inevitably, I would be accused of bias having chosen to angle the book from the perspective of the Second Republic.*

But no way do I want to suggest that the only atrocities committed in the gory Spanish Civil War were the responsibility of the Nationalists.

The Republicans' list of shame records that they had killed 55,000 Nationalist-sympathising civilians. Termed as the Red Terror the Republicans controversially attacked the Catholic Church which supported the Nationalists. Nearly 7,000 clergy, priests and nuns were murdered. In the Andalusian town of Ronda 512 Nationalist supporters were massacred in the first month of the war. Many repressive actions were committed by the Republican political police in detention centres nicknamed Checas. There were 229 such checas in Madrid where Nationalist prisoners were tortured and 12,000 executed.

The Nationalists on the other hand executed Republican school teachers, trade-unionists and many Republican sympathisers. In 1936, under the orders of invading General Juan Yagüe, it was estimated that Nationalist soldiers massacred nearly 4,000 citizens while seizing the city of Badajoz-Yagüe. He went down in history as the 'butcher of Badajoz' The Nationalists' most notorious war crime was the terror-bombing of the innocent town of Guernica by their Nazi allies.

But no Spanish Civil War atrocity transcends the human rights crimes committed under the orders of General Franco.

At least 150,000 children, it is believed, were incarcerated into Nationalist orphanages after Franco's troops and police had executed their parents.

In 2009, a Spanish court magistrate, Judge Baltasar Garzón, asked the nation's judges to add the missing children to more than 136,000 cases of people who disappeared under the Franco regime.

An unknown number of children were stolen from Republican families by Franco's supporters, and in 2009 details of individual cases have been sent to courts in Madrid, Barcelona, Bilbao, Valencia, Burgos, Málaga and Zaragoza

Campaigners claim thousands of children were taken from mothers , especially those in jail, and handed to orphanages in the early years of Franco's 36-year dictatorship.

Nearly all had their surnames changed and were never seen again!

As for our heroine, the iconic La Pasionaria, I have heard several Spaniards claim she had blood on her hands. But I have never come across any documentary evidence proving that Doña Dolores Ibárruri Gómez did anything worse that rouse her compatriots to fight for their rights.

But then.

Who would want to malign the character of a feisty woman who was a legend in her own lifetime?